Raves for Zach's Previous Adventures:

"No one who got two paragraphs into this dark, droll, downright irresistible ~~could half-~~ ~~bear~~ to pu~~~~ ~~~~ Zach is off~~~~ ~~~~ is no way h~~~~ ~~~~ ger. This is ~~~~ ~~~~ who enjoy~~~~ ~~~~ the occasio~~~~ Blonde and a cold one and just see when you manage to pull your peepers away from the page again. On second thought, John Zakour and Lawrence Ganem are too damn good to be interrupted for something trivial; skip the cold one and save yourself a trip to the can." —*SF Site*

"I had a great deal of fun with The Plutonium Blonde and have been looking forward to the sequel ever since. Well, it's finally here, and it's a good one. This is more ~~~~ ~~~~ detective story, although Johnson and HARV ~~~~ ~~~~ good pair of investigators as well as downright f~~~~ like your humor slapstick and inventive ~~~~ ~~~~ furth~~~~

"It's ~~~~
renc~~~~
The ~~~~
our ~~~~
The ~~~~
Red ~~~~
ers ~~~~
ficti~~~~

"A ~~~~
ougl~~~~

"It's ~~~~
way ~~~~
orf Z~~~~
show~~~~

The SAPPHIRE SIRENS

JOHN ZAKOUR

DAW BOOKS, INC.
DONALD A. WOLLHEIM, FOUNDER
375 Hudson Street, New York, NY 10014

ELIZABETH R. WOLLHEIM
SHEILA E. GILBERT
PUBLISHERS
http://www.dawbooks.com

First Paperback Printing, December 2009
1 2 3 4 5 6 7 8 9

DAW TRADEMARK REGISTERED
U.S. PAT. AND TM. OFF. AND FOREIGN COUNTRIES
—MARCA REGISTRADA
HECHO EN U.S.A.

PRINTED IN THE U.S.A.

To all my loyal readers.
You know who you are.

Acknowledgments

To keep it simple: Betsy Wollheim for taking a chance and publishng this crazy offbeat series. Joshua Starr for all his great edits and suggestions. Joshua Bilmes, my agent, for keeping track of me. Debra Euler for her help with the final edits and making sure I did a dedication and wrote my acknowledgments. Scott Roberts for his help editing. For my wife Olga and son Jay just for putting up with me. And to Carolina, Natalia, Ron, Mara, Luciana, Liana, Elena, Halee, Tom, Rob, Ohm and everybody else I based a character on.

Chapter 1

I am Zachary Nixon Johnson. I am the last freelance PI on Earth. It can be a tough job. It can be a dirty job. But it's a job somebody has to do. Might as well be me.

I was sitting in my office on New Frisco Bay, watching the world go by. When you're the last freelance PI in the world, you often have the time on your hands to do nothing. And when you watch the world stroll past, it's via holographic projection from your outside security. When you're me, office windows are a risk. You never know who may want to take an easy shot. That's why I cherish the quiet times. While they may not be the stuff great adventures are made of, they let me recharge for the more "interesting" times.

It had been a while since I had a big case, but that was okay by me. I knew my history, and it was bound to repeat itself. Once a year or so, whether or not I'm ready, whether or not I want it to, the world comes knocking at my door, needing me to save it.

I'm not sure why the universe always drops its troubles off at my doorstep. I'm just a slightly above-the-curve joe who happens to be as unrelenting as a door-to-door virtual encyclopedia salesman trying to make his quota on the last day of the month. Some folks call my dogged perseverance a flaw. Others say it's my strongest trait. I don't really know what to think. I do what I have to do to get the job done. My techniques may not always be smooth or by the book, but the book is boring.

"Zach, Zach, Zach, you're contemplating your place in the world again, aren't you?" asked HARV, my holographic cognitive processor. He's probably my greatest ally and my best friend. Like I said, my life is different.

"Nope, not at all, HARV."

HARV looked at me with more disdain than usual. "Zach, I am connected to your brain. I know when you are lying. You see, when you are lying, certain regions of the brain become much more active. For instance . . ."

"Yes, I was thinking about it," I said sharply, just to avoid the physiology lecture.

"That's okay, Mr. Zach," said GUS, the intelligent weapon that I keep up my sleeve. "One of the things I like best about you is how you look at the big picture."

I popped GUS from up my sleeve into my hand. Sure, I could have talked to him through my neurolink via HARV, but I preferred to look at him directly when we talked. I liked looking at what I was talking with, even if in this case the other end of the conversation was a long, plastic-looking cylinder.

"Thank you, GUS," I said.

HARV rolled his eyes. I wasn't sure if he was rolling them at me, at GUS, or at both of us. As you can see, the machines and cognitive processors in my life are far from run of the mill, even for the 2070s.

Before I could contemplate all the complicated machines that had become too much a part of my life for too long, my assistant, Carol, strutted into my office. This was a nice change, as Carol was much easier on the eyes than HARV or GUS.

"What's up, Carol?" I asked.

"Just checking in for the morning," she said, humming a tune out loud as she talked to me. I recognized the tune. It was a classic from long ago, and by classic, I mean classically bad.

"Ah, the 'Macarena,'" I said to Carol.

Carol popped her PIHI-Pod (short for Portable Interactive Holographic Interface Personally Optimized Device. P-Pod for really short) off her ear. "You've heard of it?" she said, with surprise in her voice.

"It was big hit about eighty years ago, then forty years ago, then twenty years ago. It's the song that just won't die."

"Oh," Carol said, her voice dropping. "I thought it was new . . . Now I'm not sure I like it as much."

"There isn't much new these days," I told her.

HARV appeared in front of us. He was dressed in a tweed suit. I assume he considered this his professor mode. A holographic blackboard appeared. HARV cleared his throat to make sure he had our attention. "In fact," he said in a slow precise manner, "the top five downloaded songs of today are all remakes from the last century."

The song titles: "YMCA," "Tiptoe Through the Tulips," "Itsy Bitsy Teeny Weenie Yellow Polka Dot Bikini," and "Monster Mash," appeared on this board. Being a sort of throwback to the old days, I tend to appreciate and understand earlier music and customs better than most from these days, but I found the entire list—except for "Monster Mash"—to be, well, scary.

"You're kidding," I said to HARV.

His eyes lowered. "I wish I were."

"I've downloaded them all," Carol said, now not sure if she should be happy or ashamed. The expression on

her face suddenly shifted from confusion to concentration. "I'm picking up some weird vibes coming this way,"
she said, eyes squinted.

I should mention that Carol happens to be a class I
level 7 psi. Which means not only do you want to stay
on her good side, but that it's never good news when she
starts picking up weird vibes.

"Can you be more specific?" I asked.

Carol shook her head, tossing her long blond hair
over her shoulders. "Not much." She paused and took a
deep breath. Her chest rose and then slowly fell as she
took another breath. Not only was she world-class psi,
she was also a world-class beauty.

"*Hey, remember Carol is your girlfriend, Doctor Electra Gevada's, niece, and a good deal younger than you,*"
HARV lectured in my brain.

I refused to dignify that remark with a response. Instead I remained concentrated on Carol.

"Anything is better than nothing," I said to Carol.

"Brilliant," HARV said, arms crossed, frown running
down and off his face. (He never let me forget that he
was a hologram.)

"I thought so, too," GUS said, not recognizing the
sarcasm dripping off HARV's words.

Carol closed her eyes, concentrating. "I just keep
picking up, *I will convince him, I will convince him, and
I will convince him . . .*" Her eyes opened wide, so wide
even HARV had to comment.

"*I must say, Carol does have the most beautiful green
eyes,*" HARV said in my brain. "*I don't ever wish I were
human, but if I were . . .*"

"Don't even think about going there, HARV," I
told him. Yep, that's how beautiful Carol was. Even a
mega-ultra-advanced holographic cognitive processor
noticed.

"So these thoughts are coming our way?" I asked.

Carol nodded.

I popped GUS back up my sleeve. Sure he looked more like a remote control than an überpowerful weapon, but if things did get nasty, the more surprise I had on my side the better. Like my old mentor use to say: "*Surprises are good; at least when you do the surprising.*"

"Let's meet and greet them in your reception area," I said, walking toward Carol's desk.

My office was filled with antique real wood furnishings. They make me feel the way my gumshoe predecessors did a hundred years ago. An actual desk made from oak, a big comfy leather chair behind that desk, and another leather chair, just not as big and comfy (or quite as expensive), in front of the desk. There was a real wood coat rack in the corner. It was a hundred-year-old antique and was barely noticeable, yet it somehow made me happy. Except for the holographic projector on the ceiling, and the information monitors on the walls, everything in my office was older than I was. That means everything is quite costly, and I can't afford to keep replacing them.

Carol and I entered her work area. It was much more modern and sparsely decorated than mine. A simple chair that looked like a tripod to me, but that Carol insisted was way more comfortable than it looked. A long, narrow, almost transparent sliver of a monitor desk, a couple throw rugs and a couch for potential customers to wait on, and that was it. Carol even had the wall information screens replaced with actual walls, as she said too much info was blocking her chi. The good thing was, nothing in *here* would be hard or expensive to replace. The desk and the chair were made by our personal fabber machine. I was pretty certain the computer stuff was all mass produced by robots on Mars colony.

"How close are they?" I asked.

There was a knock on the outside office door.

"Very close," Carol said, though my keen sleuthing skills had figured that part out.

It was a good sign that they were knocking. Very few actual killers knock before they burst into the room—at least none of the good ones do.

"I am accessing the security cameras now," HARV said.

The holographic image of a short but pleasant enough looking black woman appeared. She was standing outside my office door politely knocking. Behind her stood two "men." One of them was big and thick, well over 2.5 meters tall, and a simple glance could tell you he never got shortchanged at a meal. His skin had a weird, barf-greenish tint to it. I figured he was a mutant. He looked about the right age.

The other was short, stocky, and stiff, and his skin had an orange metallic look to it. Together these facts tipped me off that he was an android.

"Can you identify her?" I asked HARV.

"Of course," he answered.

I waited. More knocks but no info from HARV.

"And she is?" I prompted.

"Her name is Lemme Grabo," HARV said slowly. "She is an employee of Entercorp. She's a lawyer and head of their sequential art purchasing department."

"Well that would explain the chaotic thoughts and the backup bodyguards." I thought for a nano. "Sequential art?" I said.

"I believe the term in the popular vernacular is comic," HARV said.

"I know that," I said.

"I didn't," GUS mumbled from inside my sleeve.

"Me either," Carol said.

"What do they want with me?" I asked.

"I suggest you open the door and ask," HARV said, turning away from me.

I knew that HARV knew something he wasn't telling me. He had a giveaway when he wouldn't tell me something: he couldn't look me in the eyes. It was very humanlike, almost too humanlike. Experience has taught me it would be far easier to ask Lemme and her friends than it would be to drag the words out of HARV.

"Let them in," I said pointing to the door.

My door popped open. Lemme entered the building, followed by the mutant and the android. To others this might have been strange. To me it was just another day at the office.

Chapter 2

Lemme Grabo walked up to me, head high, hand extended. "Mr. Johnson, it is a pleasure to meet you."

"Please, call me Zach," I said, shaking her hand.

Lemme took a step backward. "I'm not sure I can do that."

"Try," I said.

"Oh, okay, Mr. John–I mean, Za-ch . . ."

"See? That wasn't so hard," I said.

She smiled ever so slightly. "No. No, I guess not," she said softly. Looking me in the eyes she said, "I am sure you have had your computer scan me, so I am sure you know that I am from Entercorp."

She touched the diamondlike P-Pod she was wearing on her ear. A holographic business card appeared in front of my face. It read: LEMME C. GRABO, J.D., ENTERCORP.

"Wow, most of the lawyers I meet these days call themselves greeting card salesmen," I said.

"Yes, I know. Some of my brothers in the field are still uneasy in public, but it has been decades since the Great Lawyer Purge," Lemme said. "Now that our numbers have been thinned, and we are so heavily regulated, I believe people are more accepting of us again."

"Perhaps," I said.

Lemme cleared her throat. "But enough about me. I have come here to make you an offer."

"Me?"

"An offer you can't refuse," the hulking mutant in the back mumbled, just clear enough for me to hear.

I turned to HARV and Carol. "See, I told you the big guy could probably talk. You owe me ten credits." Okay, it probably wasn't the best move, egging on an overgrown mutant muscleman, but I don't like being told what I can and can't refuse.

The big guy's skin tone changed from greenish to bright red. He moved past Lemme to the forefront, blocking Lemme from my view.

"Now, Hans," I heard her say from behind him. "Our boss wants us to handle Mr. Johnson—I mean Zaaa-ch—with care and compassion."

"So I'll be careful not to kill him," Hans said, licking his lips. "He'll be much more amenable to our deal after I soften him up some, literally."

The thug wasn't as dumb as he looked. Years in the business have taught me that more often than not, things are not that deceiving. The big, dumb-looking thug usually doesn't have a Ph.D in astrophysics and isn't just playing dumb to throw me off course. The years have taught me to see a spade as a spade. The problems come up on those rare occasions when you think you're looking at a two and it turns out to be an ace. I wasn't yet sure if here I was dealing with a joker. A wise man would have backed off. But I was a little bored.

Pointing behind Lemme, I told Hans, "Listen buddy, do what your keeper says and back off, before I forget my manners." I stepped toward Hans and gave him a little friendly shove to the side. Ignoring Hans, I asked Lemme, "So what is this all about?"

Interestingly enough, Hans didn't come after me. He was, indeed, smarter than he looked. That could be good, that could be bad, or it could be megabad. Time would tell, and it wouldn't be much time.

"We want to make you an offer," Lemme said.

"What sort of offer?" I asked.

"On your graphic novel series," Lemme said, as if I should know what she's talking about.

I looked at her with surprise.

"I don't have a graphic novel," I said.

"Yes, you do," both Lemme and, surprisingly (though I guess I shouldn't have been surprised), HARV said.

"Excuse me?" I said.

"The graphic novel about your life that you write, draw, and publish on ItsAmazingImStillBreathing.com," Lemme said.

"There is also an alternate site name: AISB2071. com," HARV added.

"Excuse me?" I said again.

Lemme shook her head. "For such a creative writer, I am a bit surprised you are so redundant."

"Let me jog his memory some," Hans said.

I didn't even have to look to know he was coming after me. I felt a hand come down on my shoulder. Before I could do anything about it, I found myself flying across the room and into the wall. I hit hard. If my underwear wasn't reinforced with nanomesh armor (no, I am not making that up) I would have taken some damage. Instead, the initial attack had only hurt my ego a bit. Of course Hans was bearing down on me, hoping to hurt a lot more.

"Sorry, tió, I can't stop him," Carol said in my brain. *"He must be wearing a psi blocker."*

"Hans!" Lemme shouted. "You know the boss wanted

us to be civilized first." Lemme sighed and then spoke. "D4Q1, can you stop him?"

"You know how he gets," an android voice responded.

I tried pushing myself off from the wall, but Hans leaped over Carol's desk, grabbed my throat, and pinned me back to the wall before I got too far.

"You know, you find yourself in this situation an awful lot," HARV said inside my head. He was correct, but not at all helpful.

"The little mind bender won't work on me," Hans said. Pointing to his brain with his free hand, he added: "They made me immune to mind tricks."

Hans was fairly intelligent and way strong, but that made him cocky, and that was something I could use to my advantage. He, like many before him, had underestimated me.

"GUS, I am going to pop you into my hand in a second."

"I'm ready when you are Mr. Zach!" GUS said excitedly. *"Do you want me to blast him in half?"* he said, even more excitedly.

"No, I don't want you to fire at all. I'll ram you into his solar plexus then pop you back up my sleeve."

I wanted to beat the guy down without him knowing I had help. Knock his ego down a couple of notches. I moved my wrist in just the way that pops GUS into my hand. At the same time though, I flung my fist forward fast, really fast. My body armor is also connected via HARV to my nervous system, allowing me to move much more rapidly than I otherwise could.

I slammed GUS in Hans' midsection. That buckled him over, knocking the wind out of his lungs and his sails. Not giving him any chance to recover, I kneed him in the groin. He fell to the ground panting and moaning.

I looked at Lemme and her android backup.

"Now are we going to talk or fight?" I asked.

Lemme just shook her head. "Sorry, about him. He's nonunion and a bit of a hothead."

"I guess that means we talk."

Lemme cleared her throat. "Our boss insists that we buy rights to your comic from you."

"It's a graphic novel," HARV corrected.

"Whatever," Lemme said. "She wants it."

"Who's she?" I asked.

"I am not at liberty to say," Lemme said.

I knew that at one time Entercorp was owned by one of my famous ex-clients, Ona Thompson. Ona was one of the Thompson Quads, four (according to their press releases) awesomely powerful and devastatingly beautiful sisters. Ona was the oldest and was a playgirl businesswoman, but she had recently met with an unfortunate accident.

Last year, while taking on another superbabe, a flaxen-haired one, Ona got the short end of the stick; her mind was totally erased. As far I know, she's now on life support; she couldn't be running any company. Her sister, Foraa, tried to destroy the world a few years back, and I personally put her out of business. The two remaining sisters, Twoa and Threa, are still around. Only thing is, Twoa, who fancied herself an actual superhero, was so taken aback by her encounter with the flaxen-haired beauty Natasha that she moved to New Old Tibet. That meant only one of the quads could possibly be running the company: Threa. Of course, Threa considers herself to be a fairy princess. She even lives in her own realm, called Incognito. I didn't think she'd want to be running a business. Of course if she did, I guess comics would be right up her alley.

"Let me guess. It's Threa Thompson," I said.

"Well . . ." Lemme said meekly.

"Oh, I so hope not," Carol said.

The temperature in the room started to rise. Looking up, we all saw a familiar energy bubble appeared. It was all too familiar; I recognized it as a personal teleporter. The energy bubble crackled and then dissipated. There before us stood Threa Thompson in all her glory. She was over two meters tall, with more curves than you'd find on a really long geometry test. She was naked, with only her long golden-blond hair curling down over her body, covering her ample breasts and other ... personal areas.

"Zach," she said. "Long time no see."

Chapter 3

To say Threa Thompson dominated a room is like saying I've been known to brawl on occasion. Carol and Lemme were both sitting on the floor, legs extended, sucking their thumbs, totally mesmerized by her presence. Threa gave them each a little dismissive pat on the head as she walked past them to me.

Behind me, Hans started to stir a little. Threa casually waved her toes under his nose. He smiled, stopped stirring, and plopped back down on the floor. Threa hadn't even touched him and he was out colder than a block of ice on Pluto.

Truthfully, I was surprised not to be stunned by Threa's abundant physical and mental charms. Maybe my exposure to her was making me immune.

"I am blurring the image of her and dampening your sense of smell," HARV said to me. *"That's what's keeping you from purring at her feet."*

Okay, maybe it was that.

"So Threa, you've taken over your sister's company?"

I asked. Though the answer was pretty obvious, it still seemed like a good conversation starter.

Threa nodded. "Yes, despite my duties as a former leader on the World Council, and queen of my own realm, I thought it fitting that I continue for my poor sister Ona. It was the least I could do."

"Plus Entercorp turns a four-billion-credit profit a quarter," the android behind her said.

Threa turned and glared at the droid. "I did not ask you for your input, machine," she spat. On hearing those words the android melted into a pool of goo. "Well, ex-machine now," Threa, said.

"Phew, I am glad I didn't correct him and tell her it's a 4.1-billion-credit profit," HARV said.

Threa held out her hand and I kissed it. Better her hand now by choice than her feet later. Believe me, I've dealt with Threa enough to know what was coming if I didn't cooperate.

"Zach, I've read your comic," Threa said.

"Graphic novel," HARV correct.

"Graphic novel," Threa said. "And I loved it. I want to buy it for my little company. Name your price, and if it's reasonable it's yours. Of course, if it's not reasonable you will become my lapdog's lapdog."

Taking a step backward, I said slowly, "Threa, I have no idea what you or anybody else is talking about."

Walking forward, Threa smiled at me. "Don't play coy with me, Zach. I invented coy. Okay, I didn't invent it, but I copyrighted it."

Threa put her finger over my head and started twirling it around. As she spun her finger I spun around and around, faster and faster, turning into her personal human top.

"Weeeeeee!" Gus said in my brain.

"This is an interesting experience," HARV agreed.

"Thr—ea ... I—real-lyyy—ha—ve—no—idea ..." I said.

The spinning stopped. I was facing Threa, eye to eye. Well, actually, my eyes to her breasts, but I forced my eyes upward.

"Really?" Threa said.

"Really," I said.

"How strange," she said.

You know your life is weird when a superhuman woman who considers herself a fairy princess thinks things are strange.

Threa motioned to Lemme, who was still sitting contently on the floor, sucking away. "Show Zach the comic," she ordered.

Lemme touched her P-Pod with the hand she wasn't sucking the thumb of. An illustration of me, HARV, and Carol appeared. Well at least an artist's rendition of what HARV, Carol, and I would like if we were comic book heroes. I was still me, with my strong jaw, my roman nose (that has been broken at least two times too many), and my dark hair with just a touch of distinguished gray. But I was also much more buff than I am in real life. I'm a tough guy who can take a punch—you've gotta be when your me—but I'm not nearly as chiseled from new-improved-granite as this image of me.

The image of Carol looked pretty much like Carol really does; after all, no artist can improve on nature's best work. About the only noticeable change was that, as drawn, her bra size was probably one size greater than the actual Carol's. Her dress was cut higher, and her blouse unbuttoned lower than I (or her aunt Electra, the love of my life) would allow in the office.

As for HARV, he still had his snobbish British butler look, only this butler looked like he worked out in the gym eight hours a day, seven days a week. Also, HARV liked to present himself as balding with a touch of gray on the sides, but this HARV had a full crop of jet black hair on top of his head, and a dark handlebar mustache under his nose that helped accent the goatee on his chin. The title on the page read: *The Adventures of Zachary Nixon Johnson, PI 4 $$*. Underneath the title it said: "written, illustrated, colored, and inked by Zachary H. Johnson."

I pointed at the signature. "This isn't me. I'm Zachary *N*. Johnson. Not H." I turned to HARV. "You know more about this than you're letting on."

HARV looked down, but he couldn't conceal the smile on this face. "Perhaps."

Now this was going to get interesting, and by interesting I mean odd. The good thing was, at least for the moment, nobody was trying to kill or maim me.

"HARV, you are going to elaborate," I coaxed.

HARV stood there silently, hands behind his back, letting us stew in our own anticipation. It couldn't have been what it looked like it was going be. Yes, that was a confusing statement, especially coming from a PI, but this was an extra confusing time.

"Well . . ." HARV said slowly, bending toward us, hands still behind his back.

"Spit it out!" I ordered.

HARV arched his back away from us, "You don't mean that literally, do you?" he asked. He knew I didn't. He knew I knew he didn't. He was just looking for any opportunity to drag this out.

Threa curled her fist and glared at him. "Tell us now, or so help me I will generate so much heat, I will melt your holographic image."

HARV looked Threa in the eyes. "To generate that much energy, you would wilt a good portion of the province of New California . . ."

Threa leaned into him. "I am quite willing to risk it. Sometimes you need to crack a few eggs to make a holographic image talk."

I gulped, and I am pretty certain I caught HARV gulping. HARV stuck a finger in his collar and loosened it. "I did it."

"You did it?" Threa said.

"Yes, I wrote, drew, lettered, inked, and marketed the entire thing," HARV said, chest extended.

"But you're a machine," Threa said.

"So are you," HARV replied. "You just happen to be an organic one."

"Touché," Threa said. "So this is all your creative effort?" she asked.

HARV simply smiled and nodded. To prove that the work was indeed his, he held his finger out in front of him. Using it as a paintbrush, he started to draw a 2-D holographic image. Starting from the top, the image took shape—a shapely shape. He was drawing a comic book version of Threa. Until that moment I didn't think it was possible to make Threa any more over the top than she already was, but he did it. He managed to make her lips fuller and her body rounder, yet not too much rounder, making a sexy pseudo-goddess even more alluring.

"I'm impressed," I said.

HARV looked at me. "I found I needed an outlet for my creative urges. Comics seem to be the perfect medium. Plus, the ad revenue makes us both some nice extra cash."

"Us both?"

HARV nodded. "Since, like it or not, you are the inspiration, I give you twenty percent."

I wasn't surprised at all by HARV's business sense, but his creativity—that was a whole new ballgame. Still, I was pleased to see him growing. At least, I was pretty certain I was pleased.

"Wow," Carol said, snapping out of her Threa-induced stupor. "Nice art."

"Thank you," HARV said. "The art was easy, and the

plotting was easy as well. I find writing the dialog to be the hardest part, though. Much of what Zach actually says is too far out there even for the funnybooks."

Threa looked at her newly drawn image and smiled. "You captured the real me."

"I will include you in the next issue," HARV said. "I plan to publish weekly. Being an ultramegasuperintelligent cognitive processor and holographic interface, I could of course produce more material at a greater frequency, but I don't want to flood the market. I like my readers to salivate some."

"Name your price," Threa told HARV. "I want all rights. I will, of course, give you a generous percentage of future profits from other media."

HARV shook his head no. Carol and I each took a step away from HARV. "Sorry, Threa, this is my baby, my creation, my outlet. For now I want all—no—I need all control. It's not for sale."

Threa pointed at Carol and me. "What if I wilt them if you don't agree?" she said.

HARV stood steady.

"Hey," Carol said, moving toward Threa. "I don't wilt easy. I went toe-to-toe with your sister Twoa last year."

Threa rolled her eyes. "Perhaps, but my sister and I both learned a lot from our encounter with that Natasha girl last year. It taught me to embrace my true power."

"How is Twoa doing these days?" I asked, desperately trying to get Threa to forget about threatening to wilt Carol and me.

"She's in the monastery now. She's making quilts. Lots and lots of quilts," Threa said, looking at me ignoring Carol.

"I didn't think there were any monasteries left." I said.

"There weren't. She started her own. The Sacred

Order of Women Who Want to Find Themselves And Not Wear Any Makeup: SOW³FTANWAM."

"Oh . . ."

"She's very happy there," Threa said. "Now no more trying to get me off track." Locking in on HARV, she said: "So HARV, name your price."

HARV stood steadfast. "Sorry, my art and talent are not for sale. At least, not until I decide to sell out in a few years."

Threa pointed at Carol and me again. "Don't forget, I threatened to wilt these two."

"At my core processor I am basically a fancy electronic filing cabinet. I have billions of gigabytes of storage. I never forget anything."

Threa stood there, first looking at HARV, then glancing at Carol and me. Carol had taken a defensive position, but I knew better. If Threa really wanted to wilt us we would have been dust in the vacubot's filter by now. She was bluffing. Threa may have been a lot of things, a lot of really bizarre things, but she wasn't a cold-blooded killer. She had proven that on many occasions. If you got her angry enough she might rearrange your molecules and turn you into a plant, but even then she would water you every day until she decided to put you back the way you were.

Threa smiled. "Good enough," she said. She held out a hand to HARV. "As long as you promise me an exclusive when you do decide to sell."

HARV extended his arm across the room to shake Threa's hand.

"Deal," he said.

Threa smiled. She blew Carol and me each a little kiss. The force of the kiss drove us each back a couple of steps. Threa smiled and then was gone, along with her employees.

"HARV, how come you never told me about this little side project of yours?" I asked.

"Zach, Zach, Zach, I do a billion, billion things at once. I can't tell you about all of them."

"Yeah, but you can tell me about the ones that star me," I noted.

HARV sighed. It was a familiar sigh. It was the same sigh I often give him.

"I didn't want anybody to know," HARV said. "If word gets out that this is written by a nonorganic being, half the world will read it just because of that. Of course the other half of the world won't read it because of that. I want the material to live or die on its own merit."

HARV had a point, one I couldn't make a strong counterpoint to. "Fair enough," I told him.

Carol looked at our images on the east sidewall screen. "Wow, if my breasts really were that big, I'd have to use my TK powers to hold them up!"

I smiled.

"Zach, you have a call coming in," HARV told me.

"From who?"

"Dr. Pool," HARV told me.

Dr. Randy Pool was my mad scientist friend who created HARV. This call couldn't be a coincidence.

"Put him through," I said.

Chapter 4

Dr. Randy Pool's tall, lanky image appeared in front of us.

"Hi, Randy," I said. "To what do I owe the pleasure?"

I noticed that Randy wasn't tinkering with some bot or stirring some vat, which was out of the ordinary for him. Sure, his bright red hair was going in every direction except the way it should on his head. Sure, his lab coat was stained with more colors than there are in the rainbow. But he wasn't doing anything except concentrating on this conversation.

"Threa Thompson just called me," Randy said.

"Really?"

"Well not Threa at first; it was her lawyer's lawyer, then her lawyer, then after I agreed I wouldn't sue her over anything she said, Threa herself," Randy said.

"So what did Threa want?" I asked, though I had a pretty good idea what Threa wanted.

"She asked me how much it would cost to build another HARV," Randy said.

"But I am a unique, self-aware, self-sustaining, and self-growing being," HARV said. "I can't be duplicated."

"I told her that," Randy said. "So then she asked how much it would cost to create another cognitive processor like HARV."

"So what did you tell her?" I asked.

"I told her HARV was a unique byproduct of electronic, optical, and organic technologies. Then, I did what any good scientist would do, I made up a ridiculously high number and told her it would take two years and a large advance." As Randy said this, his eyes were as wide as I had ever seen them.

"I take it she agreed," I said.

Randy nodded, grinning from—even past—ear to ear. "In less than a nano." Randy paused to catch his breath. "So I had to ask her why she was so anxious to have something like HARV," he said, panting.

"Dr. Pool, you are hyperventilating," HARV said.

Randy grabbed an old paper bag and started breathing into it. He didn't let that stop him from saying rapidly, "Then she told me HARV is creating and drawing comics."

I didn't know if Randy was more excited over his windfall of cash to come, or the fact that HARV was being creative.

"Is that good or bad?" I asked.

Randy laughed into the paper bag. He took a few more breaths in and out of the bag then lowered it. "Silly layman, this is incredible. I always hoped HARV would break the creativity barrier. He didn't just break it; he shattered it. I should be able to get a bookload of publications out of this."

HARV looked at the screen. "Dr. Pool, I would prefer to remain anonymous as the author for the time being."

"Why?" Randy asked.

"So fame doesn't interfere with my creative flow," HARV said.

Randy stared blankly from the screen; the smile had melted off his face. "But what about my fame?"

"You will still get the boatloads of cash from Threa," I said.

Randy's smile returned. "Yes I will, won't I?" he said. "I can certainly live with that. At least for now."

"Thank you. I appreciate it, Dr. Pool," HARV said.

"I do too," I said.

"I still haven't quite forgiven you for stealing some of my DNA and creating a super psi," Carol said, glaring at the screen.

Carol sometimes had a problem letting go of the past.

Randy reached for a button. His image disappeared.

"Ah, bye," I said.

"That all went well," HARV said.

I guess it did go as well as could be expected. HARV had gone head-to-head with one of the most powerful people on Earth, and we all got to walk away keeping our heads. Then he managed to shock his creator so much that that said creator actually concentrated on just one project for a few seconds. Both of those, if not firsts, were surely seconds—thirds at the worst.

Sure, the computer hardwired to my brain is writing and drawing comics based on my life, but I wasn't going to think too hard about that. Knowing the way my life usually goes, I was going to have something much bigger to keep my mind occupied sooner rather than later.

Chapter 5

I deduced (when you are a PI you don't just decide, you deduce) that my best course of action would be to actually go online and read the comics HARV was writing about me—well, about us. I started with the first story, where I tracked down a killer android who was an exact copy of a beautiful, blonde New Bollywood actress. The actress android was radioactive and would go nuclear if I didn't track her down in twelve hours or less. The story mirrored one of my real life adventures without copying it. Lucky for HARV the real life story was very hush-hush. If I hadn't lived it, I wouldn't even have known this story was based on it.

HARV appeared behind me, looking over my shoulder at my desk cover screen. (Yes, there are times I still like to look at a solid screen, not a holographic projection. What can I say? I am a throwback.)

"What do you think of it?" HARV asked, with far more excitement in his voice than I am used to hearing.

"It's . . . ah . . . good . . ." I said.

"That smile on your face increased by twenty-one

percent, and your eyes have dilated thirty-six percent, which means you liked it," HARV said.

"Yes, that's what 'it's good' means. It means I liked it."

"On a scale of one to one hundred, what do you give it?" HARV asked.

"Using integers or real numbers?" I responded.

HARV rolled his eyes. "Zach, for this type of measurement it doesn't really matter. It's not like there's that much of a difference between 99 and 99.99."

"Then I give it a 93.99," I said, really just picking a number out of the air.

"I will round that to a 94," HARV said. "By most scales that means it's an A."

I had to confess I did find HARV's work to be very good. "So you did the art and the writing," I said.

"Yes, and the lettering and the inking and the coloring," HARV said proudly. "To think you humans would do comics in teams."

"We are social creatures," I said.

"You do do a lot of social slacking," HARV said.

Before I could respond, Carol's voice interrupted. "Zach, the massage therapist you ordered is here."

I didn't order a massage. Normally, an uninvited visitor would worry me, but this one was different. This one was a past client; a very special, very flaxen past client.

"That's funny," HARV said. "Checking your calendar I see no scheduled massage. Carol should have access to that calendar too. Yet she didn't seem at all worried . . . Wait a thousand nanos, is this that Nancy girl from the doomed orbiting space station? How come you still maintain a relationship with her? I am starting to surmise . . ."

HARV didn't finish that statement, as he froze in place. That pretty much confirmed who my visitor was.

Nancy walked into my office, as she does once a

month when either she needs to talk, or realizes I do. Nancy was actually Natasha, a person cloned from Carol's tweaked DNA. The tweaking made Natasha scarily powerful, more powerful than any mortal should be. If she gets in a bad mood those around her simply wilt as she absorbs their energy. I am the only person in the world who knows Natasha did not die last year in a fiery explosion on the military's orbiting space station.

Oh, DOS. Two contacts with mega-superbeings in the same morning. This was an omen; my life was about to get interesting. And by interesting, I mean an assortment of different beings will be trying to kill me.

"I thought you weren't using your powers," I told her.

"Slowing time is hardly using my powers," Natasha grinned.

When Natasha fully grasped how powerful she truly was, she decided it would be best for her and the world if she lived undercover, never using her powers. Or, I guess, hardly ever using her powers.

"Why are you here?" I asked.

"Massage time," she said. She opened her arms to give me a clear view of her white T-shirt and shorts. "See I am wearing my massage uniform. You should be glad I make house calls."

"You don't even have your massage table," I said.

A massage table appeared in the middle of my office.

"Doctor Manhattan has nothing on you," I said.

"That's a reference to the old *Watchmen* comic book," Natasha said with a smile.

"Graphic novel," I corrected. Though I was pleased she had been taking my reading suggestions.

Suddenly, I was lying facedown on the table with my shirt and underarmor off.

"You could give me a warning when you're about to do that," I said.

"Yes, I could," she said, as she started to massage my neck. It felt relaxing.

"You need to relax more," she told me.

"I am relaxed. At least as relaxed as you can be when you're me."

"Oh, please, all you are is a guy who saves the world now and then. You want pressure, try being me. One stray bad thought and poof, all of New Oferland is a pile of cheese."

"I've never heard of New Oferland," I said.

"Exactly," Natasha said, now moving down to my mid shoulders. "Your deltoids are very tight," she added.

"So why are you here?" I asked.

She squeezed my shoulders tight. It felt good. "I got a vibe."

"You got a vibe."

"A bad vibe," she said.

"Could you hone in on this vibe?" I asked.

"I could but I choose not to. I don't want to alter it with my powers. You just never know."

"Well HARV is creating graphic novels now," I said.

Her massaging slowed. "That may have something to do with the vibe, but I don't think it's the main wave." She was silent for a few nanos. "I am worried."

"Why, Nat?"

"Please don't call me that or I will turn you into a pile of cheese."

"Why, Natasha?"

She continued her massage. "I have an image in my mind of a snowball rolling down a slope, getting faster and faster, deadlier and deadlier."

"And this snowball has something to do with me?" I said.

"Doesn't it always?" she answered.

"Why are you telling me this?"

"Zach, I just want you to be aware and ready."

"I always am, my dear. I always am."

"Good," she said.

She gave me a pat on the ass.

I was back, fully dressed in my chair.

"So that is why I believe the Mets can't win the pennant this year," HARV said, clearly having no idea what had just transpired.

Had I just imagined that? My neck and shoulders felt really good, so I was pretty certain I hadn't. Still, with me you never know.

"That's weird," HARV said.

"What?" I asked.

"Your body suddenly seemed to have shifted an eighth of centimeter from were you where a second ago."

"It's called movement HARV. It's in all the physics books."

HARV shook his head. "But you did not move. Your body just seemed to shift a bit in time and space. A normal person or machine wouldn't have noticed. Have you been involved in any time-space continuum anomalies lately?"

I just stared at him.

HARV slapped himself on the forehead. "Of course, you wouldn't know a time-space anomaly if it walked up and mooned you. And then mooned you again fifteen minutes earlier."

The rest of the day seemed like it was going to pass uneventfully, even by a normal person's standards. But I knew that wasn't to be the case. Trouble was about to come knocking at my door, or smashing through my ceiling, or ripping through my floor. (Yes, I once was attacked by molemen.) It's not like I can actually go out and look for cases. That would be like looking for trouble, and trouble usually has a way of finding me without any help.

I tried not thinking much about Natasha's warning. I had been in these world-threatening positions before and always came out on top. Or at least relatively near the top. I didn't see why this time would be anything different. I checked a few e-mails. Most of them could be ignored or answered later. One was from my longtime girlfriend, Electra. Electra was away on Mars colony, giving a medical lecture on some subject or another that was over my head. Since holographic calls from Mars to Earth were so costly, she was just checking in to make sure all was well before she gave her next seminar. For a doctor and top-notch surgeon, the woman certainly was thrifty and traveled a lot. Whenever I mentioned the thrifty part, Electra would note that credits don't just grow in ATMs. Plus, when you have me as your significant other, you never know when your house or car will be destroyed in a firefight. Therefore, it's best to have a good supply of credits in the bank.

Whenever I broached the travel issue with her, she would point out that people try to kill me a lot, and she hardly ever complains about that. Then she would go on about how I have used her medical skills, and her fighting skills (she was New Central American kickboxing champ in her day) on many an occasion. At which point I would usually try to change the conversation. After that, Electra would add that she felt teaching and spreading her knowledge were part of her unwritten job duties. Her debt to the planet, which she says we all save in our own way. Yep, that's Electra; beautiful, smart, tough, and dedicated. The total package. Some would say her only flaw is me.

"Thinking about how Electra is too good for you, again, aren't you?" HARV said.

"No," I said.

HARV smiled. We both knew that he knew me too well. "If you say so, Zach." He straightened his bow tie. "Make yourself look presentable," he told me. "We have a client on the street coming toward us."

"Who is she?" I asked.

HARV looked at me. "Zach, not all of your clients are rich, powerful females." HARV stopped talking. His eyes started blinking furiously, meaning that he was processing. "Okay, maybe all of them have been lately, but this one is different."

It was times like this that I wished I had a window, an old-fashioned actual window in my office. After all, what's the good of having an office on the beautiful New Frisco docks if you can't watch actual tourists stroll by? Watching the images from my security camera didn't feel the same. Of course HARV, Carol, and Electra all convinced me that it would better if my office were totally enclosed within walls. It made it harder for those who wished me harm (and there were a good many of them) to take a free shot at me. After the second or third time my office was "remodeled" (after being shot up) I begrudgingly agreed to the no-window look.

"Zach, stop obsessing over not having a real window in your office and get your mind on the client," HARV barked. "Most people would rather have a life than a view!" HARV paused for a nano. "Besides, having a computer simulated virtual window is better. It lets you zoom in and out and do slow-motion replay. Remember my motto, recordings of life are a lot more versatile than real life."

"So, who is he?" I asked.

"Uh-oh," HARV said.

"What?" It's never good when a supercomputer says "uh-oh."

"Our potential client has been stopped by the tabloid-bot paparazzi corps."

DOS! No good news could ever follow that sentence. I shot up from the chair and headed outside.

"Who's the client, HARV?" I asked.

"Don Rickey," HARV answered. "I know you know who he is."

Of course I knew who Don Rickey was. Not only was he my good friend Captain Tony Rickey's brother, Don was a retired pro baseball player. He was a damn fine one too. In a career spanning the late 2050s to the early 2060s, Don Rickey was a pitcher/outfielder for the New New York Yankees, the New Frisco Giants, and the New Mexico City Lobos. He had a lifetime batting average of .312 and 592 home runs, plus he'd won numerous platinum gloves. After his retirement a few years ago he made even more money starting a franchise of fitness centers. If memory served me well, this year he was eligible for entry into the hall of fame.

As I passed Carol, she asked: "What's going on, Zach?" When it looked like things were going to get serious, Carol would call me Zach instead of *tió*.

"Tony's brother's Don is outside being harassed by p-bots," I said.

"He's the good-looking, macho, rich one?" Carol asked.

"I've been told some people think that," I answered.

Carol followed me out the door. "Maybe I can help," she said.

We got outside, and sure enough Don was less than a hundred meters from my office. But he and a tall, well-built blonde were surrounded by what had to be two hundred members of the press. These days most of the press corps—at least the ones who take the photos and ask the real personal questions—are bots. The networks figure it's far easier to replace a machine than a human.

(And machines complain a lot less.) Of course, there were still a few actual humans in the mix—throwbacks (mostly bloggers) who don't trust machines to ask the really annoying questions.

Don and the blonde were trying to push their way through the crowd, but they were being bombarded with questions.

"What's your favorite color?"

"What's your sign?"

"Who'd you vote for in the last World Council election?"

"Would you be interested in running for World Council?"

"Have you ever dated anybody on the World Council?"

"Did you ever use illegal implants?"

I knew that was the question that would send sparks flying. Super Ultra Micro Muscle Stimulants (SUMMS) were the hot button tabloid topic in today's sports. Originally developed for military use, SUMMS had recently found their way into a much more profitable area: pro sports. SUMMS are chips that, when surgically implanted in a subject's muscles, stimulate and enhance those muscles tenfold. They are highly illegal in sports, which of course doesn't stop some athletes who want to be more than they can be from trying to obtain them. Even after it was revealed that extended use of SUMMS leads to extensive muscle damage, those who either wanted to grab for the brass ring, or those who had the ring and didn't want to let it go, kept trying to find ways to sneak SUMMS into their bodies and into their sport. It got so bad that now players must undergo random body scans throughout the course of a season.

Still, I knew Don Rickey. He was a hard work and ethics kind of guy. He liked to win and excel, but he wanted—no, he needed—to do it the old-fashioned way:

through practice, practice, and more practice. In some ways he was a bit like me, even though he had chosen a much more lucrative field. He got where he had gotten by working harder than the next guy through sheer persistence. I knew that the SUMMS question would set him off.

Don stopped trying to work his way through the crowd of bots. "Who said that?" he shouted, his face flushed with blood, veins bulging from what little neck he had. "Who asked that question?"

Most of the bots went dead quiet. One taller bot with WSNNN (World Sports News Now Network) rolled forward. "I did," the bot beeped.

Don shot a finger toward the bot, waving it in front of its screen. "I never used any sort of enhancements!" He paused for a nano, and then added, "Unless some of you consider eight hours of practice a day an enhancement."

There was no response from the bots.

"Do you?" Rickey asked.

All of the bots shook their heads, or what passed as heads, no.

Don backed down. His face turned a lighter shade of red and the veins in his neck stopped pulsating.

A smart bot would have let the matter go, but if tabloid-bots were intelligent they wouldn't be tabloid-bots.

"I'm not saying you didn't work hard at some point in your career," the bot said. "I'm just asking if you had extra help in the later stages, when you got older. If you come clean now you will feel better."

"Really?" Don growled, turning redder again, veins throbbing again.

"I understand honesty is good for the soul," the bot said.

"You're a tab-bot," I said. "You know even less about souls than most bots."

The bot ignored me. A telescoping camera/microphone popped out of its head and snaked in front of Don's face. "Do you have a statement, or should we just assume you are hiding something?"

I'd seen this act before. "Don, calm down," I cautioned. "It's just trying to egg you on so you lose you temper and hit it, giving it a story." These tab-bots were even more ruthless than their human counterparts, as they didn't have to worry about pain or death. Being machines, they felt no pain and weren't really alive. Most of their actions were even controlled remotely by a central processing unit, usually located at their home base.

"They want a story. I'll give them a story!" the blonde said, stepping between Don and the one bot.

"Barbette, I can handle this," Don insisted.

"I know you can, dear," Barbette said. "But I'm really going to enjoy this!"

Barbette stared at the offending bot for a nano. The bot held its ground, mechanical arms crossed against its cylinder chest. "Do your best, lady. We tab-bot-2000s are built to withstand Sean Penn clones!"

Barbette simply raised an eyebrow. The bot was instantly reduced to a pile of smoking bot parts. The other bots and humans started to clamor. Cameras flashed. Barbette focused her glare on them.

"Oh, this is going to get ugly," I said to Carol.

"The woman has style, and I love her outfit!" Carol said. "She's going to melt the crowd."

"What about the organic reporters?" I asked Carol.

Carol shrugged. "They'll melt, too."

"Don't worry," HARV said. "They are all clones. I'm sure the networks have many identical copies of each of them. "

Before I had a chance to even think about the consequences, let alone attempt to try stopping Barbette, it was over. Barbette reduced them all to piles of mush with her glare. I wasn't sure if I was impressed or scared.

I watched Barbette as she stood there proudly, chest out, hands on hips, surveying her damage. "That ought to teach them a lesson," she said with a smile. "And it will keep prying eyes away for a while."

I inched forward to Don. "It's going to cost you a credit or two to replace all those bots and clones."

He nodded. "Yep, but it is so worth it for the privacy," he said.

Carol moved forward and put a hand on Barbette's shoulder. "Mega impressive," she said.

Barbette looked at Carol and smiled, "I probably could have used my hypnotic breath on the organics, but the wilting glare makes a better statement."

Carol nodded. "I've seen death-breath from Shannon Cannon, Sexy Sprocket's ex-bodyguard; but hypnobreath? That's a new one to me . . ."

Barbette patted Carol on the shoulder as they turned and headed toward Don and me. "It's kind of like the Thompson girls' pheromones. Though much more concentrated and not as icky. One puff of my breath and anybody becomes my personal, ah . . . assistant."

"By assistant she means devoted slave," Don said.

"Well not anybody," Carol said. "Some of us psis have especially strong minds."

That was probably a mistake on Carol's part, throwing down the mental gauntlet. Carol, though powerful, is still young, and hasn't learned when it's okay to push somebody's buttons and when it isn't. Hint, you never push the buttons of somebody who can wilt a flock of bots. Psis aren't like regular people who tend to get weaker with middle age. Psis tend to peak in their middle, or even later, years. Carol had already gotten lucky once today, going toe-to-toe with Threa and not having her head handed to her. If I had a farm, I would have bet it that Carol wasn't going to get that lucky twice.

"Oh really?" Barbette said, stressing the r-e-a-l part of the word so that she exhaled on Carol.

Carol didn't answer; her body hunched over and she had a weird grin on her face. Her eyes were glazed over, but locked on Barbette. To say it was a look of devotion would be a vast understatement.

"Your wish is my command," Carol said slowly but devotedly.

"Your assistant probably shouldn't have disagreed with Barbette," Don said. "I'm about the only one who can get away with that."

"Well hopefully this will be a learning experience for her," I said.

"Don't worry, if Barbette doesn't zap her again it will wear off in a day or two . . ." Don told me.

"I take it you came here for something other than melting bots and turning my assistant into your body-guard's assistant."

Don nodded. "Yes. And Barbette is my wife *and* bodyguard."

"Cool." I pointed to my office. "Let's go inside where there will be fewer distractions. We don't need Barbette melting anything else today."

"True," Don agreed as we headed toward my building. "I'm already going to have to sign a lot of autographs to pay for this . . ."

Chapter 6

I led Don and Barbette into my office building. Carol followed, never taking her eyes off of Barbette.

"Pretty special lady you have there," I told Don as we walked through Carol's area toward my office.

Don nodded. "A few years ago I advertised for a bodyguard. Over a hundred applicants showed up. Barbette put them all under the table in less than a minute. I knew she was the one for me."

"Bodyguard or wife?" I asked.

"Both," he smiled.

We reached my office. I sat behind my desk and motioned Don and Barbette to sit in the chairs near the desk. They did. Carol stood behind Barbette giving her a neck rub. I thought of trying to send her back to her office, but I've dealt with superbabes enough to know that wouldn't work. Besides, Barbette looked like she was enjoying the massage, and, being the smart guy I am, knew it was best to keep Barbette happy.

I turned my attention to Don, "So what do you need my special services for?"

Don hesitated for moment; he wanted to word this right. "Somebody took something from me and I want it back."

Leaning forward on my desk, I said, "I'm good, but not that good. You're going to have to be more specific."

"My classic baseball card collection," Don blurted out, as if he were in pain. "Many of the cards are over ninety years old. They were printed on real paper. Somebody somehow broke into our home outside New San Diego and stole the entire collection." Don pulled a piece of paper out of his pocket and slid it across the table to me.

Looking at the paper, I saw it was an old-fashioned ransom note written with letters from really old newspaper and magazine articles. The note read: *I HaVE YoUR BasEBall CarD COLlecTion. I cAN SeLL TheM oN thE StrEET 4 A MiLLION crEDits BUT I wiLl GIVE U a ChANCE to better it. I wILL CoNTacT U iN 2 DaYs 4 YOUR answer. CoNTacT ThE PoLICE anD I wILL DeSTRoy THE CaRDS.* Underneath the text was half of a 2005 Barry Bonds baseball card.

"I don't want to pay to get my own cards back," Don said.

"I don't blame you," I said. "So you want me to track down the joe or joes who stole them."

Don nodded. "Once you locate him, her, or them, I will let Barbette speak to them. I am sure we will come to a mutual understanding."

Looking over at Barbette, I saw that Carol was now putting polish on Barbette's toenails. "I'm good at getting people to do what I want them to do. But I'm not a tracker," she said, while Carol blew on Barbette's toenails to dry the polish.

Don motioned toward Carol with his head. "I hope you'll be able to solve this case without the girl."

"Can I keep the ransom note?" I asked.

"Of course," Don said. "But I would like it back once this entire messy affair is over. I can probably auction it off."

I thought about this messy affair. Something about it didn't quite click the right mouse button. I had been to Don's house once before for a barbecue; I knew his security was state-of-the-art. For somebody to break in, they had to have known an inside person. They may have even been an inside person. Thing was, there were a lot of other valuable items in that home. Most of them would have been easier to sell on the open market. Why take just the cards?

"I'll have to interview your staff," I said.

"I've already done that," Barbette said. "We only have two human assistants. I questioned them both. They are innocent."

"Are you certain?"

Barbette looked at Carol, who was now massaging her feet. "I am quite certain. The thief knew our schedules and hit the house when we and our assistants were out. They used some sort of EMP device to deactivate our bots. The rest was easy."

"So you'll find who did this?" Don asked, though it wasn't really a question. "I'll pay twice your daily rate."

I nodded. "I'll find them."

Don stood up. "We'll send your assistant back when she snaps out of it," Don told me. He looked at Barbette. "Right honey?"

Barbette wasn't quite paying attention, as she was enjoying her foot massage.

"Right honey?" Don repeated.

"Yes, of course; one, three days tops," Barbette said.

"How much of this will she remember?" I asked them.

"How much of it do you want her to remember?" Barbette smiled.

"Just enough to humble her a little," I said.

Barbette stood up. "Done."

I watched Don and Barbette exit with Carol in tow. HARV appeared next to me.

"So what do you think?" I asked HARV.

"Kind of a different case for you," HARV said. "Even I can see no possible way this could relate to the end of the world as we know it."

Putting my hands behind my head, I sat back in my chair. "Yep. Seems like it's going to be a refreshing change of pace." That's what worried me, despite the fact that I was trying not to let it. Something wasn't sitting right in my gut. I hoped it was only that instant breakfast burrito I grabbed on my way to the office.

Chapter 7

I knew the key to tracking down the cardnapper/black-mailer was in the letter. These days only grandmas and a few connoisseurs use paper for anything. I may be a throwback in many ways to old simpler days, but even I haven't written much of anything on paper for as long as I can remember.

I held the letter in my hand, studying it both with my eyes and my fingers. It had a bit of a grainy feel to it. That meant it was real paper made from trees, not syn-paper made from some sort of nanosubstance.

"Can you analyze the paper?" I asked HARV.

"Can you tie your shoes?" HARV answered, as a beam of light emitted from his eyes, soaking over the paper in my hand.

"A simple 'sure' would have sufficed," I said.

"Perhaps for you," HARV said, concentrating on the paper much more than on me. "Oh, you have a call coming in from Electra from Mars Colony."

"Put her through," I said.

"In 2-D or 3-D?"

"Surprise me, HARV. Surprise me."

"Her image will be coming up on the east wallscreen."

I just looked at HARV. He pointed to left. "That one."

I turned to see Electra's image filling up what was apparently my east wallscreen.

"Hi, babe," I said. "How's the teaching going?"

Electra smiled. It was a smile that could ignite a supernova. "Good. I love the students here on Mars. So dedicated. So willing to learn." Electra looked around my office. "Where's Carol today?"

"Ah, she's doing some volunteer work for the next few days," I said.

"Wow, nice cover," HARV said.

"Good one, Mr. Zach," GUS added.

Sure, it was a little stretch of the truth, but my years with Electra had taught me what she didn't know wouldn't hurt me. I cleared my throat. "Why do you need Carol?"

Electra looked out from the screen and smiled. "I need her to relay a message to my mom. Now that Mom is on the World Council, I can't get past her assistant's aid's screener to talk to her. I was hoping Carol could help speed the matter up a little."

"Is it important?" I asked.

There was a pause from Electra, a slight smile. "Well kind of. I wouldn't make this expensive call if it wasn't. I need to know if Mom wants anything from Mars. The holiday is coming up and I figured I might be able to get her something different this year."

"When I see Carol I'll relay the message to her," I said.

Electra's smile grew. She noticed the piece of paper in my hand. "Paper? Zach, are you going even more old school on me?"

I held the paper up by a corner and waved it in front of the screen. "It's for a case."

Electra moved closer to the screen, squinting. "It looks like a ransom note from one of those old 2-D black-and-white movies you like to make me watch."

"Exactly. Don Rickey has hired me."

"Somebody kidnap one of his kids?" Electra said, worriedly.

I shook my head no. "No, nothing that dire."

Electra focused on the screen, "Does it have anything to do with his first wife and his divorce?"

Now that was an angle I hadn't thought of yet. Looking up at Electra's image I smiled. "That's a possibility."

Electra gave me a wink. "I'm not just a pretty face," she said.

"You're not telling me anything I don't already know," I said.

"Yes," HARV agreed. "That is so obvious, Zach was able to figure it out without my aid."

"I didn't help either!" GUS shouted from up my sleeve.

Electra and I exchanged knowing glances. She looked at the old-fashioned (she is my girl) watch she wears on her arm. "My next seminar starts in ten minutes." Looking back up at me, she said, "I'll leave you to your work. I am sure between you and HARV and GUS, you'll get to the bottom of this."

"I am too," I said.

"I concur," HARV said.

"We do make a dynamite team," GUS said.

"Especially now that I've helped nudge you in the right direction," Electra said with another sly wink.

"Ms. Electra, do you have something in your eye?" GUS asked.

Electra blew me a kiss. Her image faded from the screen.

Turning my attention to HARV, I asked, "What can you tell me about Don's ex, April Showers?"

A holographic blackboard appeared next to HARV, who was now holding an old-fashioned wooden pointer. HARV tapped the pointer on the blackboard to make sure I was paying attention, even though he knew I was since I asked the initial question. A series of facts about April Showers appeared on the blackboard: model for elite agency 2050-2052, married to Don Rickey 2054, divorced 2065.

"Ah, HARV, I pretty much knew all of that," I said.

"I am sure you didn't know the exact dates," HARV said, tapping the dates with his pointer.

"True," I said. "But the exact dates probably aren't relevant here."

"I agree," GUS shouted from under my sleeve.

"See, the gun agrees," I said with a smirk.

HARV took a step. He straightened his bow tie even though it was already perfectly straight. "The gun, while adequate for blowing things up, is not the third coming of Sherlock Holmes."

"Still when it's right, it's right," I said. "I need more info. Like why did Don and April get divorced?"

HARV shook his head. "No idea."

"Where does she live now?" I prompted.

HARV's head continued to shake no. He shrugged. "She is unlisted."

"Doesn't that seem odd to you?" I asked.

"She is rich, so she doesn't want to be bothered. That is normal," HARV insisted.

"Yes, but being unlisted to the public and being unlisted to you are two different things," I said.

"Agreed," HARV said.

"Yet you have nothing for me?"

HARV continued shaking his head; only now he was shaking it yes. Usually better, but not in this case. "Yes."

"Don't you find that odd?" I continued.

Silence from HARV, then: "She obviously paid a lot to have her information hidden. Why don't you ask Don Rickey?"

Now it was my turn to be shaking my head no. "Nah, I've learned it's best not to ask a client about their ex-mates unless we have no other options. We still have a few options open."

"Captain Rickey," HARV said.

"Smart supercomputer," I said. "Connect me to him please."

Captain Tony Rickey and I go way back. We grew up playing ball together on the not very mean streets of up-state New New York. We both ventured west at around the same time. He, to become a law officer, and I to become, well . . . me. Sometimes he accuses me of coming out here just to make his life more difficult. I believe that is a mostly unfounded accusation.

HARV was now sitting at an old style switchboard and wearing old-fashioned headphones. "One ringy-dingy, two ringy-dingy . . ."

"HARV, I said please."

"I know," HARV acknowledged. "It's just sometimes I process that you think of me as nothing more than your personal operator and world FAQ."

One of the many downsides to HARV becoming more and more human was that his ego was also more easily bruised. I would have to deal with that in greater depth later, when I wasn't on the clock. For now it was patch things up fast and get on with the business at hand.

"HARV, I assure you, I think of you as much more than my own personal search engine."

HARV crossed his arms and turned the top half of his body away from me. It was a way that only a hologram had of saying, *I'm not thrilled with you right now*.

"Truthfully, HARV, I think of you as my friend. A good friend."

HARV turned half his head back toward me. Yep, now he was really taking advantage of being a hologram. "You do?"

I paused to think. The sad truth was, next to Electra and Carol and maybe Randy and Tony, HARV was one of my closest friends. Not sure what that said about me. "Actually, HARV you are one of my better friends"

"When you say 'better' do you mean in abilities or closeness?" HARV asked, face now turned totally toward me. There was an ever-so-slight smile on his face.

"Just put me through to Tony!"

"Coming up now," HARV said.

"Mr. Zach, where do I rate in your list of friends?" GUS chimed in.

"I like you too, GUS."

"Thank you, Mr. Zach. There is no other person whose sleeve I'd rather be up," GUS added.

"HARV, how're you coming with bringing up Captain Rickey?" I asked.

"Patience Zach, he's a very busy man."

"Oh please, he's probably on a soy donut break."

At my words, HARV's image morphed into that of my good buddy Captain Tony Rickey. Tony looked at me and frowned. (I get that reaction a lot.) "Zach, that is just another cop stereotype," he said. "We don't all eat soy donuts."

"Indeed," HARV said.

"Thank you HARV," Tony said.

"I have reviewed their donut purchases for the last twelve months and many of them prefer soy crullers. On occasion they even splurge and purchase non-soy donuts."

Tony cleared his throat and straightened himself in his chair. I don't know what it says about me that I enjoy seeing HARV give others the type of treatment he usually reserves for me. "The old-fashioned donuts are only for special occasions. Birthdays, big arrests . . ."

I decided to let Tony, off the hook. "Tony, I need some information from you."

Tony stared into the camera, eyes suddenly becoming smaller, eyebrows rigid. "Zach, how many times do I have to tell you I can't give you information about any of our cases?"

"This is about one of my own cases. A new client."

"Why do you think I would know anything about one of your clients? And if I did why would I tell you? Sure we're friends, but business and protocol have to come first."

In case you can't tell, I've burned Tony once or twice pumping him for information. So he doesn't quite totally trust me. But he doesn't let his men take random pot shots at me any longer, so I know we're still friends. "This is about your brother's ex-wife."

One of Tony's eyebrows rose, I had piqued his interest. "Which brother and which ex-wife?"

"Don," was all I said.

"Why did Don hire you?" Tony asked.

"He has a special job that needs my services."

"Is he in danger? Tony pushed.

I shook my head. "No." I paused, "You *have* met Barbette. Correct?"

"Oh, yeah, good point." Tony sat back and took a deep breath. "Why didn't he come to me?"

"Nothing personal, Tony. This is something he needs to keep quiet and off the record."

"Zach, I can keep things off the record."

I just stared at Tony staring back at me. Finally Tony said, "Okay, I see your point. What do you need to know about April? You mean the woman, not the month?"

"Yeah," I said.

"Not sure what you want to know ..." Tony said.

Tony knew that, on some level, I do serve society in a way that he is unable to.

"First off, why did they get divorced?"

Tony smirked. He was trying not to but failed. "You don't know?" he asked. "No, of course you don't know," he said, making his question rhetorical. "April told him she was gay."

"Really?" I said, now extra glad I didn't question Don on this.

"I wouldn't lie about something like that," Tony said, and he wouldn't.

"Any idea how much of Don's cash she took with her?"

Tony nodded his head no. "None."

"None? You have no idea or she took no cash?"

"She didn't take a single credit. She said that since it was her fault, she didn't deserve any. Besides, she had a ton of her own money from her modeling days."

That was pretty noble of her. Perhaps too noble? Maybe now she had changed her mind.

"Tony, any idea where April lives?"

Tony shook his head no again. "Sorry, Zach. Once she divorced my brother I stopped paying attention to her." Tony looked up at the screen. "I can give you this much though: you can bet she's still in New San Diego."

"What makes you say that?"

Tony smiled. "She always insisted that the New San Diego sun had the optimal tanning angle for her skin tone."

I knew he wasn't kidding. "It also looks like she changed her name," I said.

"Yes, once she discovered her true self she picked a new name for herself, May Flowers."

"Catchy," I said.

"And kind of fitting," Tony said. "Now do you need any more of my help?" Tony asked.

Tony had given me a name, a city, and a motive. I was pretty much good to go. "No, you've been a big help."

"You'll get my bill tomorrow," Tony said. He pushed a button and his image morphed back to HARV. I hoped he was joking about the bill part.

Chapter 8

Now that HARV and I had a name, well two names actually, we needed to find an address associated with that name. HARV and I needed to track down May Flowers. Yeah, I know going with the ex-wife may have been taking the easy route to the obvious choice. But common sense dictates that more often than not when there is trouble, the ex is the first place you should look. Like my old mentor loved to say: *only simpletons ignore the simplest solution.* There is no universal law that says I can't have an easy case. Or at least, if there is, they haven't told me yet.

Besides that, we really had no other leads. Even if it wasn't May Flowers, I was hoping she would point us in the right direction.

The matter at hand was tracking Ms. Flowers down. I decided to start by having HARV check the address databases. Sure, it probably wasn't going to be that easy, especially since, if you have enough credits, you can have yourself removed from address databases; but it was worth giving it a shot.

"Zach, there are currently three May Flowers listed living in the New San Diego area," HARV said. "None of them are living in an area I would associate with our May Flowers."

So much for that shot. We were going to have to be a bit more creative in finding *our* May Flowers. I looked at the ransom paper. At times like this you never know where inspiration will strike from. Maybe something in the wording would give me a clue? Maybe the letter itself? After all, who sends actual paper letters these days? I'm as much a throwback to the old days as anybody, and even I haven't sent an actual paper anything in years. Real paper these days has a double whammy: it's expensive as anything, and it has been drilled into our skulls by a publicly funded mass-market campaign that it's bad for the environment. No matter how much of it you recycled, it still didn't stop companies from cutting down trees.

This ransom note, though, was an ode or sonnet to old-fashioned paper. Not only was it composed on a piece of classic paper, but words had been formed by cutting out letters from old-fashioned paper magazines and newspapers. Nobody has published either of those on old-fashioned paper for years. After all, not only did paper kill trees, but you couldn't scale the fonts to your liking, couldn't make it interactive, couldn't customize the ads, and you certainly couldn't utilize sound and video. Paper is so last century. Except of course, to the eclectic few who clung to or cherished the old ways, insisting they were purer. These people call themselves paper lovers, but are referred to by others as tree hackers.

Strange thing was, May Flowers didn't strike me as a paper lover or tree hacker. Not that she was incapable of loving and hating. It just seemed that she would have other, more pressing matters to consider, such as the best time to turn while tanning, or which really fancy, really expensive, restaurant to eat at. Still, we all have our offbeat quirks. Gates knows I have my share of them. I wasn't one to look a gift quirk in the eye. Here, the magazines were the key.

"HARV, I need a list of all the antique magazine dealers in New San Diego," I said.

"There are only three of them," HARV said. First: "Crazy Carl's Fine Pre-read Classic Magazines. Their motto is: *Our prices are so low, we practically pay you to take our stuff.*"

"Can you access their sales database and security cameras?"

"I can. They have their database open for searches for a thousand credit charge, or I can do it illegally for free."

"Pay the charge, HARV."

"Done." HARV's eyes blinked furiously for a nano or two. "No record of May Flowers purchasing anything from them. Scanning their security cameras for the last month." There was a pause and more eyes flashing. "Still no record."

"Move on to the next one, buddy."

"That would be Dapper Dan's Magazine Wonderporium. Their claim is: *If we don't got it, you don't want it.*"

"Is their database open for a price?"

"Zach, they sell used magazines, what do you think?"

"Just scan them, HARV."

HARV's eyes flashed a bit more. "Done, and nada."

"That was fast."

HARV looked at me. "I am very efficient."

"And the third?"

"That would be Don Juan's Maga Haven," HARV said .

"What's their database look like?" I asked.

HARV shook his head.

"They don't make it available for access?" I asked.

"As far as I can tell they don't even have one," HARV said. "Apparently Don Juan is a real throwback. He makes you look like Pluck Dodgers."

"That's Buck Rogers," I corrected.

"Whatever," HARV shrugged. "According to Paper-FanBlog, Don Juan despises new technology of all kinds."

"You have his address?"

"Yes, that much I do have," HARV said.

I stood up. "Looks like we'll be making a trip to San Diego to talk to Mr. Don Juan."

"Oh joy," HARV said.

"Yeah! Road trip!" GUS shouted from up my sleeve.

Chapter 9

As much as I would have loved to take a road trip to San Diego, the drive would have taken too long. Instead, I drove my classic cherry red 1973 Mustang to the New Frisco Bay side teleporter port (the port port, as people like to call them) and teleported to San Diego. There's a port between Frisco and San Diego every thirty minutes, so that just made sense. I'm an old-fashioned guy, but I'm not stupid. A fifty credit port for a less-than-a-second ride beats a ten-hour drive when you're racing against the clock.

New San Diego is a very modern, eco-friendly town, even by today's standards. They have mass-market autos to be shared (a concept they borrowed from the Moon) all over the town. The cars are all interchangeable and stackable. They are computer driven fly-by-wire. You just get in, state your destination, and your car takes you there. It's that easy. That's what I did. I didn't even have to give the address, I just asked for Don Juan's Maga Haven. Within ten minutes the car pulled up next to a quaint little brick building in one of the older sections

of New San Diego. It was an area where a lot of mega
senior citizens live.

"You have reached your desired destination," the
car's computer voice told me. "Have a pleasant day. I, or
one of my copies, look forward to meeting your transportation needs again."

I got out of the car and looked over the building.
Nothing out of the ordinary, except for the barred steel
door. I walked up and knocked. A little slit in the door
opened. I had forgotten how seriously some paper dealers treat their trade. They see themselves as gatekeep-
ers, or guardians of treasures from the past. "What you
want?" a voice said from behind the door.

"I want to browse your merchandise," I answered.

Silence. More silence and then, "You are not one of
our regular customers."

"I am a paper connoisseur and collector from up
north," I said.

"You don't look like a collector."

"What do collectors look like?" I asked.

"Older, grayer, richer," the voice replied.

I reached into my back pocket and pulled out something I always keep there, an old ten-dollar bill. It was
my first payday, given to me by my grandfather many
long years ago, after I helped him find his lost dog. Turns
out his lonely neighbor had dognapped it just to meet
Gramps. Gramps died of a heart attack (while in the in-
timate company of the neighbor) not long afterward. I
always kept that bill in my pocket as a memento.

I waved the bill in front of the slit. I heard a gasp from
behind the door. The door popped open. I walked in. The
place was bigger than it appeared on the outside. It was
one long, stretched out room stocked with shelf after shelf
after shelf. Some of the shelves were lined with magazines;
others with newspapers. They were all quite stuffed.

"Are you here to buy or sell?" the man from behind

the door asked. He was a tall, thin blond fellow with a barely noticeable mustache.

"Buy," I said as I walked past the man.

"We have a fine selection of classic magazines; some dating back from 2011," the man said, excitedly. "We even have fresh blank paper here. The good stuff made from trees."

I turned to the man. "Are you Don Juan?" I asked.

"No, I am Don Jose, his brother," the man said. He pointed at a short, darker skinned man standing at a counter in the middle of the room. "That would be Don Juan."

I walked over toward Don. He was reading a 2012 version of *Popular Mechanics,* not really paying much attention to me.

"Don Juan?" I said.

"Yes," he said, not looking up from his magazine.

"I'd like to talk to you," I said.

"So talk fast," he told me.

I adjusted my wrist communicator and pointed it toward Juan. "HARV, show Juan May Flowers."

HARV appeared in my wrist communicator's screen, "Do you mean the actual flowers or the woman?"

"The woman, HARV! The woman." I knew HARV was just having a bit of fun with me, but it still peeved me off.

A holographic image of May Flowers projected out from my communicator. Juan glanced at it briefly, then returned his attention to his magazine.

"Pretty woman," he said.

"Have you seen her?" I asked.

"I see a lot of people," he said.

"Is she a client?" I asked.

"We never tell who our clients are," Don said. "Now I am asking you politely to leave, before I have my brothers throw you out."

Looking past Juan without really taking my eyes off of him, I noticed another man coming toward me. This man looked a lot like Jose. They had to be twins. I couldn't see him, but my gut told me Jose was also coming up behind me.

"I don't want trouble," I said.

"Then leave fast," Juan said, peeking over his magazine.

"But I need to find this woman. Fast!"

Juan shook his head. "Sir, this is not some kinky dating service."

"I'm not here for a date. I need to find this woman."

Juan looked up from his magazine. He shot a finger at me. "Jose, Diego, escort this man out! Pronto!"

The two brothers each grabbed one of my arms. I didn't want to hurt them, but I didn't want to leave without the information I needed.

"Zach, I can shock them, without hurting you or them," HARV said.

"You can?"

"Yes, they are both grabbing you in such a way that I can run electric current through your body underarmor."

"You can do that?"

HARV sighed in my head. *"If you read the memos Dr. Pool and I sent you, you would know of this enhancement."*

Diego and Jose had now started dragging me slowly toward the front door.

"Do it!" I said out loud.

I didn't feel anything, but Jose and Diego did. They instantly pulled their hands off of me, each shaking the hand they had held me by.

"Ay caramba!" Jose said.

I quickly moved back toward Juan. I pushed aside the magazine he'd had in front of his face. I stopped in my tracks. He was holding a gun, a Colt .44, and it was aimed right at me.

"Sir, please don't make me shoot you," he said. "I can't have blood splattered over all my fine paper." He shooed me toward the door with the gun.

"I just need to find May Flowers because I believe she cut up some of your magazines to make an old-fashioned ransom note," I blurted.

"Excuse me?" Juan said.

"I believe she is using it to blackmail somebody," I said.

Juan just glared at me.

"Let me show you the paper," I said, slowly moving my hand to my back pocket. I grabbed the piece of paper and unfolded it. I showed it to Juan.

Juan leaned closer to get a good look. "That philistine!" he shouted.

"So she did purchase magazines from you?" I said.

Juan put the gun down on the desk. "Yes, and that piece of paper is also one of mine," he said slowly.

I now knew that May was the blackmailer. All I had to do now was find her. "I don't suppose you make deliveries?" I asked.

Juan shook his head. "I don't." He pointed to either Jose or Diego. "They do though. I am a full service paper merchant."

"Do you have May's address?" I asked.

Juan reached under the desk where he was sitting and pulled out a small box. Opening the box revealed that it was filled with index cards. Juan started leafing through the cards. He stopped. Looking up at me he said, "I do."

"May I have it?" I asked.

Juan looked at me; a slight smile crept across his face. "It will cost you."

"I figured." I took a breath. "How much?"

"That old bill you showed my brother. Is it real?"

"It is, but it's not for sale," I said.

Juan's eyes lowered.

"I will give you two thousand credits for the address," I told him. "That's more than the bill is worth."

Juan looked me in the eyes. He held out his hand. "Deal."

I went to shake his hand but noticed he didn't want to shake. He just had a credit transfer device in his hand. I pointed my wrist communicator at the device. "HARV transfer two thousand credits to Juan."

"Done," HARV said.

Juan pulled the machine away. He looked at his view screen. His smile grew. He reached into the little box and pulled out the card. Handing me the card he said, "Here take it."

"I can have my computer make a copy of it," I said.

Juan shook his head. "No. She is no longer a customer. In fact she is dead to me. Anybody that would deface my beautiful paper like this." He paused. He spat. That pretty much summed it up.

I took the paper and turned toward the door.

"That worked out well," HARV said.

"It did," I had to agree. It's nice when things go easy.

"Nobody even tried to really kill you," GUS added.

"Yes, that was a pleasant change," I said. Of course, the day was still young. I knew these breaks tend to even out in the end. What goes down easy here will be made up for hard somewhere down the road. Some time when my defenses are down I was going to take a shot right to the head or the groin or both. For now I was lucky. I wasn't going to question it.

Chapter 10

As soon as I got outside I read the address out loud, "202 Mockingbird Lane, New Poway."

HARV appeared next to me, broadcasting himself from my communicator.

"You know, Zach, once you confirmed May Flowers wrote the note you probably didn't need her address. I am pretty certain that Don Rickey knows where his ex-wife lives."

Walking toward our public transportation car I said, "True, but we're going to get the cards and return them ourselves."

"But Don wanted Barbette to retrieve them," HARV said.

I stopped walking right alongside of the car. "Yeah, that was because he didn't know it was from his ex-wife."

HARV shrugged. "So?"

"Think about it, HARV. If the current wife, who can wilt people with her glare, goes to chat with the ex-model ex-wife, things will get ugly. And by things, I mean May Flowers. That flower would wilt, no 'may' about it."

"Good point," HARV said.

"It's one thing wilting bots and clones, but it's totally different wilting an ex-wife," I added. "If Barbette turns May into a floor stain, it will stain Don's career, too. He'd never get into the hall of fame."

HARV nodded. "Agreed."

I opened the door. "So we're going to do Don a big favor and retrieve the cards ourselves."

I sat down and told the car to start. It did.

HARV appeared next me. "Good plan. Just one problem," HARV said.

"202 Mockingbird Lane, Poway," I told the car.

"I am sorry, sir," the car said. "I do not know that destination."

"202 Mockingbird Lane, New Poway," I said. I hate the way the World Council insisted on putting "new" in front of all city names. I guess I should be thankful they just went with "new," not "new and improved," which had been bantered around.

"Sir, I am a very advanced car nav-computer," the computer hissed. "I realized that when you said 'Poway,' you meant 'New Poway.' "

"So what's the problem?" I asked.

"That is a secure, do not disturb address," HARV and the car computer both said at the same time.

Looking at HARV, I asked, "I hope this was the problem you were talking about?"

HARV nodded. "It was."

"The address does not exist in my database," the car computer said.

"Do you know how to get there?" I asked.

"No," the car computer answered.

"I can find out," HARV answered.

I liked HARV's answer better.

"Can you override this car computer's controls?" I asked.

"That would be illegal!" the car computer noted.

"Can the average ten-year-old properly Velcro their shoes?" HARV said.

"I assume that means, of course."

HARV patted me on the head. "Smart human." HARV pointed to the dashboard. "Just look into the dashboard interface so I can do my thing."

I leaned over, opening my eyes extra wide so HARV would have a clear view.

"You don't have to open your eyes extra wide," HARV said.

"I must protest!" the car computer said. "This is highly unusual and just as illegal."

"Don't worry, we aren't stealing you," I said.

"Doesn't matter. I am reporting you to the proper ..." Silence.

HARV was now sitting in the driver's seat, dressed in a brown leather driving outfit, complete with gloves. He pulled on the gloves and smiled. "Silly car computer," HARV said as we pulled away from the curb. My passenger's seat reclined a bit. "Sit back and relax, Zach. It will be about twenty minutes until we get to May Flowers'."

Chapter 11

During our ride up the hills from San Diego to Poway, I had time to think a bit how this would all play out. At first glance this didn't look it would to be too hard. After all, May Flowers is a socialite ex-model; it didn't look like she had planned this out much at all. I get there, tell May we're on to her, and she turns over the cards. I tell her I'll convince Don not to press charges and Barbette not to wilt her and we call it even. Everybody is happy.

Thing is, first glances are often quick glances and not all that accurate. Some pieces of this puzzle didn't fit unless I jammed them in. Why did May use such a traceable method to contact Don? Was she just careless or trying to be creative? Or did she want to be found? I had to hope it was the former.

What was May's motive? Did she want revenge? I didn't think so, since she was the one who asked for the divorce. Did she need quick cash? From the looks of the homes in the area, it didn't seem that May was living anywhere near the poor farm. Of course, maybe she was living outside her means. So maybe she needed some quick cash, and the thought of sticking it to her ex just sort of sweetened the pot.

The other thing I knew was that there was no way May Flowers did this job alone. I don't know her, but I'm quite familiar with her type. I was pretty certain May had to have help on this little caper of hers. Hopefully it was freelance help, not staff, or worse, live-in help. That would make this card recovery extra tricky.

"HARV, what can you tell me about May Flower's recent activities?" I asked.

"She tends to do a lot of charity work," HARV said. "She gives a lot of credits to the Save the Bald Eagle Foundation Foundation. Apparently, the foundation is in more trouble than the bald eagle right now."

"Any love interests?"

"Why Zach, how nice of you to ask. It's kind of hard for me to date, since I am a one of a kind being on Earth. Though I have to admit, I do find myself strangely attracted to Threa Thompson lately. Hmmm, the super-cognitive processor and the superbabe fairy queen . . ."

"I meant does May Flowers have any love interests?"

"Oh . . ." HARV said adjusting his tie and propping himself up. "I am going through all public records images of her for the last month." Silence, and then: "Check your communicator."

I looked at the screen on my wrist communicator. There was a picture of May Flowers with her arm around a tall woman with long blue hair and an extremely well-built body. Her bosoms were so ample I was pretty certain they needed their own zip code.

"Who's the blue-haired babe?" I asked.

"Blue-Haired Babe." GUS giggled. "Sounds like the title of some old pulp SF novel."

HARV thought about it for a nano then said, "Here's something I never thought I'd say: the gun is right.

Though I think sapphire-haired is a more accurate description."

"Who is the sapphire-haired babe then?" I asked.

"That is a very interesting question." HARV said. "The only image I have of her is the one yesterday with May. Matching her face with ID info databases gives me one hit. Her name appears to be Kiana Waters. Outside of that I get nothing. It is like she did not exist until last month."

Okay, now this case was getting interesting.

Chapter 12

Pulling up alongside of the gate to May Flowers' home, a couple of things stood out. First the fence: it was composed of dark heavy metal, and it had to be four meters high and a meter thick. The top of the fence was lined with constantly pulsating laser wire. Looking at this gate left no question that May Flowers wanted to be left alone. Supporting this idea was a holographic fog that covered the grounds, totally blocking any house that may have been behind it from view.

There was a call button and a viewscreen along the side of the fence gate. So May wasn't totally opposed to guests; she just didn't want uninvited ones. I needed to get myself invited in. My old mentor use to tell me: *If you need to make an intelligent woman feel good, tell her she's beautiful. If you need to make a beautiful woman feel good, tell her she's intelligent.* To which I would usually reply: "Have I told you lately how beautiful and intelligent you are?" To which she would knee me in the groin.

"HARV I need a holographic disguise," I said, looking out the window.

"As?"

"Make me look like somebody who'd be an assistant to Threa Thompson."

"Why?"

"Because I figure Threa is somebody May has certainly heard of. Threa is planning to get back into politics and wants to hire May to be on her staff as an image consultant."

"She is and does?" GUS said.

"Silly gun, that's Zach's cover," HARV said.

"Ah, good one, Mr. Zach," GUS said.

"Done!" HARV told me.

I didn't feel any different, but looking at my reflection in the car's dash, I looked totally different. I had long blond hair, light blue eyes, pale white skin, and—here's the kicker—wings.

"The wings are nonfunctional," HARV told me.

"Yeah, I figured," I said.

"Well, with you I never know," HARV said. "I assume this is the type of person Threa would have working for her."

Looking at my reflection in the dash again, I couldn't disagree.

"Of course, if Threa finds out what we are doing and doesn't approve, she'll probably turn you into toe jam."

Once again I couldn't argue.

"So it's best not to let Threa find out," I said.

"I won't write about this in my comic," HARV said.

"I'll leave it out of my blog," GUS added.

I sighed and got of the car.

I walked up to the fence gate. I pushed the call button.

"Yes?" a robotic voice said over the intercom.

"Hello, my name is Clarence Gabriel," I said, thinking fast on my feet. "I am here to see Ms. Flowers."

"Regarding?" the voice asked.

I straightened my back. "I represent Threa Thompson's PET."

"PET?" it asked.

"Political Exploration Team, I said.

"Wow, impressive acronym," HARV said in my brain.

"And that would be for?"

"Threa is thinking about making a run at the World Council, this time as Council President. In order to see if she is viable or not she is establishing a team of the brightest minds on this planet."

"And she wants to see Ms. Flowers?" the voice asked.

"She considers Ms. Flowers an expert on popular opinion and color matching," I said.

A pause. Silence. More silence. Then, "She does know a lot about colors," the voice said. "I will relay the message."

I stood there tapping my foot gently while humming "Amazing Grace". It just seemed fitting.

"Do you really think this will work?" HARV asked.

"I do!" GUS said.

The door popped open.

"I do, too," I said.

HARV sighed in my head.

"Please enter the grounds and wait for your escort. Do not take one step past the entrance or you will be detained in the most unpleasant manner."

"Okay," I said.

I stepped inside the gate. The door closed behind me, making a very loud thud. I peered through the holographic fog. I still couldn't see the house, but I did see two big metal objects rolling toward me. I was quite familiar with these objects—they were battlebots, not your standard guardbots that security companies and most rich people use. These were the class A++ squared bots, the kind the military used when they wanted to kill something really dead. They were tanks with clawlike arms, mechanical heads, and some personality, all of it bad.

They were no fun to deal with.

Now I could tell something really wasn't right with this case. I wasn't sure how much battlebots cost, but they were worth way more than the baseball cards May stole from Don's house. I doubted the ransom from the balls would even pay the bots' monthly maintenance fee. There was more than meets the eye here—even when your eyes are augmented by a supercomputing holographic processor.

HARV must have noticed the look on my face when I saw the battlebots rolling toward me. *"Maybe she just wants some revenge on Don for something?"*

"For what? She left him!"

"Maybe she's angry he wasn't a woman?" GUS offered.

"Maybe she just wants to screw with him?" HARV said. *"It would be a very human reaction."*

As the bots rolled closer, I had to admit this case was getting even more interesting.

"We will take you to Ms. Flowers after your scan," one of the bots said.

"My scan? I am a representative of Threa Thompson," I said proudly. "No need to scan me."

The bots were now within arm's (or claw's) reach. "Do not fear. This is just an anti-hologram scan," one of the bots said, as a long tube appeared out of its head.

I told you what "interesting" means when you're me, right?

Chapter 13

"HARV, can your holographic disguise fool battlebots?"
I asked as a beam of light from the bot on the right
coated me.

"Time will tell," HARV said.

"He's actual," the bot on the right said.

"Yes," HARV said.

"I am verifying his identity with Threa Thompson's
rep now," the other bot said.

"HARV?"

"Have faith, Zach." He paused for a nano, then added,
"But have GUS ready."

"Always ready!" GUS shouted so loud inside of my
head that I almost jumped.

A smiley face appeared on the communication interface screen on the top of the one bot. "According to Ms.
Threa's rep, a Mr. HARV-Y Wall, Mr. Clarence is legit."

"Nice name, HARV."

*"I admit picking names is not one of my stronger
points."*

The bots motioned toward the fog with their tentacles. "Walk this way."

"If I could walk that way I wouldn't need the talcum powder," I said.

The bots started rolling away, not laughing.

"Nobody ever gets that joke," I muttered.

"They get it, they just ignore it," HARV said.

"I don't get it," GUS said.

The bots led us through the fog and into the house. May's house was a seventy-year-old mansion, not one of those domed homes that are so popular today. It was a long, sprawling single-story building with high arched ceilings. It was a throwback to a time when homes where made by men, not bots. Not sure if the homes were better then, but they were certainly homier. Walking through the elegant living room, dining room, and common area showed that May certainly didn't lack for anything. The home had to be worth 40 million credits. Now why would a woman who lived in this house need to swindle her ex out a few hundred thousand?

The bots lead us out to the patio. Sitting by the pool were May Flowers and Kiana Waters. May was wearing a one-piece and looked quite conservative for an ex-model playgirl. Kiana was wearing one of those four-piece suits that are so in rage today. Of course, somehow in bathing-suit math the more pieces you have the less coverage they give. Kiana had two near-strings wrapped around her knees, another wrapped around her private area and a final one desperately trying to control her ample gifts.

May sat up in her lawn chair. She extended her hand to me. "So, Threa Thompson wants my advice?"

Out of the blue an energy ball appeared in the middle of the pool. It's hardly ever a good sign when that happens.

"NO SHE DOES NOT!" a very familiar voice bellowed.

The energy ball dissipated, leaving only Threa Thompson. A very angry Threa Thompson.

Chapter 14

Threa walked across the pool (on top of the water) toward us, pointing and glaring at me all the way. Truthfully I was surprised that I wasn't instantly wilted.

"I am shielding you," HARV said. *"She is only emitting low grade energy, but you'd still be toast if it weren't for me."*

May got up from her lounge chair. "Threa Thompson!" she exclaimed, removing her sunglasses. "So it's true! You do want my opinion."

Threa gave May a look of sheer indifference, kind of like a sated man would give a glass of water. "I have no idea who you are."

May stopped in her tracks, "But . . ."

Threa pointed at May. "I understand you are just a poor innocent victim here!"

"I am not poor!" May said.

"Sleep!" Threa ordered.

May fell back in her chair, out for the week. I looked over at Kiana. She just smiled wisely. Before I could really ponder what, if anything, that meant, Threa locked her attention back on me.

"How dare you pretend to be one of my assistants?" Threa shouted.

"Ah, Threa, I can explain," I said, holding out my arms.

Threa walked over to me. I rose off the ground without her touching me. She sniffed me. "Zach?" she said. I lowered back to the ground. "Why are you wearing that holographic disguise?"

"He is not wearing a holographic disguise," one of the battlebots said. "I scanned him."

"Do not question me!" Threa said to the bot. She snapped her finger. There was a flash of energy and the giant battle bot was miniaturized to toy size. Threa stepped forward and crushed it under her heel. Looking at the remaining battlebot she asked, "Do you have anything to say?"

The battlebot rolled backward. "No ... no ... I'm good ..." It shuddered.

Threa crossed her arms across her chest and once again looked at me.

"Drop the hologram, HARV," I said.

There was a slight shimmer. I assumed that meant I now looked like me.

"Zach, why did you impersonate one of my people?" Threa asked. "I consider you a friend, so I will give you thirty seconds to answer before I turn you into toe jam." She looked at the small sundial she wore on her wrist. "Talk."

"Threa, I needed to get in here, and I needed a name that was both instantly recognizable and carried weight," I said quickly. " I knew if I said I worked for you they'd have to let me in. After all, you are the most influential being on this planet," I added even more quickly.

Threa lowered her sundial and smiled. "That is true," she said. She paused. "So why did you need to get in here?"

"For a case," I said.

Threa eyed Kiana and the still sleeping May. "Oh, good. Glad you aren't having an affair on Electra. I like that woman. She has the patience of a saint."

"True," HARV said appearing next to me.

"Very true," GUS said.

"I've heard that as well," Kiana added.

"What case are you working on?" Threa asked.

"Blackmail," I said.

"How exciting!" Threa said. "Do you need my help?"

I looked over at Kiana. "Am I going to need to Threa's help?" I asked her.

Kiana shook her head no. "You caught us. We will give you the cards to return to Don Rickey."

I turned to Threa. "Looks like we're good."

Threa was now turning red; smoke was coming out of her ears. "Baseball cards! You stole baseball cards!" she said, pointing at Kiana. "That's outrageous!" Threa curled her fist and stomped over to Kiana. "That's—that's—that's sacrilege!"

Kiana remained lying on her lounge chair. She was a cool customer. I had to give her that.

"Why would you steal a man's baseball cards?" Threa demanded to Kiana. Threa looked over her shoulder toward me and said, "You know I pitch in my realm's league."

Threa glared back at Kiana. "Talk!"

Kiana sat up slowly in her chair. I didn't know the woman, but I felt sorry for her. She leaned forward. Speaking slowly and a bit breathily, she said, "Really, Threa, this isn't your problem. This was just a little test for Zach. So far he is passing. You can poof yourself home now." She really stressed the poof, exhaling as she said it.

I didn't like the idea of being tested, but it didn't matter because I knew nobody could talk to Threa that way and live. Threa was going to rip Kiana a new one, or two, or three. I took a step back, waiting for sparks and body parts to fly.

Threa took a step back. She looked at me with a strange grin on her face. "This isn't my problem," she said slowly. "I will now poof myself home."

There was a flash of energy and she was gone.

This was a surprising turn of events. I wasn't sure if it was for the worse, but I knew it wasn't for the better.

"Impressive," HARV said.

"Creepy," GUS said.

I popped GUS into my hand and pointed him at Kiana. "Who or what are you?" I demanded.

Kiana stood up from her chair. She was a tall woman, even taller than Threa. She smiled. "Who I am will come later. If you pass the last part of the test."

Now I shook my head as I waved GUS at Kiana. "The last part of the test?"

Kiana opened her arms freely, exposing herself to me. If it was meant to break my concentration it was effective. "The first part was finding us. The next part was getting to us. Very impressive how you got past the bots. The extra part was Threa arriving. I, of course, didn't plan that, but it was nice to see. Now for the final part. "

"Which is?"

"How you do in a one-on-one battle," Kiana said.

Somehow, I didn't think you had to be me to see that one coming.

Chapter 15

I flashed GUS up and down in front of Kiana. "Won't be much of a fight," I told her. "You may be tough, but I have the drop on you. GUS may not look like much—"

"Hey!" GUS shouted.

"Let me finish!" I said to GUS. Turning my attention back to Kiana, "GUS may not look like much, *but* he has enough fire power to take down a Godzilla-II or a squad of battlebots."

Kiana raised her arms slowly above her head. She wasn't surrendering, just trying to distract me. And it was working. "Speaking of battlebots, my bot has you locked in its sights," she said slowly, motioning behind me with her head.

"Yeah, right, the battlebot's got the drop on me," I laughed. "Why not just tell me my Velcro is undone?"

"The battlebot does have the drop on you!" HARV said.

Gates, of course it did. I wouldn't be me if it didn't. I dropped to the floor a split nano before an energy beam blasted over me. I hit the ground rolling and spun toward the bot. Aiming GUS, I fired at the bot, who I saw rolling toward me to get a better shot.

My shot hit the bot dead in the middle. The shot glanced harmlessly off the bot's metal frame.

"The bot must be extra-reinforced," HARV said. "Ironically, your Velcro is also undone."

I concentrated on the bot rolling at me. It was quickly opening and closing both of its claws, making an ominous clicking sound. I surmised that since I didn't put the bot away with my first shot, the bot had decided I couldn't do it much harm. Therefore, it would kill me by hand—well, by claw. Bots like to kill things up close and personal. HARV says they believe it's good for their cred. Whatever, it gave me an advantage, as up close I could do more damage. To top that off, I hadn't hit the bot with nearly my best shot yet.

"HARV, how reinforced is that bot?" I asked.

"No way of telling, Zach. It has obviously been improved with you and GUS in mind."

I had to give Kiana credit; she had done her homework.

"Can the bot take a high powered blast?" I asked.

"Only one way of telling," HARV said.

"GUS, heavy duty blast," I said. I squeezed GUS' handle twice. Two more shots fired across the patio. These two made contact. The bot slowed, rolled back a meter or two, then continued forward. It was dented but not discouraged.

"I have concluded it can take a high powered blast," HARV said.

The bot was now on top of me. "Prepare for a beat down!" it said, clanging its claws together.

Noticing that the pool was beside me, I quickly slid into it and dove under the water.

The bot let out a mechanical guffaw. "Foolish human, I am quite waterproof," it said as it rolled into the pool.

As the bot entered the water I swam toward it, then around it. It swatted at me with an open claw. The claw hit, but my armor took the brunt of the blow. I pulled myself out of the pool.

I pushed GUS into the pool. "Are you shockproof?" I asked the bot.

"Uh-oh," it said.

"GUS, hit the water with all the volts you've got!" I shouted.

"Gotcha!" GUS shouted back.

Energy crackled throughout the pool. The bot crackled, spurted, and then sank into the water.

"I'll take that as a no," I said.

The good news was the bot wouldn't be any more trouble. The bad news was the bot had been the least of the troubles I had. I felt something grab my right shoulder. I knew without looking it was Kiana. She spun me toward her, hitting my left wrist with an open hand. The blow stung, forcing me to drop GUS. Before I had a chance to react, she hit me with a right elbow to the head. The power of the blow sent me face-first into the ground.

I've brawled a lot in my life—kind of comes with the job—and this woman's moves were as good as any I've seen. She was strong and well-trained. Luckily for me I was experienced and tricky. I reached down for the emergency knife I keep in an ankle holster on my right leg. I keep an old-fashioned luger in a left ankle holster, but this called for the ease of a knife. I grabbed the knife with my left hand, then jabbed it into Kiana's thigh. The knife stuck, causing Kiana to stop her attack and back off.

Pushing myself up from the ground, I watched Kiana pull the knife from her thigh. She looked at the knife, licked the blood off it, and smiled.

"Nice move," she told me. She tossed the knife back

at my feet. "Feel free to pick it up and try again," she said, moving back at me.

I made a fist. "I'll play it by ear," I told her.

Kiana leaped at me. I knew it was coming, but she was so fast I couldn't avoid it. DOS, the woman was good. Placing both her hands behind my head, she pulled my head down while thrusting upward with her chest. My head met her breasts, well, head-on. That may have been the only time in my life I was smiling when knocked totally senseless.

Chapter 16

I came to and realized I was flat on my stomach. I felt the pressure on my back and felt like I was moving. The floor felt cold and artificial. Opening my eyes, I saw blue water underneath my face. Poking my head up, I saw that I was in some sort of translucent half sphere that was racing across a vast body of water. All I could see for as far as I could see was water. Had to be an ocean. Which one was hard to tell. They all look alike when you're in the middle of them.

Turning my head to the side, I saw the pressure on my back was from two high-heeled boots. Following the boots up to shapely legs I saw Kiana sitting over me, using me as her personal footrest. She looked down and noticed I had come around.

"You passed!" she said. "Rest assured the cards will be returned to Mr. Rickey. Your assistant Carol will be released from Barbette's influence. She and your weapon GUS will be waiting for you in your office when you return. GUS is far too powerful for you to use where we're going."

I shook my head back and forth some, just to shake out the last of the cobwebs. "If this is what passing feels like, I don't even want to begin to think about experiencing failure," I told her.

She grinned. It was a warm and friendly grin, but also a confident one. It wasn't the grin of an enemy, but one of a person who knew she could take me out in the blink of an eye if she needed. "If you failed you would be my permanent foot rest," she said.

She lifted her heels off of me and spun to the side, allowing me to stand. It was another move to let me know she was in charge. I wasn't ready to get up just yet though. She may have had the upper hand, but I've never been one to let that get in my way.

"HARV are you in there?" I asked.

"Yes."

"Where are we?" I asked.

Silence.

"HARV?"

More silence.

"Ah, HARV?"

"I'd say we are over water heading south," HARV finally said.

"You can do better than that, buddy," I said.

"Apparently, I can't," HARV said. *"I have somehow been disconnected from all external databases and communications systems. All I have available to me is the information hard coded into me. Which, luckily for you, is vast. Unlucky for you, though, I don't have a built-in GPS."*

Kiana looked down at me. "I assume your computer is as confused as you are . . ." she said.

"Yes," I said.

"Well, not THAT confused!" HARV said, appearing from my wrist communicator.

I propped myself up to a sitting position. "What's going on here, Kiana?" I asked. "If that's your real name."

"Oh, Kiana is my real name," she said proudly.

"Missing the main theme of my question," I said, glaring at her.

"My people need your services," she told me. "But before I brought you to them, I wanted to make sure you were, well, worthy."

"And you proved I was by beating the pulp out of me?"

She nodded. "Well not just that. It was a multiphase test. First, you had to be willing to help Mr. Rickey and my cousin, Barbette. Then you had to track down the card thieves. Then you had to fight the bots. Then you had to fight me. You did just great on all of them."

"Great may be too strong a word," I said.

"Far too strong," HARV added. "You wiped the floor with Zach. Literally, when you were dragging him away."

"Hey! I was tired from taking on the battlebots!" I protested. "Plus she caught me off guard. Plus she kind of cheated with the breast thing," I added.

"The point is Zach got that far," Kiana said. "Most humans, especially males, would have either not tried, or given up, or caused far more collateral damage getting as far as Zach did."

"I guess," HARV said. "But you still took him down in under three minutes."

Kiana nodded. "Yes, but I am far stronger and more powerful than any normal human, especially a male. So he really did exceptionally well by lasting as long as he did."

"See," I told HARV. "I am exceptional."

"You are exceptionally pigheaded and stubborn," HARV said. "I'll give you that."

"Yes, those are two of my traits that I use to my advantage," I said.

"Exactly!" Kiana agreed. "That is why you are perfect for this case. You don't let anything stand in your way, even your flaws."

"If he let his flaws get in his way he'd never be able to move!" HARV said.

Ignoring HARV I asked, "So what exactly is the case?"

"I believe somebody murdered my mother, the queen," Kiana said.

Now we were getting somewhere. I just wasn't sure where, or if it was anywhere I wanted to be.

Chapter 17

I straightened myself up and looked Kiana square in the eyes.

"Excuse me?" I said.

"My mother, the queen of our hidden ocean queendom, Lantis, was found dead in her room five days ago. My sisters and I all think it was murder. My problem is, I am the most likely suspect."

That was a lot to take in at once, especially since I had never heard of Lantis. "Lantis?" I asked. "Don't you mean Atlantis?"

Kiana shook her head. "No. That's a common mistake, though. In the old days, after we borrowed men and returned them, they would always say that they had been 'at Lantis.' A few translators got confused, and now the wrong name has gotten stuck in your lore."

"You're kidding," I said.

Kiana shook her head. "You will be amazed how often mistakes like that happen." She smiled. "Our ancestors came here roughly two thousand of your years ago.

Our first queen wanted to lead them away from a XY-dominated society."

"XY-dominated society?" I asked.

"You certainly ask a lot of questions," Kiana said.

"You don't learn unless you ask," I said flatly.

"My guess would be that she means a male-dominated society," HARV said, hands on his hips.

"Exactly!" Kiana said with a wide smile. "Our planet was dying and we, well the queen mother, blamed the savagery and greed of XYs, or males, if you prefer. She had become only a figurehead on our planet. The male leaders who grew to power started to bicker and fight over land and over ideology. People became more obsessed with what they had, not what they could do. There can be no winners in a situation like that. So our great-grandmothers packed a ship and headed here. Here we have created a near utopia where all the people have everything they need."

"Your great-grandmothers?"

"Yes," she said.

"Wouldn't they be like your great, great, great, great and a whole bunch more greats, grandparents?"

Kiana shook her head no. "We are an extremely long-lived race. We age very slowly." She spread her arms wide. "I myself am over three hundred years old."

"You don't look a day over two hundred and ninety," I said.

She smiled again, this time more with her eyes than with her mouth. "That is why I wanted you on this case. Here you are, kidnapped and being taken to a place you have never heard of, yet still you are making jokes."

"Yeah, I'm thinking of starting an act in Vegas next year," I told her.

She giggled. "Yes, now I am even more confident I did the right thing by coming for you."

"How do you know about me?" I asked.

"We are a socialistic society of all females," she said slowly, "which is good. That means we are peaceful and look to settle our disputes by finding common bonds, not by using bombs."

"That's all well and good," I said, hurrying her along with my hands. "Only that still doesn't explain how you know about me. Do you pick up our HV signals?"

"Heavens no!" she said. She put a finger to her mouth, thinking. Somehow it made her look even sexier. "I suppose we could pick them up if we tried, but we much prefer the finer arts of stage plays and books." She thought a little longer. "We also have our museums and our team sports . . ."

I held a hand up. "Fine, you're well-rounded and cultured. I get that. Still doesn't answer my question."

Kiana stood there; I could tell she wanted to choose her words carefully. "Well," she said slowly. "Some of us—well, not many of us but some of us—still prefer to, well, do some things the old-fashioned way."

"Are you not quite saying what I think you're not quite saying?" I said.

"Now and then I like a good penis!" she blurted out. "There I said it. That's another of the reasons our grandmothers chose this planet. Our early ancestors helped seed Earth with life, so we knew you'd be compatible for reproduction and recreation. Are you happy?"

Actually I was, but that wasn't important at the moment. The important thing was I had gotten her to tell the truth. Even though she had overpowered me and then mannapped me I started to like this Kiana. After all, any woman that uses her bosom as a weapon is OK in my book. "So you occasionally make booty visits to the mainland."

"I do not think you can technically call them booty visits, but yes, I do," she said. "I have been visiting for over a year now. Until recently though, I have been very low-key, under the radar and all that. But I have heard of your adventures . . ."

"And you still want him?" HARV said.

"Very much so," Kiana told HARV. "I figure any man who saves the planet is a good man, even if he is a man." She took a breath as she thought about what she had said. She must have understood that it didn't make a whole lot of sense, but she wasn't going to let that slow her down. "So I figured if Zachary Nixon Johnson can save the world, surely he can find out who murdered my mother."

"And hopefully it's not you," HARV said.

"Yes, of course," Kiana said. "You know it's not me. If it was, I would not be looking for somebody to solve the murder. I would have just run away."

"So you found your mother's body five days ago?" I said.

"Yes, but do not worry. Our doctor put her in suspended animation so the crime scene is fresh," she said.

"Smart move," I said.

"My breasts may be great, but my mind is even greater," she said.

"Just curious," HARV asked Kiana. "What would you have done if Zach didn't solve the baseball case?"

Kiana shrugged. "I have no idea. I am just glad he did."

Now this was an interesting situation, even by my standards. Mannapped by a powerful and beautiful stranger from an all-female society I didn't know existed until a few moments ago to solve a murder. There were so many potential problems here I didn't know where to start. I had to admit I was intrigued.

"So what if Zach decides not to help you?" HARV asked Kiana. I had been thinking the same thing, but was looking for a more diplomatic way of putting it, since I was, for all intents and purposes, her prisoner.

Kiana steadied her glare while she answered HARV. "I am hoping it will not come to that."

"Ah, come to what?" I asked.

Kiana took a step back and leaned on one of the floating bubble ship's chairs. "All my people have a kind of special ability with your people, especially those with mixed sex chromosomes," she said.

HARV leaned into me and whispered, "By mixed sex chromosomes she means males, like you," he told me.

I looked at HARV. "Yeah, I got that." Turning back toward Kiana, I said, "I take it this has something to do with mental domination?"

Kiana sat in the chair, legs crossed. "Mental domination sounds so nasty." She paused to think of a nicer way of putting it. She took a few deep breaths, her chest rising and falling with each. "But I must admit, it sums it up pretty precisely." She tilted her head back, searching for the right words. She looked at me and said, "To be truthful, it is more mental and physical domination. One whiff of my breath and you become my . . ."

"Slave," HARV said.

"Pet." Kiana said. "My sisters and cousins prefer to think of you as pets. It just sounds so much cuter."

"So those are my choices? Do it of my own free will, sort of, or do it under your command."

"She may be bluffing!" HARV said.

Kiana remained cool. "I assure you, HARV, I am not bluffing. You saw how my cousin so easily overpowered your assistant Carol."

"True," HARV said with a nod. "But Carol, while powerful on some levels, is young and naive and perhaps overconfident on other levels." He stuck up a finger, "Plus, I would like to add, she does not have me protecting her brain."

"HARV! What are you trying to do to me?" I shouted in my brain.

"Trust me, Zach."

Kiana exhaled softly. "I would so prefer to have Zach do this of his own free will. Not only would it make me feel better about myself, but also I think he would perform better. Pets tend to be a bit—how can I say this—dull in the brain."

HARV stood there, arms crossed. "Well you don't have to permanently zap him, do you?" he said to Kiana.

Kiana stood up from her chair. She sighed. HARV has that affect on a lot of people. "I suppose a little demonstration is in order."

I instinctively took a couple of steps backward, bumping into the wall of the bubble ship.

"Don't worry, Zach, it won't hurt it all," Kiana said, walking toward me. "In fact, you will find the entire process quite enjoyable."

"Don't fight it, Zach," HARV said in my head. *"I need to analyze this so I have a better way of boosting your defenses in the future."*

"Is that all?"

"Plus I have to admit, I am fascinated by the thought of you being a pet," HARV added.

Kiana reached over and put her hands on my shoulders. "Just be calm," she said to me slowly. "I promise it won't hurt." She turned to HARV. "Now I could do this with either a breath or kiss, but the breath is less potent. Unless I've had garlic for lunch." She turned her head, cupped her hand to her mouth and breathed into it. She smiled as she returned the hand to my shoulder. "Nope, I'm good. Therefore so are you."

For a nano I considered protesting, but I've been down this road before, many times. I knew it wouldn't do any good. When superbabes and supercomputers get something in their minds and processors, all I can do is ride it out. I was pretty certain it wouldn't kill me and would, with some luck, benefit HARV—and therefore me—in the long run. Of course, my old mentor used to say, *"In the long run we're all worm snacks."* But she was a negative sort of gal.

Kiana inhaled slightly, then puffed a little breath on me. My knees buckled and I started to fall over. She caught me though, and straightened me out.

"How do you feel?" she asked, her voice ringing in my ears, all the way through my consciousness like a choir of well-practiced angels.

I smiled at her. I didn't mean to; I just did. I couldn't help myself. I hadn't felt this good, since, well, ever. Maybe the first time I had a crush? Maybe the first time I kissed Electra? Maybe the last time I kissed Electra? No, all those feelings were strong, but this feeling was stronger. It wasn't a natural feeling; it was kind of forced, like being drunk, yet I didn't mind. In fact I preferred it. This took all the pressure off me. All I had to do was relax and obey. No thinking needed. I only needed to do as I was told. Yes, life was much easier when you simply needed to do without thinking. Thinking is way too overrated.

I looked at Kiana, soaking in her every feature. She was the most beautiful being I had ever laid eyes on and I have laid my eyes on many really beautiful beings. Her long sapphire hair curled down her shoulders, dancing lightly over her breasts. Ah, and what breasts they were; they put mountains to shame. Her eyes, her nose, her lips, all cut to perfection. No, perfection was too weak a term; she was past perfection.

"My, you are gone," HARV said in my head, but I ignored him.

"Sit!" Kiana said, pointing to the ground.

I dropped to the ground as fast as I could, just hoping I did it fast enough for her. Looking up at her she was smiling brightly at me. Smiling is good. I made her happy. Happy is good.

"Roll over," Kiana said.

I dropped back and rolled over, once again as quickly as possible.

"Now I see why you call them pets," I heard HARV say.

"Yes," Kiana said. "He will do anything I ask of him."

I looked up at her from the ground. "Not anything," I said.

"Really?" she said, eyebrow raised.

I smiled. "I couldn't not love you even if you told me to!" I said.

"I take it back," HARV said. "He's worse than a pet."

Kiana turned her attention away from me to look at HARV. I didn't like that. "Now do you believe me?" she asked.

HARV nodded. "Sadly, yes." HARV looked at me, shaking his head. "How long until he comes back to normal?"

Kiana looked at me and shrugged. "Until I bring him out of it."

I rose to my knees and clasped my hands. "Don't ever bring me out of this!" I pleaded.

HARV shook his head. "Bring him out of it before I barf data bits . . ."

Kiana had a wink in her eye when she said, "Say please."

"Please!" HARV and I both said.

Kiana reached down and gently pulled me to a standing position. I leaned over on her and let her support me. Our eyes met. Hers were a lovely sapphire color that matched her hair and put jewels to shame. "Are you ready?" she asked.

I would follow this woman anywhere. I would do anything for her. No task was too great or too menial.

I simply bobbed my head up and down in agreement. In the background I heard HARV complaining about something, but I ignored him. He was just jealous that he couldn't experience this type of experience. Did I just think 'experience this type of experience'? Guess I did. Oh, well . . .

"Are you really ready?" she asked again. She was being redundant, but I didn't mind at all; in fact I liked it twice as much the second time.

"Yeessss!" I shouted. "I am ready for anything!"

She quickly jutted her knee up into my groin. The pain doubled me over then dropped me to the ground. I couldn't see him, but I heard HARV laughing behind me.

"Now that is something I like!" HARV said.

Kiana knelt down beside me. "Sorry, Zach, I've found nothing snaps a man out of it faster than a good swift knee to the balls . . ."

I wasn't going to argue with her. Not because I was still under her control, but because I was in too much pain to do anything but moan.

"I hope you learned something from all this!" I thought to HARV.

"I did. I learned I like physical humor. I am now going to download the entire collection of Earth's Funniest 3-D Videos. *I understand they have an extensive collection of men getting hit in their personals."*

"*I hope you learned something else,*" I said.

"Time will tell," HARV said. *"But I believe so. Her mental attack is a cross between the Thompsons' pheromones that stimulate the pleasure centers of the brain and a psi attack that controls the executive function areas of the brain. I could explain this in greater detail, but the details would be lost on you."*

"Yeah, I pretty much stopped paying attention after 'I believe so.' "

The good thing about HARV's rambling is it managed to take my mind off the pain in my groin. Not thinking about it reduced the level of discomfort from searing to just annoying.

"Just be glad your underarmor protects you, or you'd be able to audition for head soprano of the New Vienna Boys and Girls Choir," HARV added.

I slowly straightened my legs. I grimaced, expecting it to hurt. It did hurt, but not as much as I had anticipated.

Kiana rubbed me gently on the shoulder. "Once again, sorry."

"About the mannapping or the knee?" I asked her.

"Both, but more about the latter."

I took a deep breath. Most of the pain had subsided. HARV was right, my armor had helped soften the blow. I turned over on my stomach. I gingerly pushed myself to a standing position.

Kiana looked at me with her head tilted back. "I am impressed that you can rise to your feet so quickly."

"I'm tough," I said bluntly.

"Plus you wear heavy-duty armor," HARV reminded me, even though he knew I didn't need the reminder. But HARV needed to constantly reinforce to himself how important he was to me. I was just glad he didn't blab about the armor to Kiana. I needed to keep some secrets.

I straightened myself up. It still hurt some to put pressure on my leg, but I wasn't going to let Kiana know that.

"I can stimulate the opiate receptors in your brain to reduce the pain," HARV said to me.

"No, I can handle it," I insisted. I wanted the pain as a reminder not to let my guard down at all around Kiana.

"So, Zach, now you will find who killed my mother?" Kiana asked.

"I don't see that I have much choice," I said.

"True," she said. She turned her wrist so she could see her communicator bracelet. She looked at me. "I figure this will take no more than a week of your time. Would two hundred thousand credits cover your fee for the week?"

"I believe so," I said slowly.

Kiana waved a green crystal she wore around her neck at her communicator. "Fine. I am transferring the credits now. If the case runs longer I will transfer more money."

I noticed that besides the green crystal, she also was wearing blue, yellow, and red crystals around her neck. Yeah, I should have noticed that sooner, but it's been a weird day.

"You have that kind of credit?" HARV asked. "From the data you gave me on Lantis, I thought it was a non-monetary society."

"It is," Kiana said, "but your society isn't. We are a wise and powerful people. We understand the need to have some wealth for our visits to your land."

I put my hand on her shoulder. "You know, Kiana, if you led with the two hundred thousand credits in advance, you could have saved me a lot of pain."

She lowered her head. "Sorry, sometimes I am bit naive in the ways of your XY world . . ."

"That's okay," HARV told her, as he patted her on the shoulder. "It was worth that much to me for the entertainment value alone!"

Chapter 18

Here I was, on a strange bubblelike ship in the middle of some ocean. I was being forced (for the price of two hundred thousand credits) by a beautiful superhuman woman to go to an all-female colony that I never knew existed until a few hours ago to solve a murder. In other words, business as usual, when the holographic sign over your door reads ZACHARY NIXON JOHNSON, FREELANCE PI.

No matter what the flicks and blogs say, a PI's best weapon is information, and right now I wasn't packing enough of that to stop a lazy, three-legged bunny. It was time to remedy that situation with a good old-fashioned Q & A. I sat in a chair next to Kiana. She was gazing out at the vast blue of the sea. I decided to lead with the big question and see where that brought us.

"So, Kiana, you say your mother was murdered and people believe you have the most to gain by her death. Why is that?" I asked.

"Because I am her oldest daughter, her successor," she said without looking at me. "I would take control of Lantis." She pointed to the small console in front of us. HARV was holding his hand over it. "I have given HARV access to the ship's database, so he may learn about our society and relay that information to you."

"That's all fine and dandy, but I'd still rather hear things from your lips," I told her.

"Why?" She replied.

"For one, you're a lot easier on the eyes and brain than HARV," I said.

"Thank you," she said with a wink.

"Hey! I resent that," HARV said. "I've been told I am quite fetching."

"Yeah, well the opinion of the toaster doesn't count," I told HARV.

Keeping one hand over the console, he put the other on his hip. "It wasn't just the toaster, it was the vacuum and most of the household appliances."

"They're just sucking up to you," I said. "Especially the vacuum."

"Yes, I like that. You also have to admit that Threa Thompson and I have a connection," HARV said, pointing at me.

Ignoring HARV, I locked my gaze on Kiana. "So tell me your story, doll face."

"You call me doll face again and I will smash in *your* face," Kiana told me.

"So please tell me your story," I said.

Kiana stood up and walked over toward me. Putting her hand on the back of my neck she said, "If I truly killed my mom, why would I go to your world and bring you back here to hunt down the murderer?"

"Maybe you're just trying to make yourself look good?" I said.

"Maybe you think Zach is a incompetent dope who doesn't have a chance of solving the case?" HARV added.

I glared at HARV.

HARV held an open hand toward me. "Hey, I'm just throwing out ideas. It's not like she'd be the first."

HARV did have a good point, so I let it pass. Concentrating on Kiana, I said, "You realize if I do find you guilty, I will turn you in."

"I wouldn't have it any other way," Kiana said. "Besides, if I were guilty I would have just stayed hidden in your world."

"In our world you aren't queen."

Kiana smiled. "Trust me, I could be if I wanted to be."

Somehow I knew she wasn't far off on that one. So what was Kiana's story? Was she the innocent daughter and future queen just trying to do what's best for her people? Did she have something more in mind? Time would tell. For now, my best bet was to believe my client was innocent and start learning as much about the situation as possible.

"So who else would gain from your mother's death?" I asked.

"All of Lantis loses." Kiana said. "She was a great queen."

"Can the canned responses," I told her. "Certainly somebody or somebodies other than you could potentially benefit from her death," I insisted.

Kiana put a finger to her bottom lip, thinking. "I suppose any of my sisters that may have disagreed with my mother's politics could gain from her death. Perhaps they feel they would benefit from mine . . ."

Now this had potential. "How would your policies differ from your mom's?"

Kiana looked down and away from me. "My mother was never a fan of your world." She paused, carefully choosing her words. "Even though as queen she was allowed to reproduce as much as she wanted, she rarely visited the XY society."

"What do you mean 'As queen she was allowed to reproduce as much as she wanted'?"

"Lantis is a closed society," HARV said. "They keep the population between nine thousand nine hundred and ninety and ten thousand."

"We cannot just reproduce whenever we want," Kiana said. "We do have a sperm bank, but even access to that is limited. And quite frankly, it's just not all that fun."

"What good is being queen if you can't have fun?" I said.

"Exactly," Kiana said. She looked at me. "Do you think somebody may have killed my mother because they wanted to reproduce and she wouldn't let them?"

I shook my head. "Don't know. Don't know enough yet about your society and your people and your customs to make a conclusion like that. But I wouldn't rule it out. The urge to reproduce can be a strong motivator. I'll know more when I meet the others involved and check out the crime scene."

Kiana pointed to a tree-covered island that was coming into view. "It won't be long now," she told me. "We are almost home."

"So everybody in Lantis speaks English?" I asked.

"Of course," Kiana said. "And Chinese and Russian and French and Polish and . . ."

"I get the point."

Kiana laughed. "Yes. Our great intellect and mental abilities make us naturals to speak all languages."

Chapter 19

We arrived at a long, winding pier. Our ship was greeted by two tall, sword-wielding, shield-bearing Lantian women dressed in blue leather armor. Doesn't matter what the culture is, security people always wear blue. The door to the ship popped open. One of security people reached in to help Kiana out. Kiana took her hand and exited the craft. She turned to me without really looking at me and said, "Out now, man!"

I hunched my back and meekly followed Kiana out on to the dock.

"I see you brought a pet man back with you this time," one of the guards said.

Kiana simply nodded.

The other guard looked me over from toe to head. She was a woman that looked like she could play defensive end for the New Green Bay Robotic Packers. "Kind of scrawny, isn't he?" she said.

"I like them that way," Kiana said, grabbing me by the collar.

"What if you break him?" the guard asked.

"I'll just find me another," Kiana answered, pulling me along the dock.

"Would you like us to summon you an auto-chariot to the main city?" one of the guards asked.

"No, it's only a league. We'll walk," Kiana answered, dragging me behind her.

"A league?" I said.

"Our city is very well designed," Kiana told me as she pointed down the road. "So we need very few automated vehicles. Everything is within walking distance."

"It's not that bad," HARV whispered in my brain. *"The exercise will be good for you after a long trip."*

As we walked, the city of Lantis came into view. Well not the city itself, but a tall skyscraper that dominated our view.

Kiana pointed to the tall building. "That is the royal home. We call it the Ivory Tower."

"Of course you do," I said for lack of anything else to say. We were still too far to notice much about it, except that it was taller than the surrounding area.

"Where exactly are we?" I asked Kiana.

"The Lantis docks," she said matter of factly.

"Yeah, I gathered that, I am a PI. But where exactly is Lantis?" I asked. I really didn't think she'd answer, but I've learned it usually doesn't hurt to try.

"It's a secret," Kiana said.

"How do you keep it hidden?"

"We are in the middle of nowhere, and we have a force field and a cloaking device over the island."

"So your people can terraform?" I asked.

"You know, for a pet man you ask a lot of questions," Kiana said.

"I'm not really a pet man," I told her.

"Yes we can terraform if needed," she said. "But we didn't. When our foremothers came here years ago, they borrowed an already existing island. Far more efficient."

As we walked, I continued to prompt Kiana for information about her people and their origins here. Kiana was resistant at first, but I insisted that the more I knew about their society, the greater chance I would have in solving the murder. I learned that while Kiana's people were aliens, they were very closely related to us humans. They knew of Earth's existence, Kiana claimed, as they had originally helped seed Earth. Kiana's ancestors' home planet had become warlike and violent, though. The founders of Lantis were a group of female leaders and scientists who realized their home planet was doomed. They blamed the planet's downfall on the violence of men. They weren't speaking figuratively; they actually blamed males. Kiana said this was because males always wished to prove they were the best, that they were superior. Males want to conquer. Females want to unite on common ground. Kiana's great-grandparents decided they would be better off without males for the most part.

They picked Earth because, at the time, the population was relatively primitive, as they had no technology and would leave them alone. They also knew they were genetically compatible with Earth males and could control them with their voices. This gave them a ready supply of mating material if they needed it. It all made sense in a very scientific sort of way. Or maybe I just thought that because most of the scientists I know are mad ones.

The original population of the colony was five thousand, but they had let it double since then. Why? Well, mostly they discovered that it was fun "repopulating" with what they considered to be extra-primitive males, so in the early centuries the population swelled. Later though, they determined the resources of the island were best maintained with a population of close to ten thousand. That's where they stood today.

Just off the dock, we were in the outskirts of the main city: all rolling farmlands. Lantian women worked the fields, accompanied by a few bots here and there. There were rows of corn, wheat, and a few plants I didn't recognize. I wasn't sure if they were alien in origin, or if I just didn't know that much about plants. It could have been both.

Kiana pointed to a couple of women hoeing the field. "Each Lantian takes a turn milling the fields. We feel it not only helps us appreciate the land more, but it's good for the arms and abs."

"When is it your turn to man the hoes?" I asked. Fortunately, she ignored how weird that sentence sounded.

"Being a member of the royal family, I don't actually work in the field itself," Kiana admitted. "When I do my volunteer time in the field, I act as a director to the other workers."

"So what you're saying is that royalty is royalty no matter what the culture."

"No, what I am saying is that somebody has to lead, and I am born and trained to be that somebody."

I simply looked at her, as we walked on.

"Look, being part of the royal family means I have to wear these sapphire silk gowns most of the time I am here. Do you have any idea how hard it is to get sweat stains out of silk?"

"I have no idea," I said.

"It's quite hard," HARV said. "Though I understand that using either vinegar or nanobots can do the trick."

We walked a bit farther into the main part of the city, or community, or country, or whatever you wanted to call it. As we walked, many of the women looked at me and stared, some with approval, many not so much.

Kiana picked up the pace but turned her head slightly to talk to me. "Remember, you are my pet man, so walk three steps behind me."

"Yes, master," I said, making sure she could hear the sarcasm in my voice.

"And hunch your back and grovel more," Kiana half suggested, but mostly ordered.

"Am I man or a gnome?" I asked rhetorically.

"You are a man of course, but my man for now," she said.

"So I should be proud and happy," I insisted. "No reason why a pet can't be happy."

Kiana slowed down her pace. That had gotten her thinking. "That is a good point," she said. "I see why you come so highly recommended."

"Thanks," I said.

She looked back over her shoulder and said, "You can smile, but keep your head down and don't get too cocky."

"Sure," I said. I lowered my eyes, focusing on her shapely behind. Hey, if I was going to play the role I might as well have some fun.

"And don't focus on my ass," she added.

"Wouldn't think of it," I said, raising my head.

"You are a cad," HARV said.

"Nah, just male," I said.

"Pretty much synonymous," HARV said.

We continued our walk.

"Have you Lantians ever considered using horses for transportation?" I asked.

"Zach, we are an advanced people—of course we considered it. But we concluded that would be taking advantage of the poor animals."

"So you will use males as pets but won't ride horses?" I asked.

"Exactly!" she said.

We reached a couple of long three-story stone buildings, one on each side of the road. They looked like a cross between a military barracks and a storage house.

They were painted light blue, but it still didn't give them even a hint of personality.

"What are those buildings?" I asked Kiana.

"You ask a lot of questions for a pet," she said.

"Ah, not really a pet. Really a PI. We need info."

"Right, I forget. Sorry, I got a bit too into the role," Kiana said. "Those buildings are the living centers for the masses. They house the sleep pods, the eating areas, and, of course, the baths."

"So you all eat, sleep, and bathe together?"

Kiana nodded. She must have noticed the smile on my face. "But not in a kinky sort of sexy way." She paused a finger to her lips again, and then added, "At least not most of time."

"I may have to check it out," I told her.

"I bet you will." HARV said. *"By the way, I am taking notes for Electra."*

We continued walking past the buildings, but they were still a topic of interest to me. "So the royals have their own quarters and dining areas and baths?"

Kiana nodded again. "We do. We find it is easy to relieve the pressure of leading if we do so by separating ourselves from our people. We become closer to them that way."

I didn't say anything as we kept walking. Apparently, though, my silence said it all.

"I know what you are thinking," Kiana said. "But we really do separate ourselves to clear our minds so we can lead better."

"Okay . . ." I said, using a dry tone that suggested "I don't really believe you, but if that's your story I'll let you keep it."

Kiana stopped and turned to me. "My mother, sisters, aunt, first cousins, and I are good leaders. We each try to eat one meal a day in the common area. We even bathe once a week in the common baths."

"That's all you bathe?" I asked. I knew that wasn't what she meant, but just because I was playing a pet didn't mean I was going to be a submissive one.

"No, of course not," Kiana said. "We bathe much more than that. It's just . . ." she noticed the smirk on my face and stopped talking. She pushed me. It was mostly playful, but it still stung a bit. I wasn't going to let her know that, though.

"You do see how that could breed resentment?" I said.

Kiana keep walking. "In your world, yes, but not in our world. My people understand that we need our space at times, to think clearly, to make the important choices that come with running Lantis."

"Such as?"

Kiana held out a hand. "What plays to have at the theater. What crops to plant. What sports to suggest for staying fit. Picking the daily menus. Suggesting proper exercise routines. Deciding what goals we should pursue with our research. When to use the weather control system to make it rain." She stopped in order to let what she'd told me sink in. I guess I was meant to be impressed. "We do a lot. You wouldn't understand."

Kiana turned away from me and walked faster toward the tall Ivory Tower.

"I wouldn't understand because I'm a commoner?" I asked.

Kiana shook her head no without turning to face me. "It's because you are male."

"And you are pretty dense," HARV added.

We walked the last few hundred meters, past a majestic red stone amphitheater. Then we passed a pleasant enough looking, L-shaped art museum made from red bricks. The museum's grounds were filled with many women painting away on canvas. Next we passed the stone stadium. The stadium reminded me of a smaller

version of the Roman Colosseum. Not the new improved version in New Vegas, but the original one in
Old Rome.

"For being on an island, you have a lot of resources,"
I said to Kiana.

"Yes. We used our original spaceship to collect and
transport the raw materials," Kiana said. "We stress both
athletics and art. We believe a healthy mind and body go
hand in hand."

"I can't argue with that."

"We also have no HV entertainment, and don't pick
up any from your XY world. So we amuse ourselves
with daily plays and athletic events and art showings."

"You're kidding, right?" I said.

Kiana shot me a glare. "Really, Zach, we believe your
society took a turn for the worse when they invented the
remote control and hundreds of channels."

I decided to change the subject a bit. "Where's the
spaceship your foremothers came on?"

"They destroyed it. So none would be tempted to return," Kiana said.

"Wow, kind of harsh, don't you think?" I said.

Kiana shook her head. "No, not all. They built a perfect and peaceful society here. Here, everybody has
what they need."

"Easy for you to say, since you're part of the group
running the place."

"Trust me, Zach, this is all the people have known.
They are happy."

"Well, somebody isn't," I said.

We walked in silence, as Kiana wasn't thrilled with
me right then. I knew that was because she saw at least
some truth in my words. She just couldn't quite admit
that to herself. After all, she can think whatever she
pleases, but the bottom line was the royals here had better treatment than the workers. I had no doubt she was

right, and the workers had it good, but still others had it better. If somebody else has more than you have, it's human nature to want more, even if you have enough. I was guessing that the near-human nature of these Lantians wasn't all that different.

That was part of the reason why I prodded Kiana so much. When you knock off the person on top that means somebody somewhere is looking to improve their position. It could have been a commoner but it also could have been a royal. After all, the royals had more to gain. I had to see how Kiana reacted. She claimed to be the innocent party here, the one searching for the true killer. I needed to learn all I could; about not just her society, but also her personality. I wasn't about to make myself an accessory to a crime by helping Kiana get off the hook for a murder if I thought she was the one who committed it. The good news was she seemed sincere. The bad news was the bad ones who are good at what they do always seem good at first.

Chapter 20

We neared the double doors to the tall Ivory Tower that served as the royals' home and headquarters on Lantis. It was by far the tallest building on the island. I'm not sure if the Lantians appreciated the irony of their home for the elite being a literal tower of ivory, but I certainly did. The two blue-leather-clad guards who were flanking the door raised their swords and saluted.

"Welcome back to the IT," one of the guards said.

"We have announced your return to your sisters," the other guard added.

We walked past the guards and the doors slammed and locked behind us. We had entered into a large, rounded entrance area. The room had a shining marble floor, a big red carpet traversing its center, and not much else. It was a big room full of basically nothing. A true sign of power is when you can use space for just space.

"If Lantis is so peaceful, why have guards?" I asked Kiana.

"Tradition," she answered. "It's a great honor to guard the IT. The guards change every hour."

"So you call it the IT," I said walking into the room.

"Yes, our people actually invented the acronym," Kiana said.

"Ah, inventing IT for Ivory Tower isn't much to brag about," I said.

Kiana stopped in the middle of the room and turned to me. "Silly man, we were the first people to use acronyms. We, being a highly advanced race, were the first to realize that being an advanced race, we don't have the time to say a bunch of words when initials will suffice."

I looked at her looking at me. "You're kidding."

She didn't blink. "You can look it up."

"No, I can't," I said.

"In that case you must assume I am right," Kiana said.

Before I could say anything to refute her, three other sapphire-haired women entered the room. The only similarities they shared were the hair color and the fact that they were all striking.

Kiana pointed to the approaching flock of women. "Zach, these are my three sisters. They know why I've brought you. I will let them introduce themselves."

One of the women, a tall, powerfully built lady with curly hair, led the pack. She was dressed in a purple, sleeveless armored top, purple shorts, and high purple boots. She carried a sword by her side.

She reached out and took my hand; I could see the muscles rippling through her arms. If I had seen a man with more muscles, I couldn't remember him. She was tall, even by Amazonian standards.

"Greetings, Mr. Johnson, I am Andra," the woman said as she shook my hand, almost lifting me off the ground with each shake. "I am head of security here on Lantis."

"A pleasure," I said, hoping she would release her grip soon, as it was starting to hurt. I just couldn't show it.

I wasn't sure if this was Andra's normal grip, or if she was just trying to prove a point. After all, she was head of security and I was sniffing around her territory. Not sure she was happy about that. If she was anything like the hundreds of other security people I've met in my career, she wasn't thrilled by the prospect of my kibitzing here. I know if this were my turf, I wouldn't want the outside help. Certainly not right from the start.

The shortest of the women moved forward quickly, and tapped Andra on the hand she was using to shake mine. "Andra, loosen your grip," she said, also quickly. "He can't lend us a hand if you break it. Remember, he's only a man. He doesn't have our tolerance for pain," she said even faster.

Andra released me. She took a step back and gave me a smile; I wasn't sure if it was sincere or a crocodile smile. "Sorry, don't know my own strength."

The woman who caused Andra to release me took my hand. She was a thin, smaller woman, at least smaller than most of the women I'd seen on Lantis. Her hair was short and straight, just covering the tips of her shoulders. She had a dark complexion and a piercing in her nose, which made her nose much more noticeable that it otherwise would be. Her eyes were small, dark, and constantly darting. She was dressed in a sleek red outfit that was some kind of cross between a lab coat and a track suit. She jutted out a hand to me.

"Mr. Johnson, I am Mara, the science minister here," she said, again quickly. Mara seemed to have two speeds: fast and faster.

"Call me Zach," I said.

"I will, at least when there aren't other non-relatives around."

"Yes, in public she will have to refer to you as Kiana's pet," Kiana told me.

"Yes, of course she will," I said.

I heard HARV snickering inside my brain.

"It was Mara's idea that I should recruit you, Zach," Kiana added.

"Yes, being a social, medical, and physical scientist, I have taken great interest in your world," Mara told me.

"Well, we are an interesting world," I told her.

"Yes," she said, smiling, but looking away from me so I couldn't tell if she was laughing at me and not with me. She took some deep breaths, then returned her focus back to me. She patted me on the back about a hundred times. "I just hope your experience in your world will be able to help us here in our world."

"You drink a lot of new improved caffeine, don't you?" I said to her.

Her smile, and the focus of her eyes changed; now she was being more sincere. "No, silly! I tend to move really fast. It's my gift."

"If you say so," I said.

A third woman stepped forward. She took my hand, looking me right in the eyes. She had a warmth and sincerity to her that the other Lantians I had so far met were lacking. "Zach, I am Luca, the minister of EEP, Entertainment, Enjoyment, and Pleasure."

"The pleasure is mine," I said with a slight bow, and more of smile than I probably should have.

Luca was certainly a pleasure to behold. Tall, but not so tall she was intimidating. She had long hair that fell down her shoulders, sapphire-colored like her sisters', covering the upper portion of her back. Her skin tone was dark golden, rich and appealing. Her facial features were all smooth and symmetrical, making her very warm and comforting. She was also very calm and serene, the antithesis of Mara.

Luca released my hand. It made me feel a little sad. (I'm not so macho that I can't admit that.) "Zach, all direct relatives of the queen have our unique special gifts,"

Luca said. She nodded to Mara with her head. "Mara's is super speed."

I looked at Mara standing there in front of me. She gave me a wink and was gone. Before I really realized she was gone I felt a tapping on my shoulder. I didn't have to turn to know who it was, but I did anyhow. Yep, it was Mara. I looked back at Luca. She just smiled.

"My special gift is that I am extra charming. All Lantians can charm, but my charm is far more powerful," Kiana said.

Andra flexed her muscles. "My special gift is that I am extra strong."

"How strong?" I asked.

Andra put her hands behind her back, feigning coyness, "Once I visited the XY world and, for fun, challenged the New Green Bay Zappers of the pro rugby league to a match."

"That league went out of business after their first year," I said.

Andra grinned. "Yeah, they couldn't afford the insurance after I decimated their champions."

I didn't want to think about that for too long, so I turned my questioning back to Luca. "So what is your special ability?" I asked.

"Gift! Special gift!" HARV screamed in my brain.

"We call them gifts," Luca corrected, much more gently than HARV.

"So what is your special gift?" I asked.

Luca put her hands behind her and took a step backward. Head lowered, she said, "Ah, it's not nearly as exciting as my sisters' gifts."

I didn't think she was being coy or falsely modest. She thought her gift didn't compare to the others. My gut told me she was underestimating herself.

The words *middle child syndrome* rolled across my eyes. At times HARV had interesting ways of delivering data to me. I was betting he was dead-on with his assessment.

"Why don't you let me be the judge of that?" I said to Luca.

Luca looked over to Kiana, who nodded her approval. Luca looked back to me and held out her hand. "Please give me that knife you carry in a holster on your right ankle," she said to me.

Now I took a step backward. "Knife?"

Luca gave me a dismissive little wave. "Please, Zach, don't play coy with us. Kiana searched you very carefully before bringing you here. We know you carry two extra knives on you. That's okay, we like knives."

I glared at Kiana.

Kiana shrugged. "I did a thorough body search," she said.

"Phew, good thing you weren't wearing your classic Star Wars *underwear,"* HARV said.

"I don't have Star Wars *underwear!"* I shouted back mentally.

"Zach, I made the bids on e-square-bay myself!"

"I don't wear them . . . I collected them as an investment."

Forgetting about HARV, I looked at Kiana. "Why did you body search me?"

"Had to make sure you didn't have anything that could do too much damage. Like that fancy GUS," Kiana said. "I let you keep that cute little old-fashioned gun and your knives."

"My .44 Magnum is not *cute!*" I told the ladies. "It been slightly minimized for easy hiding and access, but it has a nasty kick."

"If you say so, Zach," Kiana said.

HARV appeared via my wrist communicator. "Believe me, ladies, considering Zach's way with people, he needs to carry at least that many weapons."

Luca glided toward me and stretched out her hand. "Your knife please, Zach."

Figuring I had nothing to gain from denial, and lots to gain by gaining their trust, I reached down, rolled up my pant leg and grabbed my knife.

"Great mother of Earth!" Andra exclaimed. "What skinny legs you have."

I ignored Andra and showed the knife to Luca and the others. It had a wood-trim handle and a two-centimeter improved steel blade. It glistened from the light in the room. The glistening made me smile. It probably shouldn't have, but it did. I've learned to live with my little knife fetish.

Luca gingerly took the knife from my hand. "Metal is so yucky," she said.

"Well, it does have its place," I told her.

Luca lifted my knife to her mouth and promptly took a bite out of it. She chewed, swallowed, then smiled. "Much better," she said, handing the knife back to me.

"So that's your gift? You're a knife eater?" I asked.

"It's more than that," she insisted.

"You can eat all metals?" I guessed.

Luca pointed to my lips. "Try the knife yourself."

I shook my head no. "Sorry, metal leaves a nasty aftertaste of blood in my mouth."

"Zach, just do it for me," Luca smiled.

I drew a deep breath. I placed the knife in my mouth then bit down. Much to my surprise, I bit through it. Much to my pleasure, it tasted like chocolate. I must have been smiling.

"I can rearrange the structure of matter," Luca told me.

"Oh, is that all," I said with a mock yawn.

DOS, if she thought that was a little gift, I was afraid to see what she considered a big gift. That was the sort of power only the strongest psis back on Earth or the Moon had.

My initial take on the situation was that while these women shared a common mother and special abilities, they were nothing alike. Andra was the strong, overconfident one. I have seen her type a lot in my life. Quick to anger, quick to throw the first punch. The good thing about her type was that I knew I could handle her.

Luca, the meeker, seemingly less than confident one. I haven't dealt with her type as much, but I am wise enough to know that sometimes the quiet exteriors only mask the raging volcano underneath. If she did erupt, I needed to make certain I wasn't downhill.

Mara was the classic overachiever. The type of woman who wanted to do it all and felt cheated if anything threatened to slow her down or get in her way.

Any of these women would be formidable opponents against me, or valuable aids in my upcoming investigation. I just needed to deduce which would be which.

Looking at Kiana, I said, "Now that the formal introductions are out of the way, I believe you said something about meeting the queen . . ."

Kiana pointed to a door at the end of the room. "Yes, come this way. We'll take the elevator to the penthouse." She looked at me. "Unless you would like to take the stairs? It is only seventeen flights."

"The elevator works for me," I said.

Chapter 21

The elevator brought us up directly to a small hallway, or entryway, that led to a pair of double wooden doors. Kiana waved a yellow crystal at the door handles. The doors creaked open. We walked into the queen's bedroom. It was a large bedroom, certainly bigger than most I had been in, but it didn't scream "queen slept here." The only distinctive feature of the room was that it had a wood theme. The room's floor was of wall-to-wall wood. I wasn't sure what kind of wood it was, but I knew it was a good one from both its shine and the way it felt firm and strong beneath my feet. The room had a wooden table surrounded by wooden chairs with no cushions. There was a large wooden dresser with a wooden stool next to it. The bed had a dark wooden frame that was covered by a wooden canopy. There were small wooden nightstands on either side of the bed. Even the full-length mirrors on the wall were framed in wood.

Lying motionless in bed was the queen. She was a tall woman whose most striking features were her thick lips and curly sapphire hair. The queen looked older than the sisters, but by no more than a few years. Two Lantian women were kneeling beside the queen. One of the women, a younger looking Lantian, was tall and slim and had Asian features. She was dressed from head to toe in a brown leather jumpsuit. She had a sheath for a sword, but it was empty. There was also a clipboard attached to her belt.

The other woman was a shorter, slightly heavier-set woman; her pale skin was nicely contrasted by her big dark eyes and her darker sapphire hair. The eyes were round and alert. The hair was up in a bun. She was wearing a long white robe with many pockets. She looked older than the queen, but once again by no more than a year or two.

Walking toward the bed I noticed a large wooden cup had fallen to the floor, spilling its dark, viscous contents all over. There wasn't much leakage, so I figured that the queen had drunk most of it before she dropped it. The queen and the area around the bed were surrounded by a pulsating electric field.

Reaching the pulsating field, Kiana said, "Zach, I would like you to meet my Aunt Poca." She pointed to the rounded woman. "Poca is the queen's personal physician."

Poca bowed and said, "I am also the senior medical researcher of Lantis."

Kiana motioned to the tall Asian looking woman. "This is Ohma, my mother's personal aide."

Ohma bowed deeply. "And that is my only position, sir."

Kiana glanced sadly at the body and pointed, "And this is my mother, Queen Ella."

"I surmised that," I said.

"Normally, one should curtsy in her presence, but we'll waive that for now," Kiana said.

"I put her in a stasis field the moment I found her.

I figured you would want the crime scene to be clean," Poca said. "I've read many of your XY world pulp novels," she added.

"Smart lady," I told her.

I gave the scene the once over a few times, seeing if either HARV or I could pick up any clues before we disturbed the scene. Nothing immediately sprang into sight as an obvious sign of wrongdoing. You didn't need to be a highly trained PI to figure out that the queen had been drinking something and died while drinking it. If I had to guess, which I didn't, I would guess there was poison in the drink. Like my old mentor used to say: *"Just because it's obvious doesn't mean it's not right."*

"Who was the last person to see the queen alive?" I asked.

Ohma meekly raised her hand. She didn't raise it very high though. She looked like a person who wasn't sure her deodorant nanos were still working.

"What was she drinking?" was my next question.

"Hot cocoa with a touch of peppermint," Ohma said. "It was her nightly favorite."

"Who brought her the cocoa?" I asked.

Once again Ohma meekly raised her hand.

"Yes, but Kiana prepares the cocoa," Andra said, shooting an accusatory gaze at Kiana.

"It is the tradition of the oldest daughter to make the cocoa," Kiana said defensively.

I again noted the hostility between the two sisters. You could see it in their faces; they didn't do each other's toenails and hold gab sessions at night. Was it sibling rivalry, or was it something more? Time and talk would tell.

"Can I see video from the room's surveillance cams?" I asked.

They all shook their heads no.

"Why not?" I asked.

"We don't have any surveillance cameras," Andra said. "We are not a paranoid society like yours."

"And even if we did, we wouldn't give you access to them," Mara added. "They would have been filled with images of the queen in her private moments."

Andra turned to Mara. "You didn't need to tell him that."

Mara crossed her arms. "I thought he should know the truth."

"How does that help?" Andra asked her sister.

"He should know that the queen is above all to us," Mara said. "That's why this crime is so unthinkable."

"You say this happened five days ago," I said.

"Yes," Kiana said. The others all nodded.

"Don't the people miss the queen?" I asked.

"Our official announcement is that the queen is finally taking a well-deserved vacation to visit the XY world," Mara said, quickly.

"I thought we should have said she is on a meditation retreat," Ohma said meekly. "After all, in a way she is . . ."

"That is why you are a cousin and not in line for the crown," Andra told her. "You don't think like a queen."

Ohma dropped her head and dropped back a step.

I stepped forward. "Okay, I am going need you to drop the stasis field so I can examine the body and evidence."

Poca turned toward me. "Are you a doctor and do you have a forensic lab?"

"Not exactly, on both counts," I said. I lifted my arm to show them my wrist communicator. I pushed a button on the communicator to activate HARV. It was a faux gesture, but I wanted to put on a good show. HARV appeared. "But I have the next best thing," I said, finishing my statement.

HARV looked at me. "Please, you are making me blush."

"Ah, yes, your legendary computer," Andra said in an unconvinced tone.

HARV turned to the ladies and curtsied. "I am more than up to this task. Don't doubt me because I am a machine."

"It's not so much because you are a machine," Mara said. "It's because you are a male machine created by a male."

"Actually, being a machine, he's not technically a male," Luca said.

HARV looked at Luca, "I assure you, young lady . . ."

"I am two hundred and seventy-five years old," Luca told him.

"I assure you, young-looking lady, that while I may be a holographic representation of a male, I am currently *all* male. The algorithms and heuristics that compose my neuron net are modeled after summarized data of over ten thousand males. Physically, my simulated right inferior parietal lobe is much larger than my left, much like a male's. I could go on and on. But to put it simply: if I peed, I would do it standing and with the seat up." HARV paused for a nano. "But being a gentleman, I would always lower it again after use."

"None of the seats on the relievement vestibules here go up," Luca said. "But I stand corrected."

HARV moved forward, passing through the stasis field. "I assure you, the fact that I think and act like a male, a very superior male, is a good thing here."

"Are you saying that males are better than females?" Andra asked. She jabbed a finger into my chest. "Is he saying that?"

"Not at all," HARV said, appearing in front of her

while also examining the body. "It's just that males think and process information slightly differently from females. With all these female minds at work here, looking at the matter from a different perspective can only be a good thing." HARV held up a finger. "Remember, I am not saying better, I am saying different."

Andra backed down. "I suppose . . ." she said.

The other ladies all nodded in agreement.

"Can you lower the stasis field please?" I asked.

"Of course," Poca said. She reached into one of her pockets and pulled out a long yellow crystal shaped like a rod. She pointed the crystal at the field and vibrated it up and down. The pulsating energy disappeared.

I moved forward to examine the body. There were no bruises or signs of trauma on her face. I started to pull the covers back to reveal more of her body.

"What are you doing?" Andra screamed. She leaped forward, grabbing me by the shoulder and spinning me toward her.

"I need to examine her entire body," I said in my calming voice.

Andra made a fist with her right hand, "I will not allow that. You are a man!"

She swung that fist wildly. I ducked under the punch. My initial instinct was to spring back and give her a HARV-enhanced punch to the solar plexus. I fought back that reaction. Hitting her would only spur her and the others on. I needed to gain their trust first, and then their respect. Instead of punching, I curled and quickly moved forward, darting toward Kiana for cover. I reached Kiana, slipped behind her, and then spun around.

Andra was coming at me, fists clenched. "Fight like a woman, you coward."

Andra lunged at me, but was cut off by an elbow to the nose from Kiana. The blow drove Andra to her knees. She looked up, grabbing her nose to halt the rush of blood.

Kiana shot a finger at her. "Zach is here to help us. We must cooperate!" she said sternly to Andra.

"But he is a man, and she is the queen. He may not look at her body without permission."

"What if I have HARV do it?" I asked. I was looking at Andra, but addressing all the women.

"I don't know," Andra said. "He's still kind of man, he said so himself."

"'Kind of a man' isn't a man," I said.

"Believe me, Andra," HARV told her. "I have no carnal interest in your mother the queen. I will be looking purely for signs of a crime."

Andra stood up slowly, one hand still cupped to her nose. "I don't know . . ."

"I vote it is okay," Kiana said.

"I agree," Mara said.

"I do too," Luca said.

"I see no other way," Poca said.

"I agree with the majority," Ohma said.

"The sisters, aunt, and cousin have spoken," Kiana said, looking at Andra, but really addressing me. "HARV may examine the body." Kiana turned to me. "Zach, spin around and cover your eyes."

I did as I was told.

"Okay, HARV, you may perform your examination now."

I couldn't see HARV but I could hear him.

"Please remove the covers," HARV said. There was a slight pause, then: "I am scanning her upper right quadrant, now her upper left quadrant, now her lower right quadrant, now her lower left. No signs of trauma detected there. Now scanning her right upper extremity, now left upper, now left lower, now right lower. Once again, no signs of trauma. Please turn her over."

There was a slight pause. I heard some shuffling, then HARV started talking. "Now examining her dorsal side. Now rescanning her upper right quadrant . . ."

"HARV, no need for the play-by-play. Just give us the final score," I said.

"If you insist," HARV said.

"Oh, men and their sports talk," Mara said.

A few seconds of silence, then: "My scan is complete. I find no evidence of physical harm," HARV said. "Please cover the body again."

I heard a little more rustling.

"You can turn around now, Zach," HARV told me.

I turned and looked at the queen's face. She seemed content, happy. There were no signs that she'd been surprised or startled. I pointed to the cocoa on the floor. "Examine the cocoa for poisons."

"I did that before I put the queen into stasis," Poca told me. "I found nothing. Just as my examination of her body revealed no physical harm."

HARV walked over and dipped his finger into the cocoa. "My analysis agrees. There is no known poison here."

I turned to Poca. "So why are you so sure she was murdered? Why can't this be from natural causes?"

"Because she was barely a thousand years old and didn't look at day over eight hundred. Nobody here just dies," Poca said. The other women nodded in agreement. "It had to be foul play."

"So do you people live forever?" I asked.

All the woman and HARV laughed at me. "No, silly man," Mara said. "Once we reach a certain age and have seen, learned, and experienced all we wish to, we will ourselves into a lasting sleep."

I pointed at the queen and said, "How do you know she didn't do that?"

Kiana stepped forward and looked me straight in the

eyes. "Because she is the queen. Queens do not do that. Not without telling the people."

I couldn't argue with that logic. Largely because there didn't seem to be much logic there to argue with.

Luca stepped forward and gently took my hand. "Zach, we know it doesn't seem like murder, but it must be murder. That is why we brought you here. Not only because we needed an unbiased opinion from someone with nothing to gain but the truth, but also because you are much more experienced with this sort of thing than we are. I know you can find the killer. Please tell me you can." She spoke as much with her deep searching eyes as she did her mouth.

Looking into those eyes, I knew I couldn't let her, or them, down. I had to figure out who did this and how they did this. I had two courses of action: I could look for a motive and try to match that motive to a person. Once we got the who, the how could fall in place. Or, I could take the opposite approach: find the mode of killing, then match that to the person most likely to use that mode. I decided for now to follow both lines to see where they brought me.

"Who would want to kill the queen?" I asked.

"Nobody," Kiana said.

"She was loved by all," Luca said.

"She was a great queen," Mara said.

Okay, looking for the who wasn't going to be easy at all. If I was going to have any chance at all of solving this case, any chance of finding out whether there *was* a case, I was going to have to get to know more of Lantis.

"I need to see more of your society and your people," I said.

"That can be arranged," Kiana said. "I will take you around as my pet man, but for now we could both use some rest. It has been a long day.

"So it is settled. I will have Ohma take you to your

quarters, and then I will come for you in the morning. Is that acceptable?"

"Quite," I said.

The day had been long, even though I was out cold for some it. I could use the downtime to put some of the pieces together. I wouldn't be able to solve the entire puzzle, but hopefully I would get the edges—which always makes filling in the middle easier.

Chapter 22

Ohma led me to my room, a floor below the queen's. The room was simple as can be: a bed on one side, a shower, toilet, urinal, and sink on the other, all surrounded by windowless, dark blue walls. One of the walls had a few pegs where I guess males were supposed to put their clothing.

"This is where Kiana's pet men stay," Ohma said as we walked into the room. "It is just down the hall from her room."

"Nice," I said, cynically.

Ohma picked up on the tone of my voice. "It's not meant to be long-term, Zach. It's just a place for her men to rest and clean when, and if, she needs a break from them."

I walked over and sat on the bed. "I get it, they're supposed to be so honored they're with Kiana, they don't mind the conditions."

Ohma shook her head. "Nah, she just wears 'em down so much, they never even notice." She looked at her watch/communicator. "I have many duties to attend to, planning the funeral." Ohma started toward the door. She looked back at me and asked, "Do you need anything?"

"I could use a little something to eat," I told her.

Ohma reached into her pocket and handed me a couple of long thin wafers. "The kitchens are closed now, but these energy wafers should tide you over until breakfast."

I took the wafers. "Thanks."

Ohma pointed to the sink in the bathroom. "If you need water, the sink works just fine." She paused. "Do you need anything else from me?"

"Just a little information. You are a cousin, correct?"

Ohma nodded. "Yes."

Okay, so she wasn't all that talkative. "Is Poca your mother?"

Ohma shook her head. "No, Poca is ... well, the queen's youngest sister. The queen never allowed her to bear children. The queen insisted Poca was too important as is."

"So where is your mother?" I asked.

"Once the queen had her daughters, my mother knew she would never be queen. So she asked the queen's permission to leave the Ivory Tower and live as one of the people."

"Really?"

Ohma shrugged. "I have no reason to lie to you, Mr. Johnson. My mother, Juuda, figured that if she couldn't be queen, she might as well live the simple life."

"But you stay here in the Ivory Tower with the royal family."

"I am one of the royal family. I feel it is my duty to honor my duty." Ohma said.

"You are a woman of honor," I told her.

She smiled. "I like to think so. I am loyal to my heritage. Besides, I have to admit, I like having my own room and being—well—special."

If Ohma was anything, she was honest and straight. I liked that.

Ohma looked at me guilelessly. "Do you have any other questions for me?"

"Not right now," I said.

"Am I a suspect?" she said.

This caught me off guard. Most people don't like to bring themselves up as possible suspects, as it might make them look guilty. Ohma wasn't most people.

"Truthfully, right now everybody is a suspect," I said.

Ohma lowered her head. "I understand."

"But right now you are way down my list," I assured her.

Ohma looked up at and gave me a weak smile. "Do you need anything else?"

Now I shook *my* head. "For now I'm fine."

"I will check in on you from time to time to assess your needs."

Ohma gave me a polite bow, then left the room, closing and locking the door behind her.

Though I wasn't thrilled about being locked in, it was good that I was alone. HARV and I needed to talk, and it would be best if it were done in private.

"What have you got for me, HARV?" I asked.

HARV appeared from my wrist communicator, sitting on the bed, legs crossed. "No need for mental communication, Zach. I have scanned the room and there are no eavesdropping devices."

"Are you sure, HARV?"

"As sure as I am that the one thousandth prime number is seven thousand nine hundred nineteen," HARV said.

"Can't you ever just say yes?"

"Apparently not," HARV smirked.

"So what have you got for me?" I repeated, this time out loud.

"Good news which is interesting and that may lead to bad news," HARV answered.

I sighed. I hated when HARV did commentary on his information. Of course, that was better than when he did commentary on my life. "What's the good news?" I asked.

"Ohma keeps quite complete records of the queen's comings and goings and her meetings. And for all of Kiana's talk about this being an open society, for the last three days of her life, the queen only met with the six women you've met so far."

"So one of them is most likely the killer. If she was killed," I said.

HARV smiled. He knew something. "Oh, she was killed. I lied about the cocoa."

"Why didn't you tell me sooner?" I asked.

HARV shook his head. "Because I was afraid if I told you in the presence of the ladies your reaction, however subtle, might tip off the killer that we were on to her."

I had to give HARV credit there—he was right. I've been in the business a long time, and I'm still alive with all my original body parts, so I'm good. But, I'm also human, and there may be times when I make a subtle facial tick or gesture that may reveal my true feelings to a well-trained mind. We all make these subtle motions hundreds of times a day. I stay ahead of the game by reading them in others. That still doesn't mean others can't read them in me.

"So what was the poison?" I asked.

HARV lifted a finger. "This is the interesting news. There were traces of XTC-69 in the cocoa. It's only made in one lab on Earth . . ." HARV paused for suspense.

I hated when he did that. "Randy's lab in New Frisco," I blurted, killing the suspense.

HARV frowned. *He* hated when *I* did that. "Yeah." He paused. "I checked Randy's records over the last few months, and there is no record of any of our ladies being there."

"But ..." I said.

"But since Randy is my designer, he is able to shield certain things from me, unless I really poke around. So it is quite possible that one of them visited him."

I knew Randy well. He had a big weakness for beautiful babes. I guess we all do, but in Randy's case it was extra bad. Breasts were like kryptonite to his common sense.

"We do know Kiana has been in the general area," I said.

HARV nodded. "Hence, the interesting news. I currently rate her as the most likely killer. She had the motive: becoming queen. She had the means. It all adds up."

"Sure, it adds up, but who knows who's been feeding us the numbers," I told him. "Try to contact Randy. See if you can get better data from him."

"Now that won't be easy," HARV said. "The Lantis force field blocks all incoming and outgoing transmissions."

"I thought you specialized in doing what others couldn't," I told HARV.

"You are just flattering me," HARV said.

"True."

"I have to admit I like it," HARV said. He sighed. "I am starting to think I have been connected to your brain for too long."

I smiled. "I know. That's why it allows you to think outside of the cube."

HARV looked at me. "Zach, sometimes you think so far outside of the cube, you and the cube aren't even in the same time zone." A slight delay. "DOS, you're not even on the same continent." Another pause, then a smile. HARV lifted a finger. "I may have found a workaround."

"I knew you would," I said, patting him the shoulder.

"Oh, interesting just got more interesting. And by interesting, I mean bad for you," HARV said.

"You usually do. Did you get through to Randy?"

HARV shook his head no. "Unlike you, I am able to process many streams of incoming information. While I haven't been able to ping the outside world, or worlds, yet, I have found the queen's online diary."

"She kept an online diary?" I said.

"Why are you surprised?"

"I thought she'd be more of a 'write it on good old-fashioned paper' type of queen."

"Zach, they aren't primitives," HARV said. "Every queen writes in this diary to share their knowledge with those who follow. From what I gather, she used a crystal to record the information, or wisdom, on an e-tablet."

"So what did you find, buddy?"

"Most of it is quite boring. Tips like: *A queen must love herself to love her people. Never eat too many onions before a formal dinner. Don't forget the people's wishes are important but your wishes are more important. You are born to lead, so lead.*"

"Yeah, words to rule by," I said.

"But it's the last phrase she wrote that sticks out," HARV said. He paused again, knowing there was no way I could ruin his suspense this time.

"Which is?"

"She wrote in big bold letters: *I DON'T TRUST MY OLDEST DAUGHTER.*"

There it was. All the signs pointed to Kiana, my client. Problem was, they were too obvious. Sometimes the obvious choice is the right choice. There are times when, yes, the butler with the bloody knife in his hand *is* the killer. I just needed to figure out if this was one of those times.

I laid down on the bed. I didn't realize how tired I was

until my head hit the pillow. It wasn't a very big, comfy pillow; but it still felt good. Getting beat up, knocked out, and dragged to unfamiliar society to solve a murder is surprisingly tiring. And I still had to figure out if Kiana really wanted me to solve this murder or just to somehow find a way of convincing people she was innocent.

I wanted to yawn. I tried to fight it off, but the harder I fought, the greater the urge to yawn. I gave in and felt better. Some fights are more worthwhile than others.

"HARV, do your best to contact Randy. We need to know if any of the ladies have been there," I said.

"Working on that now," HARV said. "What are we going to do if it turns out Kiana is the killer?"

I stretched out on the bed and kicked my shoes off. "We'll leap over that ravine when we come to it."

If Kiana was the killer, then I was going to need allies here. That shouldn't prove too difficult. Luca seemed like the type who wanted to do the right thing. Andra seemed like the type who wanted to do whatever Kiana didn't want. So she would certainly be up for putting Kiana down.

Of course, first I had to determine if Kiana really was the guilty party. She had the motivation and the means. Her argument, that she would never have hired me to solve the crime if she was the killer, didn't hold water. If she truly wanted to take a shortcut to the top, the kill and run technique wouldn't work. She would need me, or somebody like me, to get her off the hook. And if that was true then she was simply using me. I fell asleep thinking that if she was using me to help her cover up a crime, then she was in for a nasty unveiling.

Chapter 23

I woke up the next morning. For the first few nanos I didn't recall where I was. The bed was cold and stiff, not like my bed at home. Then I remembered I was in Lantis. A place that, a mere twenty-four hours ago, I didn't even know existed. I felt a body by my side. That wasn't right; Electra wasn't here.

My first instinct was to go for the gun I always keep under my pillow. Not my pillow, not my bed. The gun wasn't there. I quickly reached down to my leg to go for my first knife. Ah, DOS! Luca had turned that into chocolate. I reached for my backup knife. It was missing. My hand darted to my other leg. I searched for my backup .44-Mag-version 2A. It wasn't there. DOS! I don't sleep with that gun.

I rolled out of bed then sprang to my feet. My old-fashioned weapons may have been gone, but I still had HARV wired to my brain. I was sure we could come up with something to give this intruder as much trouble as he was planning to give me.

"HARV, are you there?"

Before HARV could answer, I saw that my intruder was Kiana, who was now propping herself up on an elbow on my bed. She was balancing my backup knife on a finger. My .44-Mag was next to her.

"Wow, talk about weird morning wake up rituals," Kiana told me.

"Of course I am here, Zach. Why do you ask?" HARV said.

"You could have warned me about Kiana," I told him.

"I would have, but she didn't appear to be a threat, so I wanted to study her studying you. I thought you would have been pleased."

His logic may have made sense, but I still didn't like it. I shot a finger at the smiling Kiana, who was lying there like an overconfident cat that had just gotten the jump on a drunken mouse. "What's the meaning of this?"

She shrugged with one shoulder. "No meaning. I just like watching men sleep. You are all so cute with your snoring and all."

"I don't snore," I said.

"Would you like a replay?" HARV said, not proving to be helpful at all. At least not to me.

"I don't snore loud," I said.

Kiana laughed as she rolled off of my bed to her feet. Pointing to the shower she said, "It's late by our standards. One hour after sunrise. Shower, then I will feed you and show you around." She pointed at a set of clothes hanging on the wall. "I had Ohma bring you suitable clean attire."

Stretching, I told her: "I don't need clean attire. My gray PI suit has nanotechnology that always keeps it clean."

"Perhaps but it is still not suitable," Kiana told me.

I walked over and examined the outfit. It was blue shorts with a sleeveless blue vest. There was also a pair of worn leather sandals on the floor. That was it. I grabbed the hanger and showed the outfit to Kiana. "You expect me to wear this?"

"Standard pet man attire," she said.

I had three problems with this attire: First, it was ugly as sin. Second, it was way too revealing. It made me look easy. I am not easy. And third, and probably most important, wearing shorts and no sleeves would certainly expose the underarmor I wear and weapons I carry.

I put the outfit back on the hanger. "I can't wear this," I said.

"You can and you will," Kiana said, in a strong, forceful voice.

"I can and I will," I repeated.

"After you undress and shower," Kiana added, once again in the strong forceful voice.

"After I undress and shower," I repeated.

"HARV she's using the voice on me," I said.

"I know."

"I thought you were coming up with some defense for that," I said as I dropped my pants.

"I am," HARV insisted. *"I just don't want to tip Kiana off. I figure you need a shower and you need to blend in. So no use trying to break her control of you now."*

"What about my underarmor?" I asked, pulling my shirt over my head.

"As always, we will find workarounds," HARV assured me.

I turned and headed to the shower. I knew Kiana was watching me. I knew HARV was getting a kick out of this, at least on some level. I knew Electra wouldn't approve, but she would also understand I had no choice. Like my old mentor used to say: *"If you can't swallow your pride then you'll choke on this job."*

I straightened my back and walked as purposefully as I could. I tried to walk as if to say *I know you are watching and I don't care.* But I wasn't flaunting my stuff, because that's something a true gentleman never does. Besides, HARV was probably recording this and would replay it for Electra.

I reached the shower. There was only one knob. I turned it, and I got doused with cold water. Not the best feeling, but it did wake me up.

"Here on Lantis we believe in only cold showers," Kiana called to me. "It's good for the soul."

If that was their reasoning for an island of all women always taking cold showers I wasn't going to argue. At least not now. I quickly lathered up and rinsed. I got out of the shower and started toweling off. Looking at Kiana without really looking at her, I saw she had a smirk on her face. Not sure if she was smirking at me, or with me. I choose to believe the latter.

"Hurry up, pet man," Kiana said. "I am getting hungry."

"Still not really your pet man," I said as I grabbed my clothing—such as it was.

"Just getting into character," Kiana said. "Besides, you could be if I so desired it."

Taking the hint, I hurriedly put on my pants and shirt. At least the cloth wasn't scratchy. I slipped into the sandals.

Kiana examined me. She pointed at my wrist communicator. "You can't use that here."

"It's how I communicate with HARV," I said.

She shook her head. "No. My people here know men only serve one purpose: to serve us. You have no need to communicate with others."

"But I need to communicate with HARV," I insisted.

Kiana walked up to me and gently stroked my arm. Leaning over, she whispered in my ear, "Just use the interface in your brain."

"Oh, right, you know about that," I said.

Kiana grinned. "Of course I do."

I slid the communicator band off my wrist and let it drop to the floor. Strangely, now, for the first time, I felt naked.

Kiana lead me by hand down the hallway to her room. Her room was about the same size as the queen's, maybe a little smaller. It was also much softer and warmer. The floor was blanketed with thick red carpet. The windows all had long, red silk drapes. The bed was a mega king-size canopy with thick plush red and pink covers. There was even a stuffed teddy bear sitting there, leaning against the pillows. The room screamed feminine so loudly a deaf man would have to cover his ears. This was a bit of a surprise to me. I never pegged Kiana as a girly girl.

Kiana took my hand and led me over to a table in the middle of the room. The table was covered with a nice, white linen cloth. On top of the cloth was every type of breakfast food a man or Lantian could want: pancakes, bacon, sausage, eggs, ham, hash browns, and fresh fruit.

Kiana pointed to the table with an open hand. "I take it you will find something here you like."

I pulled up a chair and sat down. I hadn't realized how hungry I was until I saw, and more important, smelled the food. None of the senses are as primal as smell. Smell really tells it like it is. It doesn't analyze. It doesn't have a lot of gray areas. Smells are usually bad, which means "avoid," or good, which means "go for it." I was going to go for it.

I looked up at Kiana. "You really know how to make a man happy," I said.

"In many more ways than just this," she said, sitting down beside me.

Kiana picked up a sausage with her fingers. She put it to her lips and slowly but surely sucked it in. She began chewing, wriggling in her seat just enough to make me squirm. I don't know what I found more impressive and appealing, the fact that she could inhale a sausage, or the fact that she seemed to enjoy it so much.

"Keep your mind on the ball, big guy," HARV said to me. *"Okay maybe ball wasn't the best choice of words there. Keep your head in the game. Okay, maybe head wasn't the best choice of words either."* HARV inhaled deeply, and then shouted, *"ELECTRA!"*

That worked. I looked Kiana right in the nose. (Her nose was her least sexy part.) "You know, right now I have to consider you to be my number one suspect," I told her.

She picked up another sausage and dangled it in front of her. She bit of the top off it, tilted her head, then dropped the remaining part into her mouth. She looked at me. "I know."

"No amount of flirting is going to stop me from finding the killer," I said.

"I know," she repeated. "That's why you need to start learning about us quickly. Soon the people will ask about the queen and discover she is dead. You will not be the only one to point an accusing finger at me."

I took a bite of toast. "Why is that? Simply because you're the oldest and next in line?"

Kiana looked away. "If only it were that easy." She took a sip of orange juice. "My mother and I have had some very public debates in the past."

"Over?" I asked.

"The XY world," Kiana said. "Your world."

"Yeah, I kind of figured that. Who was pro and who was con?"

"I wanted to establish relations with your people. We've been in isolation long enough. We are strong, powerful women. We have no fear of being dominated and ruined by men again."

I took a bite of bacon. "So your mom had other ideas?"

Kiana looked down. "She thought you would corrupt us. She liked the status quo."

"Most people in charge do," I said.

"How true," Kiana told me. "You are wise, for a man. My mother was afraid I might try to take power early."

"And would you consider it?" I prodded.

Kiana looked me in the eyes. "No."

I wasn't sure if Kiana was guilty or not. I hoped she wasn't. My gut was telling me she wasn't, but I wasn't sure if big breasts and/or a big paycheck were influencing my gut. I am only human, and male. If I was going to find Kiana innocent, I needed to start zeroing in on other potential killers.

"Who is next in line to the throne after you?" I asked.

"Luca," she said.

"Do you trust her?" I asked.

"Of course. She is my sister."

I looked at her with a lifted eyebrow. "Yeah, sisters never fight."

"Of course we fight. We're Lantians. We're fiery, independent spirits. But you've met Luca. She's as pure as virgin snow before it hits the ground."

My first thoughts on Luca mirrored Kiana's. The catch is that sometimes a sweet and innocent exterior is masking a much darker, more dangerous interior. I needed to make sure that Luca wasn't just a really good actor.

"You know it had to be you or one of your sisters or relatives," I said.

Kiana nodded. "Yeah."

"So which one of your relatives is more likely to kill your mom?" I asked. I didn't expect a direct answer, but sometimes you can learn a lot from an indirect answer or from no answer at all.

She looked me in the eyes. "I don't know, Zach. That's why I brought you here."

Surely by now Kiana had an idea which one of her sisters was more capable of murder than the others. I wasn't sure why she wasn't willing to rat her out.

Chapter 24

Kiana and I finished eating, and she took me for a tour of the city. The tour was actually at least as much to learn about Kiana's personality as to learn about the city itself. Still, why accomplish only one thing when you can do two at once?

I had to give Kiana credit. On the outside at least, the city of Lantis did seem much like a utopia. The streets were clean, well manicured, and lined with fresh flowers and tall flowering trees. All of the buildings were made either from stone or wood, and had to be a couple thousand years old; but like the women who built them, none of the buildings showed cracks in their facades or other signs of aging. Everybody we passed greeted us with a hearty hello and a bow of respect.

Looking around, I saw women and low-level bots working together, painting and touching up the city's many smaller museums. None of the women were as tall as the royal family, but they all seemed extremely healthy and in great shape.

"As you can see, we are all very fit," Kiana said.

"I noticed."

"It is from a proper exercise program and diet. Poca, Mara, and their aides have nearly perfected the food, so we get the optimal benefit from it."

"Very good," I said.

Kiana pointed to the building being worked on. "That is museum of sculpture. Do you wish to go in there?"

"Ah, not really," I said. "Not a sculpturing kind of guy. For now I prefer just to walk around and soak up the sights."

"Our museums act as our cultural and education centers," Kiana said proudly. "We believe the body and mind should both be well-sculpted. Sometimes a woman teaches, sometimes she learns."

Kiana motioned toward a large, red brick building with a domed roof. "That's our public library," she said proudly. "We invented the public library," she said even more proudly.

"I thought Ben Franklin invented that," I said.

"Benny was one of our guests," Kiana said. "He liked the idea so much, we let him keep the memory."

"Oh . . ."

"Neat," HARV said.

"So you read books from our world," I said.

Kiana laughed. "My family and I do, but the common people do not. We have more than enough Lantian literature to keep them busy. We encourage all of our citizens to write a book every few years. We still publish our books on paper, the way books are meant to be read."

We continued our walk. Kiana told me more about her land.

"As you can see, we have bots handling most of the day-to-day grunt work: the farming, the collecting, the cleaning, and the manufacturing of goods. This frees the citizens of Lantis to spend their time learning about the world—writing, painting, sculpting, doing craftwork. Or they work on their bodies. Or, if they feel like it, just meditating and relaxing."

I pointed to a couple of women up on scaffolding, repairing a window. "Those aren't bots working there."

"Wow, Zach, you are so smart," HARV said in my brain.

Kiana smiled. "No, of course not. Each woman on the island has one day out of every ten where they do community service and help the bots out. It is good for the soul. We are not like a mixed society where competition spurs greed. We are all equal."

"Oh," I said as we continued to stroll. "When is your day again?"

Kiana's smile flattened out just a little. "Zach, we've been over this. The royal family has other duties."

That's one of the problems I have with socialistic societies. As much as everybody claims they want to be equals, they don't. Humans and near-humans always want more than the next guy has. It goes back to the days of one caveman wanting a bigger cave than his neighbor's. No matter how much a society claims to be equal and fair, there are always some who have more than others. And this imbalance is bound to upset those on the lower part of the scale.

"Do you really believe you're equal to the people who serve you?" I asked Kiana.

Kiana kept walking. "In most areas, yes. I have extra duties, so I need extra attention. The trappings of power come with costs, and vice versa."

"So the masses are equal, but you and your sisters are above them?" I asked.

She nodded. "Yes. Everybody cannot be totally equal or else nothing would ever get done. Some people have to take charge. Those who are taking on more responsibility deserve a bit more attention. We have taken socialist ideals and made them work here. Everybody knows her place. Everybody is happy."

"Well, not everybody is happy, or else I wouldn't be here."

"Zing!" HARV said.

"Yes," she admitted. "You can never keep all the people happy unless you use mind control or drugs on them. Mom wasn't for that at all."

Kiana and I now came to a little park by a stream. It was a pleasant area, filled with lots of rolling grounds and just enough trees dotting the landscape to give some shade. Every few hundred meters there was a covered park bench and wooden picnic table. Next to the tables were open roasting pits for barbecuing. At least that's what I hoped they were for. It was a calm relaxing place.

For the first time since I arrived here, I noticed two young girls; one of them a tall skinny blonde no more than twelve, and the other a short brown-haired girl, maybe five or six years old, still carrying her baby fat. The young girls were running up and down, flying a kite as if they didn't have a care in the world. Ah, how I missed those days.

I pointed to the girls, just in case Kiana didn't see them. "You have children here?" I said.

"Wow, very good, Captain Obvious," HARV said in my head. *"Now what's that big yellow orb in the sky?"*

HARV was becoming more and more of a wiseass. Yeah, he'd been wired to me for too long.

Kiana lifted her fingers to her mouth, attempting to suppress a giggle. She didn't completely succeed. She was more diplomatic than HARV though. "Yes, we do keep our population regulated, but on rare occasions we lose a member. When that happens, we replace the sister who left us with a new life."

"Clones?" I asked.

Kiana stopped walking. She looked at me, eyes wide open. She put her hand to her chest and took a deep breath. "No, no, of course not. We feel cloning is unnatural. And no fun at all."

Now I was grinning. "Well put. So some of the men you borrow become fathers?"

Kiana started walking again. "Like I told you before, we do have a nice sperm bank, but sometimes we like to leave some things to chance and use a live being to help us create another live being."

"You don't find that at all wrong?" I asked her.

"No, of course not. We think of them as happy sperm donors." Kiana stopped walking and turned to me again. "Believe me, Zachary, none of them ever complain."

"Do they even remember?"

Kiana shook her head. "No, not really. We are just an occasional smile they get out of nowhere." Kiana touched me playfully on the shoulder. "Have you ever had one of those moments, where you just smiled and didn't know why?"

I didn't answer. She was playing with my mind now. I've been played with by the best of them. I've learned it's best to ignore the goading and focus on the line of questioning.

"So how do you decide who gets to do the deed?"

Kiana placed her hands on her hips. "I don't get your drift."

"Who has the baby? The queen?" I asked.

"The queen gets first choice, being the queen and all. If she isn't in the right mood, then my sisters and I get the next choices."

"Have any of you had children yet?"

Kiana gave me one of those dismissive waves I was getting so used to. "No, silly. None of us are even four hundred years old yet."

"So if you gals and the queen pass, then who's next?" I probed.

"Everybody who wishes to reproduce signs up for a lottery," Kiana said.

"So it's random," I said.

Kiana shook her head again. "No, not at all. The queen picks the one she feels is most deserving."

"So, why do you call it a lottery?" I asked.

"Do you realize you've just started three sentences in a row with 'so'?" she asked.

"So what? Now it's four. What's the answer?"

"Zach, calling it a lottery sounds so much nicer than saying queen's choice. That sounds so ... so matriarchal."

"What happens if one of you has a baby boy?" I asked.

Kiana laughed.

"Zach, you are embarrassing us," HARV said.

"We have evolved so the physical environment of our wombs is hospitable only to X sperm," Kiana said.

"Well duh," HARV said. Then he sighed. *"I don't believe I just said 'duh' ..."*

"I understand," I said.

I looked at the two girls running back and forth, flying the kite. "Cute kids. How old are they?"

"I believe Kia is eleven and Saya is six," Kiana said.

"When where they born?" I asked.

Kiana looked at me like I was a bit dim. "Kia eleven years ago, Saya six years ago."

I shook my head. "I thought you people aged slower?"

"Zach, Zach, Zach," HARV said in my head.

"We age normally for our first twenty years before the slowing process begins."

"I guess that makes sense," I told her. "Nobody wants to be a teen for a hundred years."

"Exactly!" she said.

Kiana sat down, kicked off her heels, and dipped her feet into the water. She patted the ground for me to sit beside her. I did.

"Once we reach slowing age, we all age at the rate we choose. We age at varied rates, based on our needs, stresses, and metabolism." She touched her chest. "I age at the rate of about one year to every twelve of your years."

"How often does one of you die?" I asked.

"Maybe once or twice every couple of years," Kiana told me.

"How do they die?"

"My, you do ask a lot of questions," Kiana said.

"Can't learn unless I do," I told her.

Kiana took another deep breath. "On occasion, on very rare occasions, one of us will be killed in an accident. We can get a little rough in our sports."

"Oh . . ."

Kiana continued. "The number one cause of our passing is boredom. Sometimes after living for a thousand years, some of us decide we have seen and done everything there is for us to see or do on this plane."

"You mean planet," I said.

"No, I mean plane of existence. Once that happens we let their soul pass to a higher plane of existence."

"Oh," I said.

"It's really a happy time for all. We get a new member of our society, and one of our older members gets to explore new dimensions."

"Interesting," I said. "How often do you lose people to our world?"

Kiana touched me again on the shoulder. "That's a very good question, Zach."

"Yeah, well, I'm the best," I told her.

"*And the most modest*," HARV said.

"Well you already met Barbette. Over the last ten of your years we've lost ten others. The one you know as Shannon Cannon is one of us."

I nodded. That explained a lot about Shannon Cannon.

"Before that, defections were rare. The one known as Oprah was the most famous. She was in line to be queen here, but decided she could be so much more in your world."

"So not everybody is happy then?" I asked.

"Everybody is happy, but a rare few are even happier elsewhere."

I heard footsteps behind us. I turned to see three rather large women coming toward us. They were wrapped head to toe in black ribbon and brandishing clubs in each of their hands.

"Ah, speaking of people not being happy," I said.

Kiana looked over her shoulder and saw the three approaching women. You didn't need my keen PI mind to tell that they didn't plan on using those clubs to play us a tune on the rocks along the stream.

Kiana stood up and held out her arm. "What is the meaning of this?" she demanded.

"This is nothing against you, Your Highness," one of the ladies grunted, stepping toward me.

"We are doing this for your own good," another of the ladies said.

Ah, yes, when you're me, a day wouldn't start off right unless somebody tried to kill you. Once again my keen intellect wasn't needed to know that they'd be making a beeline right for me. No gun, no knife, no GUS. Just my wits, muscle, and, of course, HARV.

"HARV, you can pump me up, correct?" I asked, jumping to my feet and taking a ready stance.

"I can, but I think I can do better," HARV said. *"I've been studying neurology and old military techniques. I*

compute that I have found how to transmit a pulse of light through our optic connection to temporarily short circuit a human brain."

"Well I hope it works, because I've seen hungry cats around gimpy birds that didn't look as anxious as these three," I said.

"When have you ever seen that, Zach?"

"Waxing poetic, HARV. It's what I do."

The three women in black robes lunged toward me. Kiana wasn't about to let them have their way with me, though.

"Nobody beats my pet man but me!" she shouted, right before she leaped across the field, barreling into two of the women and tackling them.

The other woman managed to avoid Kiana's attack, swinging down at me with the club in her left hand. I darted to the right and avoided her first attack. Undaunted, she swung across her body with the club in her right hand. I ducked under this attack, countering with an upper jab to the solar plexus. She took the blow and staggered back maybe half a step. Reaching forward, I grabbed both of her arms, pulling them down so she couldn't club me again. Acting fast, I forced her arms together to the middle of her body to take away her power. She was shockingly strong, pushing outward and forward to break my hold on her. I had gravity and HARV on my side. I hoped that was enough.

"HARV, this trick of yours better work!"

"Zach, it's not a trick. It's a technique I have developed after minutes and minutes of theoretical testing."

"Minutes and minutes?"

"Zach, I am a megasupercomputer. I do more in minutes than most do in a lifetime."

"Theoretical?" I asked.

"Yeah, you got me on that one. I figured people might

*get upset if we tested it on them in real life. Still, I am
ninety-nine percent confident it will work."*

Great Gates. Now HARV, like his creator, Randy
Pool, was using my body to field test his ideas. I just
had to hope it worked, like most of Randy's products.
I cocked my head forward, opened my eyes wide, and
locked them with my assailant's. She had deep brown
eyes. I might have found them attractive if they weren't
bloodshot out of hate for me.

"Fire, HARV!" I shouted in my brain.

"I did, over a hundred times," HARV said.

Oh, that was so not good. Before I could reflect on
how bad it was, my attacker tilted her back, then shot it
forward into my head, butting me to the ground.

Standing above me, she smirked. She dropped both
of her clubs. Rubbing her hands together slowly, she
said, "You are a weak man. I need no weapons to take
care of you."

"HARV, what's going on?"

"You're going to find this funny."

"I don't think so, HARV."

"Well, maybe interesting then?"

"HARV!"

*"I failed to take into account the differences in the
Lantian brain and the human brain. Lantians and humans are very close, but different. Luckily for us, the Lantians have made in-depth studies of their brain activities,
so I have been able to recalibrate."*

"Yeah, just what I was thinking. How lucky I am . . ."
I said.

My assailant reached down, grabbed me by both sides
of my vest, and yanked me back to my feet.

"I want to see the look on your face when I smash it
in!" she said, as she slowly drew her fist back. "You will
stand there and take this!" she ordered.

"She was using the mind control voice on you," HARV said. *"I think I blocked it . . ."*

Two good things were happening here. First, she had no idea that HARV was able to block her attempt at mind controlling me, putting her totally off guard. Second, by getting a good look at my face, it gave me a good look in her eyes.

"Fire now, HARV!"

"Done!" HARV said.

I studied my attacker. She still had her fist locked and drawn back, ready to clock me. Checking out her eyes, I noticed they weren't blinking. It had worked. I reacted fast, clenching my right hand into a fist. I jabbed it into her face. Her head shot back. Sure, I felt bad hitting a defenseless woman, but I would have felt worse getting beat up by a not so defenseless woman. Not wanting to give her any chance to recover, I hit her with another right. This time a fast jab to the nose. My punch drew blood, but she kept to her feet. DOS, I had to admit this lady was tough. I needed to put her down before she recovered.

Stepping forward, I hauled off, hitting with a left hook, a haymaker to the jaw. This did the trick, sending her crashing to the ground. Not having time to bask in my victory, I turned my attention to Kiana and her attackers.

I guess attacker was too strong a word. They were both lying facedown on the ground, motionless. Kiana was standing over them proudly.

"I am not just a pretty face," she told me. Kiana pushed a button on her communicator. "I will have security come and put these three away until they cool down."

"Why did they attack us?" I asked as I walked over to her.

Kiana looked down at the two ladies. "They are man-haters."

"Man-haters?"

"A part of our society, a small part, doesn't think we should have anything to do with men. They think men are too violent and competitive. They think all men should be killed," Kiana told me.

"They don't think that in itself is violent?" I said.

"They believe violence in the short term will lead to a better world in the long term."

"So the end justifies the means," I said. "And the meanness."

Kiana put her arm around me. "My, Zach, you are a smart man!"

Chapter 25

Kiana and I sat by the stream waiting for security to come and take away our assailants. During that time, the two assailants that Kiana had handled stayed stiffer than a frozen rope on Pluto. When Kiana put you out you stayed out.

The one who attacked me did start to stir after a few minutes, but, almost as an afterthought, Kiana pressed her foot against the side of my ex-attacker's neck, dropping her cold.

After around fifteen minutes, Andra showed up dressed in full battle gear, not the purple leather stuff she wore yesterday. This was thick blue metal armor. You knew she was serious as it even covered her legs and midsection. Andra was backed up by six armored security women, each bigger than the last. Luca was also there, with a look on her face that was a cross between sad and worried.

This didn't feel right. Why send eight people to take away three people Kiana had clobbered? Why were both Andra and Luca here? Something bad was up.

Before I could say anything, though, Kiana got up to greet her sisters and their backup.

"Sisters, how good of you both to come," Kiana said, then paused and added, "I am touched by your compassion, but really, I am fine."

Andra pointed a finger at Kiana. "You are under arrest for the murder of our mother, the queen."

Oh yeah, I could have seen that one coming.

"You can't be serious," Kiana said.

"I am deadly serious," Andra snarled.

"We are," Luca said, eyes lowered.

"On what grounds?" Kiana demanded.

For all her bravado, this couldn't have been a total surprise to Kiana. She had to at least know that her sisters, or at least Andra, would suspect her. Yet, like a true leader, Kiana wasn't about to admit that her opponents' actions might have been reasonable.

"Mara expanded the parameters of our poison scanning devices," Luca said.

"We found a poison in mother's cocoa," Andra said, almost licking her lips. "One found only in XY land."

Kiana took a step backward. She knew where this was going. She had to have suspected this might happen. I guessed, though, that she didn't think it would happen so soon.

"I am not the only of us who visits that land," Kiana protested.

"This poison is a very specific poison found only in one lab," Luca said.

I was surprised that the Lantians had figured this out so quickly. It was impressive. Unless, of course, it was a setup.

"The poison is found at AMP labs. A lab owned and operated by a Dr. Randy Pool," Andra snarled.

"So?" Kiana said.

Luca took a blue crystal from her pocket. "This holographic crystal says it all," she said, eyes lowered.

A holographic image of Kiana entering AMP labs projected from the crystal.

"This image was captured from AMP lab's security cameras ten days ago, at 12:01 P.M., their time," Luca said, sadly. "Can you explain it?"

Yeah, I was interested in hearing this explanation too. Surely Kiana knew Randy and I were friends. She should have at least mentioned their meeting to me. I knew a woman like Kiana could wrap Randy around her little finger and get him to do anything. DOS, a woman just a quarter like Kiana could have her way with Randy.

Andra shot an accusing finger at Kiana. "Arrest . . ."

"Everybody but Zach, FREEZE!" Kiana shouted.

Everybody within shouting distance, except for Kiana and me, stopped in their tracks, becoming living mannequins.

I turned toward Kiana. "Impressive."

Kiana looked at me with those big sapphire eyes. "It is my extra special gift. I can't hold them long though. Zach, you have to believe me. I didn't kill my mother."

"Why didn't you tell me about your meeting with Randy?" I demanded.

"I didn't think anything of it. Mara told me of his work, so I thought he might make potential mating material. Then I met him and figured, no way. I made an excuse and left."

I looked at her. No noticeable facial ticks or changes in expression.

"Her breathing pattern and heart rate did not change," HARV told me, further confirming that she was either telling the truth or was a hell of a liar.

"Still, you are smart, lady. You had to know it was important that you met with Randy. Even in passing."

Kiana looked down and away from me, slumping her

shoulders. "I was afraid if you knew that you wouldn't take the case."

I shook my head. "I seem to recall I didn't have much choice but to take the case."

Kiana looked back at me without quite looking at me. "Yes, but if you thought I was guilty you wouldn't try very hard to prove otherwise. You would turn me over to my sisters. I wanted you to get to know me better; to realize I could never murder my mom."

The rest of the ladies became unfrozen, seemingly unaware they had ever been.

". . . her!" Andra finished saying.

The six security women cautiously surrounded Kiana.

"I will not fight," Kiana told them. "I am sure the court will prove my innocence."

One of the security women pulled Kiana's arms behind her back and bound them. Another guard stuck a long piece of adhesive over Kiana's mouth.

"Take her away," Andra ordered loudly.

The security women saluted, then led Kiana away, leaving me with alone with Andra and Luca.

Andra approached me, once again licking her lips. "What do we do with this one?" she asked Luca, though she never took her eyes off of me.

"He is innocent," Luca said. "I will put him on a bubble back to his land and wipe his memory."

Andra got so close I could smell her breath. She leaned in to me.

"Trying to smell what I had for breakfast?" I asked her, not giving any ground.

"No, trying to see if you smell guilty," she said.

"Well, do I?" I asked.

Andra shook her head. "Nope. You are free to go."

Luca came up to me and took my arm. "Come, Zach. I will escort you out."

I gently slipped my arm out from Luca's grasp. "I'd like to stay."

"Why?" Luca asked.

"No way," Andra said.

"I'd like to make sure Kiana is guilty," I said to Luca, ignoring Andra. "If she used me, I want to know."

Andra stepped forward, grabbing my shoulder. "Trust me, you've been used. Get used to it. Men did it to women for centuries, so turnabout is fair play. Now, time for you to get off our land."

Andra was too anxious to get rid of me. That wasn't kosher. That made me more anxious to stay.

I twisted away from Andra's grip. "If she really is guilty, what's the problem with me staying around?" I asked, purposely raising an eyebrow.

Andra took a deep breath. I was getting on her nerves. I liked that. Of course, there was a fine line between getting on her nerves and having her rip out my spinal cord. I had to be careful here. She took another breath this time, looking away from me. Andra was no shrinking violet. She was trying to think of a reason to get rid of me.

"It is for your own safety," Andra told me.

"I'm touched," I said with a false sigh. "But I am big boy. I can take care of myself."

Andra shook her head. "In your world maybe, but here, without your fancy weapons, you wouldn't stand a chance." She puffed out her lips to show she was amused by my statement. "I could kill you with a fart in your general direction."

"Now this is girl you want to bring home to mother," HARV said.

Luca leaned into me and whispered, "Don't challenge her on that one, Zach. Please!"

"I'm a lot tougher to kill then people think," I told Andra.

Andra smirked at me. "Let's see if that's true."

Luca stepped in between us, spreading her arms apart to separate us even more. First she turned to Andra. "Sister, Zach just wants what we all want: a fair trial. Please be patient with him. He is our guest."

Andra shook her head no again. "He's not my guest."

Luca puffed out her chest and stood up on her toes. "Well, he's *my* guest," she said loudly. "And I am now next in line to be queen." She accented this statement with a stomp of her foot.

Andra backed down.

Luca turned to me. "Zach," she said in a lower, calmer tone than she used on her sister. "It's only a matter of time now until the general public learns of our other mother's demise. Since Kiana had a pro-man agenda, many of our people may wrongly blame you. We couldn't protect you."

"I can handle myself," I stubbornly restated.

Luca nodded. "Yes, in your own environment, I am sure you are quite formable."

Andra mumbled something under her breath. I couldn't make it out, but I knew it wasn't a compliment.

Luca shot Andra a look, then turned her head back to me. She had a smile on her face that was sweeter than nectar. "I am also sure you could handle yourself against one, or maybe even two of our citizens." From the slow, uneven tone of her voice I knew she didn't wholly believe those words, but she wanted to stroke my ego. "But only the Thompson sisters on Earth could stand up against four or five angry Lantians. Maybe a very powerful psi like Elena on the Moon could stand up against three. But you, Zach, no way."

Luca put her arm around me and started to lead me away from Andra. "Now, let me take you to your room to get your stuff. Then I will escort you to the docks to make sure you are safe."

I didn't want to leave. In fact I knew I had to stay, but this wasn't the place to plead my case. Not only would it be good to get as far away from Andra as possible, it was also better to get out of the public's sights for now. Luca wasn't nearly as wild or explosive as Andra; I might be able to reason with her. But first I had to get her alone. I let Luca lead me away toward my room.

Chapter 26

As Luca hurriedly pulled me back to the Ivory Tower we didn't talk much. I needed to think. Sure, Kiana had the motive and the means to kill the queen. She had certainly had the most to gain, but she also had the most to lose. Kiana would eventually become queen, so why rush the matter? From my contact with her she didn't seem like she was in much of a hurry to become leader. Even if she did have issues with her mother's politics. I thought Kiana would have been content to wait the queen out, and then implement her own policies when she became queen.

I needed to find out what Kiana did when she met with Randy.

"HARV, you have to contact Randy and let me know what he knows about Kiana."

There was silence. Then, *"Zach, I've tried over a billion times. I am ashamed to admit I can't figure out a way to transmit to our world. Their defenses preventing communication with the XY world are quite good. It's weird, their systems are over two thousand years old, yet in some*

*ways they are more advanced than our regular Earth sys-
tems. In other ways they aren't. They are quite different
and therefore difficult."*

Now this was different. I had never seen HARV so
stumped and frustrated before. At least not when dealing with technology. People, especially me, frustrated
him, yes, but not machines. HARV was normally a master at getting what he wanted from other machines. But
not this time, with his normal method. This was going to
take a different approach. A more off-world approach.

"Try to contact Elena. Maybe she can help us," I told
HARV.

"Moon Elena?"

*"Yes, Moon Elena. Luca mentioned her, so they obvi-
ously have some contact between the Moon and Lantis.
Neither group quite trusts regular humans."*

The Moon colony, while being an official colony of
Earth, isn't exactly close to Earth. Due to a series of selective breeding and genetic tweaking, much of the population of the Moon has become powerful psi females.
In fact, they had a lot in common with Lantians. It would
make some sense that they had some contact with each
other.

"The Elena who threatened to turn you into a turnip?"
HARV asked.

"Yes, that Elena."

"Okay, I am trying. I will let you know if I get through."

"Good," I said.

"Zach, you look pensive," Luca said to me.

"No, just thinking," I said.

Luca slowed her step. "Ah, Zach, I don't know about
your world, but here in Lantis, pensive and thinking
mean about the same thing."

I smiled. Someday, somebody was going to get that
joke. "Just a little joke," I told her.

"Nobody is ever going to get it," HARV said.

"I don't want to leave just yet," I told Luca.

We reached the bottom level of the IT.

Luca looked at me with sad eyes. "Ah, you've grown accustomed to Kiana. How sweet."

"Not Kiana. The truth."

Luca was silent until we entered the elevator. Once the door closed, she said, "Zach, it doesn't matter what the truth is. Once the word is out that the queen is dead, and Kiana, a man sympathizer, is the suspect, it will not be safe for any man here. Thank the mother of us all you are the only man on the isle right now."

The first thought that ran through my mind was, *Wow, I am the only man on an isle with ten thousand women.* I wasn't sure if this was a dream come true or a nightmare in the making. That wasn't all that useful a thought. My second thought was much more practical.

"What if I could stay and not be a man?" I said.

Luca looked at me with tilted head. "Zach, we don't have time for you to undergo an operation now."

"*HARV, toss a Lantian holodisguise over me,*" I said.

I saw the room shiver. Looking at Luca, her eyes were now wide open in surprise.

"What the Hades?" she said. She thought for a minute. She pointed at me. "You look like one of us now. You must be wearing a holographic device."

I nodded—that is, my image nodded. "Sort of. I have my computer connected directly to my brain. It allows both of us to do all sorts of things."

HARV appeared from my optic lens in full butler regalia. He bowed. He was such a ham. "I am not his computer. I am a cognitive processing entity that just *happens* to be hard wired to Zach's brain." HARV looked over his shoulder at me. "If anything, he is my human."

"So it's safe to assume that Kiana didn't tell you a lot about me," I told Luca.

Luca nodded, mouth open some. "No. She just said you were stubborn and persistent and could take a punch."

"I prefer to think of him as dogmatic, pigheaded, and just plain lucky," HARV said. "Mostly lucky he has me."

The elevator stopped. The door popped open. Luca walked out; I followed her in disguise.

"Just say yes. I can stay and help find the truth," I said.

"Your voice even sounds like us," Luca said.

"I have a very advanced holographic interface," HARV said. "It took me a while to figure out how to change Zach's voice, but let's say they are audio simulations."

I softly placed my hand on Luca's shoulder. "Please let me stay."

Luca looked up at me. She smiled. "Well, I suppose now that my mother is dead and my oldest sister will be on trial, I could use a personal bodyguard."

Right then and there I knew one thing. Luca's willingness to play along and let me stay meant that I could drop her if not off the suspect list, then way down on the list. If she worried about being connected to the murder, no way she'd want me sticking around, especially after she saw what I—well, HARV and I—were capable of.

"Then call me Zena, bodyguard to the queen-to-be."

Luca smiled. "Zena it is."

Chapter 27

First we stopped at my old room, where I was able to pick up my clothing, weapons, and underarmor. Even with a holographic disguise over me, I still felt better in my pants and shirt. Plus, if my past history was any indication, the armor and weapons would come in more than handy.

Next, Luca led me down a different hallway to her room. It was a large room, much like Kiana's, just a bit fluffier here and there. More throw pillows. In fact, it looked like a giant throw pillow-eating beast had barfed in the room.

Ohma was in the room with a duster. She was fluttering from bed to desk to nightstand, frantically dusting away. She didn't even notice that we had entered the room. She was clearly nervous, like a wounded bird at a cat show.

Luca cleared her throat. It didn't catch Ohma's attention. She glided over to the window shades, dusting them back and forth, up and down.

Luca coughed intentionally. It was a loud cough. At first I thought it had done the trick and gotten Ohma's attention, as she stopped her dusting. Instead, she pulled another duster from her belt and started dusting her duster with it.

Finally, Luca gave up her subtle attempts. "Ohma!" she shouted.

Ohma stopped dusting her duster. She turned around. Her eyes opened wide and her head lowered when she saw Luca. "Your Highness, I am sorry. I was just cleaning."

"I can see that . . ." Luca said.

Ohma scurried over to us, her head a bit lower with each step. "I am sorry I stated something so obvious. I am sorry I didn't see you come in. I am sorry that . . ."

Luca reached forward and patted Ohma on the shoulder. "It's okay, old friend."

"It's—it's—just—just . . ." Ohma panted, sweat formed on her brow.

"Slow down, breathe," Luca said. "That's a royal order."

Ohma tilted backward a bit, arching her back. She took a deep breath. Then another. She wiped the sweat off her brow. "It's just, you are going to be queen now. At least until after the trial."

"I am aware of that," Luca said.

Ohma started to pant again. "And we don't how the trial will go. The thought that your sister, my cousin, killed your mother, my aunt, our queen, saddens me. The thought of how the people will react when they learn what happens saddens me. The fact that your mother, our queen, is no longer with us saddens me deeper. The fact that I couldn't protect her . . . that I brought her the instrument of her demise . . ."

Ohma couldn't take it any more—not that she was taking it too well to begin with. She threw herself down to the floor, wrapping herself around Luca's knees and just weeping, wailing, "I am sorry. I am sorry."

Luca gently bent over and put her hand under Ohma's chin. She used her hand to gently bring Ohma up
to a standing position.

"You did nothing wrong," Luca assured her.

Ohma resumed her weeping; only now from a higher
position on Luca's shoulder.

"Now, now, this will not do," Luca said, rubbing Ohma's shoulder. "I need you to be strong. We all need you
to be strong."

Ohma couldn't hear Luca's words over her wailing. She
was deep in regret. I had seen this before. Didn't know if
it was guilt or sorrow. Or sorrow brought on by guilt.

Luca shook her head slowly. She grabbed Ohma by
the shoulders and looked her dead in the eyes, sapphire
to sapphire. "There is only one thing to do when you get
like this."

Luca darted forward, smashing her elbow into Ohma's face. The blow knocked Ohma flat on her back. It
also took me aback. I wasn't expecting that.

Ohma lay on the floor for a nano or two, eyes shut.
She started to blink. She opened them. She pulled herself up to a sitting position.

"Thanks, I needed that," she said to Luca.

Luca looked over her shoulder at me. "A good leader
does what's best for her people, no matter how much it
may hurt."

Luca reached down and pulled Ohma up to a standing position. Ohma for the first time noticed I was in the
room.

"Excuse me, and you are?" Ohma asked me.

*"Zach, the standard greeting is a fist pump, then a
shout of your name,"* HARV told me.

"You're kidding, HARV."

"Believe me, I can't make this stuff up."

I made a fist, held it out, and shouted. "My name is
Zena!"

"Zena will be my private bodyguard," Luca stated.

Ohma shook her head. "Strange . . . I've never seen you around."

"Do you know all ten thousand of us by name?" Luca asked Ohma.

Ohma lowered her head. "No ma'am, I should. But I only know nine thousand three hundred seventy-three by name. You must be so ashamed of me."

Luca smiled. "No, of course not. That is why I have Zena here. I wanted new blood, somebody not in the inner circle."

"I have spent much time in the XY world," I said as Zena. "I just recently returned when I decided all men are scum." I accented my words by spitting. Not very ladylike, but I figured it worked here.

"How did you, a non-royal, spend so much time in the XY world?" Ohma asked.

"Spitting, spitting in public," HARV said. *"That gets you banned here."*

"I spat in public once a hundred and fifty years ago. And Luca saw me. As punishment she exiled me to the XY world."

"Oh, I see," Ohma said. "How did you become friends then?"

"Since her return, we have been playing rugby together," Luca said quickly.

"I want to make up for my indiscretion," I said in a firm tone.

"She is a fierce competitor. She will have my back," Luca added.

Ohma looked me over, head to toe. "Really? She looks a bit soft."

"Zach, you have to prove yourself to Ohma," HARV said.

"Really?"

"Really. I am pumping extra blood to the bones and muscles in your right arm now."

I felt the surge HARV was talking about and went with it. I moved forward and hit Ohma with a right elbow to the jaw. I didn't want to hurt her, but I didn't want her asking too many questions.

My blow sent her stumbling back. She wobbled, but stayed on her feet. She steadied herself and smiled. "I was wrong. You throw a decent elbow." She ducked her head down and turned away from me. "I do believe you will be a worthy bodyguard."

"Of course she will," Luca said. "Now go prepare a room for her." Luca pointed to the door, just in case Ohma had forgotten where it was.

Ohma just stood there, hands to her sides. "Ah, my future queen . . ."

"Yes?" Luca said, hands on hips, leaning into Ohma. She was leaving no question as to who was in charge here.

"Isn't it both customary and safer for those who need bodyguards to have their bodyguards with them at all times?" Ohma asked, though it really was a rhetorical question.

"Well, yes," Luca said, slowly. "But I feel safe in my own room."

Ohma stood silent for a moment or two, biting her lip. "But wasn't your mother, our queen, killed in her own room." It may have been worded as a question, but it was much more a statement of fact.

Now it was Luca's turn to bite her lip, as she stood there thinking. "You are right," she said to Ohma. She pointed to the door again. "Now go find Zena a bed and linen."

Ohma bowed her head. "Yes, my future queen."

Luca and I watched in silence as Ohma left the room.

The door shut and Luca turned to me. "I am sorry, Za—Zena. You must sleep in here with me."

"No problem at all," I told her. "I'll adjust."

"Remember you are almost married," HARV scolded in my mind.

"I remember," I said.

"Plus, this girl is too young for you," HARV added.

"HARV, she's close to three hundred years old."

"Yes, she's too old, too," HARV said. *"So don't get any thoughts."* HARV thought for a nano. *"Well, you are only human. Thoughts are okay I guess. Just don't do any actions."*

"Got it," I said.

It was time to get on the case, so I could get HARV off my case.

Chapter 28

I sat down on Luca's bed. The mattress was much firmer than I thought it would be. I patted the bed. "Come, let's talk for a moment before Ohma comes back."

Luca looked at me. She slowly started to walk toward me, eyeing me carefully. Then her eyes lit up. "You think I may be involved in my mom's killing."

"I wouldn't be doing my job if everybody wasn't a suspect," I told her, trying to sound as macho as a guy disguised as a woman could. I didn't really think she was a suspect, but the PI in me still needed to pry a little. Never know when a little push can lead to a big aha.

Luca sat down gently on the bed about a meter from me. "I would never kill my mom," she said. "I would never kill anything. I do not even kill insects. I trap them and set them free outside."

"She died drinking cocoa, and I do believe you said you make the best cocoa," I told her.

Luca turned her gaze from me. "Yes, I did say that."

"For all I know, you could have used your powers . . ."

"My gifts," she corrected.

"You could have used your *gifts* to make the cocoa lethal," I said.

Luca sat there in silence for a nano or two. She turned her head back toward me. "I never thought of that."

"You seem sweet and caring on the outside, but I've heard Jack the Ripper could be quite the charmer."

I needed to push her to see how she reacted. Then I could gauge her response.

Luca looked down. "Yes. I remember that," she said.

That was interesting, 'cause I was just making that Jack the Ripper stuff up.

Luca tilted her head toward me. Her eyes fixed steadily on mine. "Perhaps I should step down until this is settled?" she said. "I never wanted to rule. I never thought I would need to rule."

"Who's next in line after you to lead?" I asked.

"Andra," she said.

"Lovely," HARV said.

"Don't do anything rash," I told her.

"Okay," she said.

I really didn't think Luca was the killer. I didn't think she had it in her. Sure, the sweetness could have been an act, but if it was, it was a damn convincing one. If so, she'd make a great politician. Besides, my instincts told me we didn't want Andra leading no matter what. Andra was a "hit 'em first, hit 'em again, why bother asking questions when the hitting's so much fun" kind of person.

"Any idea why somebody would want to kill your mom?" I asked.

Luca shook her head. "No, Mom was loved by all."

"Well, obviously not all," I said.

"Okay, all minus one," she said.

"So, your mom didn't want to open relations with my people," I prompted.

Luca looked up at the ceiling. Her eyes darted back and forth like they were searching for the right words.

"No. She thought men had one purpose and one purpose only."

"Right, to open jars," I said.

Luca looked at me. "No, sex, silly. We are all really strong. We can open our own jars."

"But Kiana wanted to open up relationships with my world. Tell the world about Lantis."

Luca nodded. "Kiana thought the diversity would be good for us. That we were becoming too set in our ways."

"What are your thoughts?" I asked Luca.

Once again, Luca looked up to the ceiling, searching for the right words. "I kind of saw both their points. Men tend to be overly violent and settle arguments with their brawn instead of their brains." She smiled wistfully, "Still they do have their purposes. And even we women have our violent sides. It's different, but it's still there. So, I can see why mom wanted to protect us from that culture. I can also see why Kiana wanted us to interact more with that culture."

"Wow, you straddle the line pretty well," I told Luca. "You *are* a natural born politician."

Luca smiled. "Thank you," she said.

I didn't tell her that wasn't meant to be a compliment.

Luca stood up from the bed. "I have some of those political duties to attend to now. Will you be okay alone for a while?"

"I'm a big girl," I told her.

Luca smiled, nodded, and then left the room.

I walked over to the door and bolted it. I didn't need or want any surprises.

"HARV, drop the holodisguise," I ordered.

"Why, Zach? I think you're cute. A large and just a little on the manly side woman."

I gazed at myself in the mirror. I had to give HARV

his due. I certainly looked like a woman, but the woman did have some of my traits. My holographic nose was a lot like my regular nose; not a small nose by any means, but not a long one either. It was slightly bent from taking one or two too many shots to the head, but that just gave me character. The eyes were my brown eyes, a bit weary, but still alert. My lips were fuller and redder than normal. My hair was dark black like it was in my youth; only it was down over my shoulders, far longer than I could have comfortably worn it as a man.

The holographic image faded and I was greeted with the image of my familiar face in the mirror. I rubbed my chin. The stubble on my face was dotted with some gray specks, more than there were last week. The good news was these spots of gray were nothing a laser razor couldn't handle.

"Zach, stop gazing so lovingly in the mirror," HARV told me. "I have made contact with Elena on the Moon."

"And?"

"She'll be right down," HARV said.

I turned away from the mirror. "Excuse me?" I said to HARV.

HARV appeared before me. He pointed to a spot on the floor. The spot started to glow. "Avoid that spot."

A shapely female shape started to form on the spot. At first there was an outline only. Then the outline became a translucent figure. Then the figure became solid. Elena was standing before me. I hadn't seen the blue-haired Elena in over a year, since I made my trip to the Moon when her stepfather tried to destroy Earth. During that trip, Elena tried to kill—or at least harm—me on numerous occasions, once even threatening to rearrange my molecules into a turnip. Still, over the course of the adventure, Elena became instrumental in helping me, and others, stop her stepfather's evil plans.

Elena had matured some from those days. She was still strikingly beautiful, with long dark blue hair that draped gently over her shoulders, a pure cream complexion, and deep, striking dark green eyes. Now though, those eyes seemed to hold more soul. They were the eyes of person who had seen and experienced so much that she was more mature than her chronological age.

She was dressed somewhat more conservatively than I remembered. She was wearing a short blue dress, but it came halfway down her thighs and it wasn't split open. Her blue, high-heeled boots were high, but within reason. Finally, her blue halter top gave a hint of her flat abs without giving away the entire picture.

Elena looked at me looking at her. "I am dressing more conservatively these days to reflect my new position on the moon."

"Which is?" I asked.

"I am a senior member of the Moon Council," she said.

I was kind of embarrassed that I didn't keep better tabs on Elena and the Moon. I tried not to let my face show it. After all, most people on Earth couldn't name half the World Council members, much less name a Moon Council member.

Elena walked over to me. "Don't worry, Zach. I'm not offended that you don't know I'm on MC now. I realize you have a lot on your mind."

"And not a lot of extra room up there," HARV added.

Elena smirked. I ignored HARV. I pointed at the spot Elena arrived upon. "Did you just teleport from the Moon?"

Elena nodded. "Yes. We are making great strides in our teleporting ability on the Moon. We use a mix of technology and our advanced psi powers." She touched me lightly on the shoulder. "Only a few of us are advanced enough, or have enough control of our powers, to do it, though."

"When I asked HARV to contact you for help, I had no idea you'd actually show up."

Elena smiled. "No, of course you didn't. My people and the Lantians have a relationship. It's mostly based on a mutual mistrust of your people, but it's a relationship all the same. Still, I didn't want to risk it by communicating electronically, too easy to tap. While we have a relationship with the Lantians, that doesn't mean I trust them anymore than I do regular Earth folks."

I looked at Elena, trying to deduce where she was going with this.

She reached over and touched me gently on the shoulder again. "Don't worry, Zach. You I do trust."

That was reassuring to know. I finally had one ally on my side, someone besides HARV who I knew I could trust. True, this was an ally with a temper, but in a pinch you don't look a gift ally in the mouth.

"I'm honored you would come all this way to help me," I told Elena.

Elena walked over to the window, drew back the curtain slightly, and peeked out. "It's not just for you, Zach. It's also for me and my people, and your people. We all want Lantis in stable hands. They are a small bunch. But they do have knowledge from a very old and advanced civilization. Knowledge that should not fall into the wrong hands."

"Speaking of knowledge, did you talk to Randy Pool?" I asked.

Elena nodded, still not looking at me. "I did. I visited him before I came here."

"And?"

"He made an awkward pass at me."

"Yep, that's Randy. What happened after that?" I prodded.

Elena turned toward me, arms crossed, eyes steady. "I rearranged his molecules into chimp form."

She didn't blink. She was serious.

"How did that go?" I asked.

"He used sign language to tell me what a fascinating experience that was," Elena said.

"That sounds like Randy."

Elena walked over and sat on the bed. "So I turned him back and we talked."

"And?"

"He met with Kiana all right, but he only met with her for a few minutes in his outer office. She told him she just wanted the honor of meeting one of the greatest minds on Earth," Elena said.

"She had him pegged for possible mating material, but changed her mind when she actually met him in person."

Elena nodded. "That makes sense. You can't really experience Randy until you meet him live."

"Is there any way Kiana could have tweaked Randy's brain and made him forget stuff that happened? That way she could have stolen a poison from him."

Elena shook her head. "I scanned Randy for any signs his brain had been tampered with by anybody other than me . . ."

"And?"

"There are some residual effects from something your Carol did to him," Elena said.

"Yeah, Randy kind of borrowed her DNA without permission, and that kind of irked her," I stated.

Elena looked up, like she was gazing off into space. "Wow, cloning Carol. That would make for an interesting being."

"You have no idea," I said.

We heard a rustling at the door. Somebody was starting to enter the room. The door popped opened a crack. Only the chain lock prevented the person from entering.

"Zena, it's me, Ohma," a voice called from behind the door. "A worker and I are coming in now with your bed. You seem to have bolted and chained the door, but don't worry, I have a key for the bolt and I can teleki-netically move the chain."

"HARV, throw the disguise over Elena and me fast," I said.

"Don't bother," Elena said, standing up from the bed. "I will handle this."

The door opened wide, but nobody came in. Elena walked away from the bed and out of the room. She walked back in holding two apples in her hand, a bed rolling behind her. The door shut behind her. She tossed me one of the apples.

"Now we can talk in peace," she said with a smile.

I examined the apple: red, round, firm. I looked at Elena, who was sitting next to me on the bed again, holding the other apple. "I take it these apples aren't for eating?"

"You could," she said with a wink in her eyes.

"But ..."

"But you'd be eating Ohma's aide," Elena added.

I put the apple/aide down gently on the floor. My first instinct was to scold Elena for transmuting two humans into apples. Not wanting to be the third apple in the room I went against that instinct. Instead I got inquisi-tive. "How long will they stay like this?"

"Long enough for us to finish our talk," Elena told me.

I decided not to think about Elena being able to transmute people into apples and to concentrate on the matter at hand.

"So what's left to talk about?" I asked Elena. "We know Randy met with Kiana, but we also know she didn't take anything from him."

Elena gave me a wry half smile. The kind of smile where half the face starts to light up, only the other half tries to stay calm, not wanting to tip off an observer.

"There's something else, isn't there?" I asked.

"Zach, these women come from a society that was dealing with nanotechnology even before our societies were societies," Elena told me. "A very paranoid, advanced society," she added.

"HARV, contact Randy and have him sweep the office for any nanotechnology that isn't his."

HARV held up one finger. "One, I can't contact Randy directly from here."

"Oh yeah, good point. I guess I got caught in the moment."

HARV held up another finger. "And two, Randy sweeps his lab for nanobugs constantly."

"Yes, but those are regular bugs. These will be different," I said.

"Different how?" HARV asked.

I looked at him.

"Oh, right, how the DOS would you know?" HARV said. "I will try to discreetly scan the information I have to see if I can figure out what Randy needs to look for."

"Then if you find out, you can tell me and I will tell him," Elena said.

"Can you give him a hint now?" I asked Elena.

She answered with silence.

"I would have to port back to the Moon and then back to his lab."

"I'll owe you one," I said.

"You'll owe me more than that," Elena replied.

Elena pushed a button on her sleeve. She was engulfed in a ball of energy, then disappeared.

Everything in front of me shimmered for a nano. HARV had reactivated my holodisguise.

Ohma and her assistant transformed back into their original forms. They both looked around.

"That's funny, I don't remember walking this far into the room."

The assistant nodded in agreement.

I stood up from the bed. "That's because you two are so efficient and move so quickly, you don't even remember moving."

Ohma and the assistant just looked at each other.

"Yeah, that must be it," Ohma said. She shook her head again. "I've either been working too hard or not hard enough."

The assistant pushed a button on the rolled up bed. The bed unfolded in front of me. The assistant pushed the bed into place next to Luca's bed.

"I assume that will be fine," Ohma said.

"Yes, I am sure it will be," I said.

"Is there anything you need?" Ohma asked me.

I needed to question Ohma as one of her own people. She saw the queen more than anybody. I needed to ascertain two things. One, if she may have been the murderer or in on the murder. And two, if she wasn't the murderer or in on it, if she had any ideas on who would want the queen removed from office forcibly. It probably wouldn't be easy to get her alone or to talk, but I had to try.

"I would like to talk to you alone."

Ohma pointed to the door and said to the assistant, "You may leave now."

As I watched the assistant leave the room I couldn't help thinking that it had been a bit too easy.

Chapter 29

"So you want to talk with me alone?" Ohma asked.

"Yes," I said.

Ohma pointed at me. I went flying backward. I've been hit by enough telekinetic attacks in my time to instantly recognize them. The thing was, that while I was being telekinetically moved across the room, this wasn't with malice. I was moving softly, slowly, floating in the air until I was over the bed. Then I drifted down like a feather slowly coming to rest.

HARV snickered in my head. "I have no idea how you get yourself in these situations . . ."

I looked over at Ohma. She was floating toward me, smiling; her outerwear peeled off as she drew nearer. It was a pleasant view, but I wasn't here for sightseeing. Ohma landed on top of me and flung her arms around me. She planted a kiss on my lips hard.

"Oh, I am under so much pressure," she moaned. "I am glad we have this little release valve." She looked up at the ceiling. "Funny, I usually find myself attracted to XY's but in your case I am SO ready to make an exception."

"Hmm," HARV said in my head. *"Apparently, you are still giving off some sort of male pheromone. Not sure what I can do about that."* A slight pause then: *"Nope, nothing I can do about it. Lucky for you though, most Lantians probably won't act on it. They probably just shake it off or ignore it. Ohma must be extra lonely, or sensitive, or both."*

As HARV babbled on, Ohma kissed me up and down my neck. I pushed up, bench pressing Ohma up in the air.

"Ohma, wait, you've got this all wrong," I said.

Ohma shook her head from above me. "No, I don't think so." She pushed my hands away from her teleki- netically, then fell back on top of me. She kissed me on the neck again. She looked up at me. "Hey! What the frock! You have an Adam's apple! I can't see it." She kissed me again. "But I can plain as Hades feel it." She pushed herself off from me. "By the goddesses above and below, you are a man!"

Ohma leaped off of me. Eyes wide open, she shouted, "This can only mean one thing! You are the one who killed the queen and now you are after Luca!"

I went flying across the room again. This time, though, it wasn't gentle at all. I crashed into a far wall headfirst. It hurt, a lot. I was lucky HARV and my body armor were able to cushion the blow or I would have been out cold. Instead I was just in pain.

The good news was, Ohma's sincere rage and com- plete surprise meant I could rule her out as a suspect. She believed in her heart of hearts I was the killer. The not so good news was she was now determined to kill me.

Ohma focused her glare on me, pinning me to the wall. "I should call security, only I want to pummel you myself first!" She curled her finger into a fist and shook it at me. "Were you in on it with Kiana? Or did you somehow set her up? If you are using holographic technology that we have long banned, you are capable of anything!"

Ohma glanced over at the bed she had brought in. A devious smile crept over her mouth. "I will pummel you with the very bed you had me bring in here!"

Ohma pointed to the bed with the hand that wasn't a fist. The bed elevated off the ground. I put two and two and together and came up with grief. I struggled to break free, but my back was pinned tighter to the wall than a robo-butterfly's wings in a cyber-entomologist's collection.

Ohma waved her open hand. The move sent the bed hurtling across the room toward me. I lifted my arms to ward off the attack. Sometimes I slip by on luck. Sometimes I do it with guile. Other times I gadget my way out of jams. Sometimes I just use plain brute force. Sometimes I just have to pray and hope for the best. This was one of those times.

"HARV, drop my cover," I shouted.

"Yeah, probably a good idea," HARV agreed.

The room shivered again. I took it to mean the holo-disguise was off me. The bed was still barreling at me. I ducked my head and held out my arms.

"Zach?" I heard Ohma say.

The bed and my arms met. It hurt, but not nearly as much as I expected it to. The bed fell to the floor. I floated down and softly landed on top of it.

"Zach?" Ohma repeated. "It really is you."

I sat up in the bed. "In the flesh," I said.

Chapter 30

Ohma ran up to me and helped me off the bed. I was sore and bruised, but frankly I have gotten beaten up worse on trips to the barberbot. (Don't ask.)

"Are you okay?" Ohma asked me.

I dusted myself off. I stretched a few kinks out of my back and neck. "I'm fine."

"Why are you here? How are you here? Does Luca know you are you?" Ohma asked. Then, before I could answer, she did. "You are here to further investigate the murder. You have some sort computer interface that allows you to use holograms. Of course Luca knows you are you."

I nodded. "Yep."

"Wow, Zach, way to impress her with your use of the language and your grasp of the facts," HARV said, appearing from my optic lens.

Ohma glanced over at HARV, then back to me, then back to HARV. "Wow, fascinating," she said, passing her hand through HARV.

HARV took a step back. "Please, I really hate it when people do that," he told Ohma.

Ohma grinned. "This is so cool." Ohma concentrated her attention on me. "So you don't think Kiana did it? You feel she is innocent?" she asked, though the squeal in her voice led me to believe she was leading me more than asking me.

"I take it you don't think she's guilty," I said.

Ohma looked away from me. "It's not my place."

"Sure it is. You live here. You run the place," I told her.

Ohma curled her body away from me like a sly cat, playing coy. "Oh, run is too strong a word. I like to think of it as 'manage, with great efficiency and care.'"

Ohma was one of the overworked, underappreciated types. Experience has taught me that giving these types a little appreciation could lead to a fountain of information.

"You are the eyes, the ears, and the soul of this place," I said.

"Pouring it on a bit thick, aren't we, Zach?" HARV said.

"Without you, the queen probably wouldn't know when to pee," I told her.

Ohma giggled. "You are just trying to, how do you say it, butter me down . . ."

I stepped back and looked at her as if she'd said the sky is green, rain falls up, or all politicians are totally honest all of the time. I let my expression speak for itself.

"Don't worry," Ohma told me. "I like it." She crossed her arms. "It's about time somebody figured out all I did around here." She exhaled. "Figures it would be a man."

I sat down on the bed again. "So you don't think Kiana did this?"

Ohma shook her head no. "Not Kiana's style."

"She's not a killer then?" I asked.

Ohma shook her head no again, "Oh no, she's a killer. But she's not subtle. If she killed you, she'd want you to know she's the one who killed you. She would never use poison." Ohma looked up contemplating. "She might beat you to death with the heel of her shoe, but never poison . . ."

"Maybe she used poison to throw the others off track? Point the blame in another direction."

"I guess," Ohma said. She thought a bit more. "No, she wouldn't. Once, when we were kids studying the history of our native world, we learned that one of our leaders poisoned his rival. Kiana was appalled by this action. Thought the man was a coward."

I needed to pry a bit more. "Didn't Kiana and the queen have some slight disagreement on how to handle relationships with my world?"

Ohma looked at me like monkeys had just sprouted out of my ears. "It was more than a slight disagreement. They were at opposite ends of the spectrum. Kiana wanted to embrace your culture. The queen, Mother Nature rest her inner light, wanted to avoid it with a passion. She had been born on our planet of origin. She had seen what violent bastards men could be." Ohma looked up at me realizing what she had just said. "Oh, sorry. No offense."

"None taken." I didn't mention that she was the one who just tried to squish me like a bug with a bed tossed at me at warp speed.

"If Kiana wanted to take over, she would have done it openly. She would have challenged the queen. As the oldest, it is within her rights. Kiana told me recently she would consider this someday, once she studied your culture a bit more. She figured it shouldn't take her more than fifty years."

Ohma had confirmed my feeling on Kiana. She may have been a lot of things, but she wasn't a subtle killer. Therefore, she probably wasn't the guilty party here.

"That means somebody is setting Kiana up," I said.

Ohma put a finger to her mouth, thinking. "Yes, I am afraid it does."

"Luca?" I asked. "She's next in line and would benefit from the queen dying and Kiana being put away."

Ohma shook her head no yet again, "Luca, no. She's no killer. With her gifts, we're lucky she isn't. Besides, Luca has confided in me many a time that she is so glad she is behind Kiana. Which meant she wouldn't take over for centuries if at all."

"Yes, if Kiana had a daughter, then that child would become first in line to replace her," HARV said.

"That is true," Ohma said. "You are a very wise holographic being."

"Thank you," HARV said proudly.

I was pleased that I was able to reasonably cut the number of possible suspects in half. Sure, it was possible Kiana, Luca, or even Ohma killed the queen, but not likely at all. I wouldn't shut the doors completely on them, just in case some piece of information popped up that would blow the doors wide open. For now, though, they were on the back burner, pretty much ready to be taken off the stove.

"That narrows it down to Andra, Poca, or Mara," I said.

Ohma was silent. I prodded some. "Which one would you say is the most likely?"

"I don't like to think or speak bad of my fellow royals," Ohma said, turning her eyes away from mine.

"One of them killed your queen," I said coldly.

Ohma straightened her back. "I am sorry," she said, walking away. "Your secret is safe with me. I will not tell anybody who you really are, but I will also not mouse out any of them."

"I believe the phrase you are looking for is rat out," I said to her back.

She stopped walking and turned back to me. "Once again, we are not men, we do not turn on our own by making idle speculation."

"Can you at least schedule appointments for me to meet with each of the three? Tell them I need to discuss their new queen's protection," I said, hoping that giving her something to do along the lines of her regular duties was something she would respond to.

"That I will do," she told me.

"Thank you," I said.

"Do not thank me yet, Mr. Johnson. My cousins are not used to being questioned. They will quickly deduce what you are doing. How they will react to it is anybody's guess." She paused for a moment. "Andra certainly will not respond positively. You are stomping in on her territory, our security."

"If she was better at it I wouldn't be here. Unless, of course, she's responsible for the queen's death," I said. Right now, Andra was my number one suspect. I didn't mind tipping her off. If she came after me that would make my job easier.

"I venture the others will also be less than cooperative," Ohma said.

"That's okay. Sometimes what people don't say or do speaks louder than their actions," I said.

"I would not want to be in your shoes, or holoboots, or whatever," Ohma said.

"Very few would. This is why I'm the world's *last* freelance PI."

"Tread carefully, Mr. Johnson, or the world may soon

be without any freelance PIs." She paused for a moment. "Good day."

She turned and started to walk away. She stopped and turned back toward me. "I will come back and tell you what they say, then escort you to them."

"You could just call me," I said.

Ohma gave me a very incredulous look; as if she were forcibly willing her eyes not to pop out of her head. "Mr. Johnson. We are very civilized people who believe non-personal communication is used only in emergencies. As the queen liked to say, 'If you have something to say, say it face-to-face.' It is the only proper way to communicate."

"Okay," I said slowly.

"The queen believed strongly that, as communication becomes easy, it becomes less and less personal, and that helps lead to the downfall of society. It reduces people to symbols and makes them lazy. The queen felt true meaning could only be felt by people exchanging words in the same physical area." Ohma looked up and smiled whimsically. "It's funny. The better your society became at mass communication, the less we would have to do with them."

"Well, that is interesting," I said.

"Our queen was wise, as I am sure our new queen will also be wise," Ohma said.

"I certainly appreciate all you're doing for me," I told Ohma.

"Save your appreciation until after you see how my cousins react," Ohma said. "I feel their reactions will be less than pleasant. Again, I would not want to be in your holographic boots right now."

Ohma turned and left the room.

HARV looked at me. "She makes a valid point. These women aren't used to being questioned. There is no hint of press or media here. It would appear that the royal family is used to being able to do whatever they want when they want."

"Well that's about to change," I said.

Of course, this wasn't going to be easy. But then, I *am* Zachary Nixon Johnson. The universe never gives me easy. Where would the fun be in that?

Chapter 31

I had HARV at work trying to tap into Poca's computer records while I waited for Ohma to bring me the women's responses. HARV was growing increasingly frustrated at being unable to get very deep into the records. He kept assuring me that he could and would soon do it. I had faith in HARV, but I could hear more and more frustration in his voice.

After about fifteen minutes with no luck on either front, there was a knock at the door. I went up and answered it. It was Ohma, very prim and businesslike.

"I have talked to Mara. She will see you now," Ohma told me. "I will lead you to her lab."

I stepped out of the room into the hall. "Thank you, I appreciate it."

"We are a polite society. Face-to-face communication helps nourish that."

We started walking down the hall.

"I don't know whether that nourishes it, or if it is just that impersonal conversations kind of starve politeness to death. It's easier to be rude or indifferent when you aren't in the same room as the person you're talking with," I said.

"Oh, please," HARV said. *"You humans and human types blame all your woes on your machines. Face it, you are rude and indifferent by nature. We just help you be rude and indifferent faster. It's like blaming guns for killing."*

I didn't reply right away.

"No snappy comment?" HARV said.

"I was just thinking that trying to blame GUS for anything would be like kicking a puppy."

HARV had a point, but I wasn't going to give him the satisfaction of admitting it right away. Anyway, I needed to concentrate on Ohma. We reached the elevator and started down.

"What can you tell me about Mara?" I asked.

Ohma looked at me. "I told you I will not mouse out any of my *sisters*."

"Not looking to have them moused out. Just want to know what makes her tick."

Ohma grinned. "Oh, that is easy. That I can do. I can sum up Mara in two words: speed and science."

"That's three words," HARV said in my head.

"I've seen the speed in action, and I knew she was science minister. Can you give more details?" I said.

"She just loves making our world better as fast as she can," Ohma said proudly. "I know she is fast but she does the work of three people!"

The elevator stopped; I noticed we were on the basement level. I've never had a lot of luck in basements. The doors opened, revealing a long room. Along the sides of the room were plants of all sizes. A long lab table ran through the middle, stretching from end to end. The table was covered with various lab equipment: many different kinds of microscopes, a few small centrifuges, test tubes, burners, and various other pieces of equipment I am sure HARV could have identified if necessary. Mara was down at the far end of the room, wearing goggles and mixing the contents of a couple of test tubes together. She saw Ohma and me, put the tubes down, and streaked down to us.

She pointed to a locker by the elevator and said, "Please remember; safety first while in my lab. Put on your lab jackets and goggles."

"I will leave you two alone," Ohma said. She dropped back into the elevator. The doors closed behind her.

I walked over to the locker and opened it. There were dozens of yellow lab coats on hangers on one level, and a top shelf filled with eye goggles. I reached into the closet.

"Ah, Zach," HARV said. *"You can't actually put those on. Your actual body is smaller than your holographic body."*

"Yeah, I know that, HARV. Toss a holographic version over me."

"Pantomime the moves," HARV said.

"Really?"

"Zach, would I make you do this if you didn't have to?"

"Yes, HARV, you would."

"True," HARV said. *"But in this case you really need to do it to avoid suspicion."*

I positioned myself so the locker door was between Mara and myself. I reached in and pretended to pull something out. I arched my back like I was putting on a jacket or lab coat.

"Now the glasses," HARV prompted.

"HARV! She can't even see me!"

"Zach, we have to do this right!"

I reached up into the higher shelf. I pretended to grab a pair of goggles. I moved my hands closer to my head. I adjusted a strap that wasn't there. I turned and smiled.

"Happy?" I asked HARV.

"Strangely, yes. Just remember, you aren't really wearing goggles, so your eyes aren't protected."

"Yes, Mother."

I turned and Mara was beside me, hand extended for a greeting.

"Hello, I am Mara, fourth in line for the throne," she said quickly.

"I am Zena, Luca's new bodyguard."

Mara smirked. "I bet Andra is going to love you," she said cynically.

"I am not here to be loved. I am here to keep Luca safe. She is next in line to the crown now."

"Yes, I understand," Mara said. "Why do you want to talk to me? Surely you don't think I am a threat to Luca? I am last in line to be queen. Much would have to go wrong for me to become queen."

I—that is, my image—locked eyes with her. "It is my job to get to know everybody and, nothing personal, to make sure you never do get to become queen."

Mara shook her head. "I assure you, I have no interest in becoming queen. I have dedicated my life to making our world better through science. To me, being queen is too much administrative and PR work." She paused for a nano—she had something else to say but wasn't sure if she should say it.

"And?" I prompted.

Mara looked me in the eyes. "I feel I can accomplish so much more in my role here than I could as queen." She pointed down the room. "Look at my lab here. I am working on ways to create more food that is even more nutritious with less work. I am doing far more here than I could as queen. Being queen involves a lot of sitting around. I'm not a sitter."

"Fair enough," I said.

"So Zena, what exactly do you want from me?" she asked.

"Just to talk, to see what you do," I said.

"Why?"

"We little people don't know you royals all that well. If I am going to protect Luca, I need to see if you are the type of person who could harm her. Seeing your work will give me a greater idea of that."

"How?" Mara asked.

I pointed to the lab table. "What are you working on now?"

When we talked about her work Mara's face lit up. She took me by the hand. "Come, let me show you."

She led me to the back of the room. The table there was filled with crates of grapes, both red and green. "Right now I am working on two new wines."

"Wine is science?" I asked.

Mara looked at me. "Of course," she smiled. "It's the best kind of science. Science you can drink! And it makes you feel better. Wine has many positive attributes."

I actually knew that. But I figured Zena might not. "Oh?"

Mara smiled. "Yes. You commoners have so much to learn. Didn't you go to my talk last year on the benefits of phenols found in wines?"

I shrugged. "Sorry, must have been wrestling that day."

Mara pointed to the grapes on the table. "There is a lot of selective breeding of the grapes involved in order to grow the grapes with the most flavonoids and the best taste. I have a new variety that goes from seed to maturity in one month. It tastes great on the table, or crushed for wine."

"Interesting," I said.

"Wine is going to be especially important in these coming days," Mara said, eyes lowered.

"Zach, I have been going over their traditions. They drink a new wine whenever a new baby is born and one of their queens dies."

"Yes. So with the queen's passing, not only will we get a new queen, we will get a new life," I said, like I knew what I was talking about.

Mara looked up at me. "Actually, two new lives."

"If Kiana gets sentenced to death," HARV said.

"Oh, that's right, I forgot about Kiana," I said.

Mara laughed and patted me on the shoulder. "You silly thing," she said. "Luckily you are cute."

"Why, thank you," I said, putting my hands together under my chin and batting my eyes in jest. I got serious again. "You know, sometimes I wish to have a baby," I said.

"You do?" HARV said.

"In character, HARV."

"Oh, right."

"Well, if none of the royals want to reproduce, then maybe you will win the lottery," Mara said a bit halfheartedly.

"What about you? Do you want any children?" I asked. I was starting to think it possible that somebody offed the queen to increase their chances of being able to have children. After all, I have seen many people go to great lengths to become parents. I had to consider that many of these women had biological clocks that were ticking away. They may have been ticking more slowly than other women's, but they were ticking all the same.

Mara looked at me like I had just asked her to recite pi to the last digit. "Want kids? I am only two hundred and fifty. I haven't even begun to begin starting to possibly consider thinking about reproducing."

"I'll take that as a no," I said.

Now Mara looked at me like I was trying to count backward from infinity. "Of course you should take that as a no."

It was time to cut to the chase. I had gotten to know

Mara a little. Now I needed to see how she would react to a tough question. A question a good bodyguard
would ask.

"Why do you think Kiana killed our dear, beloved
queen?" I asked.

Mara popped a grape off its stem and ate it slowly,
thinking. "It's not important what I think. What is important is what the court thinks."

She sat down on a stool and started studying a petri
dish under a microscope. Mara was a cool one when she
wanted to be. I gave her that.

"Surely you must have an opinion. You are the smart-
est of us all." I said.

"You are just flattering me so I will talk," Mara said.
She *was* quite sharp, after all.

"No, I seriously am interested in your knowledge and
wisdom," I told her.

Mara turned back to her grapes. "In that case I'll give
you a little bit of advice: Leave the protection of Luca to
Andra and her people. Andra doesn't like people interfering with her work."

"I am not interfering, I am helping," I said. I pounded
on my chest for good measure, since it seemed like
something Zena would do.

Mara looked over her shoulder at me. "I doubt Andra will see it that way."

"I am sure I can handle Andra," I said.

Mara turned back to her work and mumbled just
clearly enough so I could hear. "That just proves you are
not very bright."

I decided to push a bit harder.

"The queen drank poisoned hot cocoa," I pointed up
and down the lab. "I would guess you have the ability to
make poisons here."

Mara stood up and shot at me in super speed. She

didn't hit me or touch me; she just stood on her tiptoes to get into my holographic face.

"I only create things that bring life," she said. Now she pointed down the table. "I have my books and computer records. You are free to look at them if you like."

It was more than apparent I had gotten all I was going to get out of Mara for now. The good news was I had the impression she was hiding something. The bad news was I had no idea what.

"No, that's okay," I said as I backed away. "Thank you. You have been very informative."

I pushed the button to call the elevator, turned and looked over my shoulder and said, "Make sure you're available in case I need to question you some more."

I probably wouldn't need to question Mara again, but I wanted to irk her a bit. History has taught me irked people make more mistakes.

Chapter 32

When I arrived back in my—that is, Luca's—room, Ohma was there, sitting at the table.

"I brought you some food," Ohma told me.

I walked over and sat at the table. It looked good: a few slices of ham and eggs and a glass of wine. I liked the way these women ate.

"I find good food makes bad news go down easier," Ohma said.

I took a bit of the ham. "Bad news?"

Ohma fingered the crystals around her neck. "First, Luca says she is sorry. She is in meetings all day, trying to prepare the proper statement on the queen's death and Kiana's trial."

"I understand."

"What about Andra and Poca?" I asked.

No answer.

"Andra says she will speak to you when she feels like speaking to you on her own terms," Ohma told me.

"Well that's not really bad news," I said.

Ohma looked away. "Andra's own terms usually mean pain for somebody else."

"Oh," I said.

"Poca has flat out refused to talk to you. She says she is far too busy. She deals with injuries, not inquiries."

"Oh," I said.

Both Poca and Andra were being too defensive. History has taught me that the innocent are hardly ever as defensive as the guilty. Of course, experience has taught me very few are ever totally innocent. Poca and Andra may have been hiding guilt over something else.

Ohma stood up. "I need to get back to the conference room to help Luca."

"I understand," I told her.

Ohma got up and I followed her to the door. I opened it for her and watched her walk away. I closed the door and locked it. HARV appeared in front of me.

"Zach, you have a message from Elena."

"Put her through," I said, walking back to the table.

HARV's image morphed into Elena.

"Hello, Zach. I was able to talk to that Randy Pool again."

"And?"

"He made a pass at me again . . ." Elena said.

"And?"

"I made him think he was a puppy dog," Elena said.

"And?"

"He said he enjoyed the experience," Elena sighed.

"Did you get anything constructive out of him?" I asked.

Elena nodded. "Yes, we reconfigured his nano-defense scanners. He found a nano-spy transmitter had infiltrated his computer systems. It was very advanced in some ways, but almost ancient in others. It appears to have been loaded by hand from one of his terminals. It went online 12:10 P.M., nine minutes after Kiana arrived."

"I hope you didn't disable it," I said. "Don't want to tip off whoever's responsible for this that we're on to them."

Elena shook her head. "No, of course not. Randy just rewrote part of his defense system so it would now feed the transmitter false information."

"Good," I said. "Could you trace where the transmitter was transmitting to?"

"He could only narrow it down to somewhere in the middle of the Pacific Ocean," Elena said.

"I think it's safe to say that somewhere is here," I said.

"Duh," HARV said. Then, "I don't believe I am saying 'duh' now."

"Second time today, buddy," I said.

HARV shook his head in dismay.

"Now I just need to figure out who planted that spy device," I said.

"Kiana seems like the most obvious choice, since she was there," Elena said.

"Thanks, Elena, you have been quite helpful," I said. I knew what she said made sense, but Elena sees the world as fairly black and white. I needed to see the world in full color.

"I was also able to contact Carol and Electra to appraise them of your situation."

"And?"

"Carol at first didn't believe me and thought I might have something to do with your disappearance. She still holds a bit of a grudge for all those times I kicked her ass on the Moon."

"If I remember correctly, Carol got in her share of licks on you," I said. Sure, Elena was helping me here, but I've always been one to set the record straight.

"That's because she had you and HARV and a bunch of others backing her up," Elena said.

"What is it with you psis? Why do you have to always prove who can spit the farthest, telekinetically speaking?" I asked.

Elena shrugged. "Just superhuman nature, I guess. Don't worry though, Carol is fine now."

"Fine now?"

Elena waved dismissively at me. "I am sure she will be totally back to normal by the time you return. She may randomly cluck once in a while, but that will go away. We're even going to have lunch sometime."

I sighed. "How'd Electra handle this? Please don't tell me you zapped her."

Elena smiled. "Nah, she was cool. Electra said, and I quote: *'Only my man can get himself into trouble that involves him being on an island with ten thousand women.'* "

"Yeah, I am talented, and somehow extremely lucky—or unlucky depending on how you look at it."

Just then there was a knock—well, more like a banging—on my door.

"Gotta go," I told Elena.

"I understand," she said. "If you need anything, just have HARV call."

Elena's image faded out as the knock grew louder. The force of the knocking was so powerful the door was practically bursting off the hinges.

"Hold on. I'm coming!" I said. I got up and headed toward the door.

I was quite sure I was about to have a little heart-to-heart chat with Andra.

I opened the door. Andra burst in past me. She was followed in by two other large women. Both had their hair up in buns, both had their noses slightly bent, each of them had slightly puffy lips. Both were wearing light chain armor that they looked like they'd been born in. They looked like sisters—and they were both the big sister.

Andra pointed behind her. "These are two of my best people: Boppa and Clobba."

Boppa and Clobba nodded.

"I am Boppa," the slightly larger one said.

"I am Clobba," the smaller one said.

"Charmed," I said.

"I am not thrilled with my sister bringing in outside protection," Andra told me, moving close enough so I could smell her breath.

"I am sure she is not thrilled to need my services," I retorted.

Andra looked away from me toward her backup muscle. "Still, Luca is next in line to be queen so I must honor her wishes."

"Okay . . ." I said slowly. I knew this wasn't going to go that easy. You don't bring extra muscle unless you are planning on using it: either to put on a hurting or to give a scaring. Andra didn't seem like the type who needed help to scare people.

"But for you to get my approval, you must pass a test," Andra told me.

"I kind of figured as much," I said.

"Zach, I have some potentially bad news for you. One of the crystals Andra is wearing around her neck seems to be a holograph detector," HARV said.

"Potentially bad news? HARV, that sounds like really bad news."

"See, Zach, you always look at the worst side of things!"

"Get to the point, HARV."

"I can block her detection."

"Great!" I said.

"Except I can only block and keep the hologram up

while fighting for one hundred eight to three hundred sixty seconds. So fight fast."

"I'll do my best."

Andra stepped back, in true royal fashion. For now, at least, she was content to let others do her work for her. Boppa and Clobba each inched forward. I chose to look upon this as an opportunity. If Boppa and Clobba got in a few good blows it would give me a chance to talk with Poca. These women may have been brawlers, but I was guessing, or at least hoping, they were used to wrestling and fighting the in the same style under very set conditions. I was about to change the circumstances.

"HARV, I want to take the first one out fast. It'll put doubt in the other's mind."

"Roger."

"We haven't seen you around the sparring ring," Boppa said.

"Well . . ." I started to say.

I leapt forward and clasped my hands over Boppa's ears.

"HARV, shock now!"

I pulled Boppa's head forward, and current shot through my fingers into her brain. She started to convulse, but I didn't stop pulling her forward. I brought my knee up, smashing it clean into her nose. That drew blood. Boppa instinctively pulled back and brought her hands up to stop the rush of blood. I clocked her with a left cross to the jaw, using her momentum to knock her down.

Clobba reacted quickly. She threw a right hook into what she thought was my head. My holographic head took the blow. Of course, it didn't hurt the real me at all, since the blow passed harmlessly over my actual head. I had faith, though, that HARV made my holographic head react as if it had taken quite a shot.

"I broadcasted the sensation that she made contact with your head into her brain," HARV said proudly.

I decided not to think too closely about what that meant. From the contented look on Clobba's face, I determined that she indeed felt she had landed a hard blow. She thought she had me stunned. I took advantage of this by hitting her dead straight in the solar plexus with a computer-enhanced punch. The blow doubled her over, her head leaning toward me. I put my arm around her neck and positioned my body beside hers. I bulldogged her to the ground, face-first. She was out cold.

I rolled to my feet. I took a fighting position in case Andra was next.

Andra merely looked at me. "Okay, you can take on two of my average people. I guess you will do." Andra walked forward and put her arm around me. "You fight good. I am surprised I never noticed you in the gym before."

"I train off hours," I said. "That is how I met Luca."

"Ah, I see," Andra told me. "You know, I always have room on my team for a girl like you. One who can kick ass."

I couldn't blow Andra off. It's common sense that the best way to get info out of somebody is to get them to trust you.

"I've known Luca for a long time," I said.

"She only likes XYs," Andra told me.

"A girl can hope," I said.

Andra patted me on the back. (It kind of hurt.) "Okay. Think about my offer."

"I will," I said.

Andra looked closely at my nose. "You should go visit Poca," she told me. "Your nose may be broken."

"I will do that also," I said.

By now Boppa and Clobba were coming around. They certainly were tough. Andra walked back to them. "Get up," she ordered. "Our work here is done."

Boppa and Clobba followed Andra out of the room. I went to the door and locked it.

"That turned out better than I expected," I told HARV.

"HARV, are we going to be able to convince Poca that my holographic head is really my head?" I asked.

"We, no," HARV said. "But I can say with a high degree of confidence that *I* can. At least for a few minutes."

I started to the door. *"Well then, a few minutes is what I'll take."*

I walked into the hallway. *"Do you know the way to Poca's?"* I asked HARV.

"Zach, you are becoming so reliant on me. Soon you will ask me if it's time for you to use the potty."

"Just say yes, HARV."

"Yes, HARV."

I just looked at him.

"I really have been hooked up to your brain for far, far too long," HARV said.

Chapter 33

I started walking down the hallway toward the
elevator.

*"You know, Zach, I can simulate some sensations to
people who touch the hologram, but I certainly can't keep
up with Poca fixing your face . . ."*

"Yes, I am aware of that," I said.

"Therefore . . ."

"I can't let Poca touch me," I said as I reached the
elevator.

I called the elevator and waited.

"So why are we going then?" HARV asked.

*"I was under the impression that you needed to get
close to Poca's system to get a cold read on it."*

"Well, it would help," HARV said. *"Press button 5."*

I pushed the button. The elevator started down.

"Don't worry, HARV, I have a way with people."

"You don't have to tell me."

*"By the time I'm done with Poca, her Hippocratic oath
will be a hypocritical oath."*

"I have no doubt . . ."

The elevator stopped; the door opened. The medical facilities, like Mara's lab, took up an entire floor. The room looked like a combination of a hospital dormitory room and a mad scientist's lab. Poca was sitting on a stool on the far side of the room, peering into a microscope while holding a golden crystal that was beaming some light into a computer.

I walked up close enough so she could hear I was in the room.

"I will be with you in a moment," Poca said, not looking away from the microscope. She spoke into the crystal, "Sample one-nine-five-seven shows no signs of abnormality, record."

"Andra said I should come down to see you," I said.

The name-dropping got a rise out of Poca. She turned to me. "Oh, it's you," not even attempting to hide the disappointment in her voice. "Andra and Mara have told me about you."

It was good she wasn't thrilled to see me—after all, I didn't want her touching me. Somehow, though, I was still offended.

"I had to teach Andra and her muscle a little lesson," I said.

Poca looked over her shoulder at me. "It looks like they got in a couple of shots, too."

I shrugged. "Yeah, three on one and they got a little lucky."

"*HARV, are you able to tap into her computer?*" I asked.

"*I need line of sight and she's blocking the system. It would be good if you could get her to stand,*" HARV said.

"*Don't worry, I am pretty sure I can spark her ire,*" I said.

"*I have no doubt you can light a fire under her ire,*" HARV said. "*Oh man, I am going to have to run a diagnostic check.*"

"I will take a look at you in a bit," Poca said. The tone of her voice made it clear that in the list of her priorities, I was somewhere behind clipping her toenails.

"No hurries," I said. "I realize my health concerns are not as important as a member of the royal family's day-to-day tasks." I was hoping this would get a rise, literally, out of her.

Poca continued looking into her microscope. "It is nice to see somebody who understands their place and role in this world."

Okay, this was going to a little harder, and potentially more painful, than I had hoped. Sometimes you have to take a wild swing at the ball and hope you make contact.

"You obviously know your place in the line of hierarchy," I said with enough intonation in my voice to make it a leading question.

"What do you mean?" Poca asked, still not really paying attention to me.

"You know your place in the pecking order. You can take pecks from them and give them to us," I said. "When you are low woman on the totem pole, you are basically looking up at all the others' asses. Lucky for you the view is so good."

Poca pulled back a bit from her microscope viewing. She took a deep breath. "I am not low woman on the totem pole."

"Sure you are. You are doctor in a place where nobody ever gets sick and dies."

"I have my duties," Poca said, slowly and deliberately. "We get a couple of sports-related injuries a week. I also do research to help us live longer and better . . . I am important around here," she insisted.

She was getting ready to spring. I liked that. I took a step back, then took my best shot. "Then how come you never got the chance to experience motherhood?" I asked.

Poca pushed away some from the lab table. "Excuse me?"

"Your sisters did. Here you are, bringing life into our world for them, yet you were not allowed to bring your own child into the world."

"I could not deliver my own child. I am good, but not that good," she said, perhaps missing the point a bit.

"Yeah, well your sister was never going to give you the chance anyhow," I said.

"In case you haven't noticed, you haven't gotten her to stand yet," HARV told me.

"So your DNA was deemed nonworthy," I said. "I can understand that. You were always my least favorite of the royals. I think the queen was wise in letting others reproduce over you." I paused. "Well, not literally of course, as that would be gross. Unless you are into that kind of thing, which would make you even less likely to be picked for motherhood."

I couldn't see Poca's face but her body was squirming. I was starting to get through to her.

"The queen must have thought you would not be a fit mother. Why else would she have four children and allow you none?"

Poca shot up from her stool and thrust a finger out at me. "You don't know what you are talking about!" she shouted.

"Vingo!" HARV said. *"Nice clear view of the monitor. Tapping in now."*

"You do NOT know what you are talking about!" Poca repeated, her face growing redder with each word.

I took another couple of steps back. "Obviously not, since I haven't sparked any emotion from you on the subject."

Poca made a fist and shook it at me. "You are lucky I am a woman of medicine, dedicated to the healing of others."

"And birthing other peoples' babies, just not your own," I added.

Poca lunged at me. She took a wild swing, which I ducked under. I sprung back up and hit her with an open palm to the nose. It was a quick tactic meant to draw blood, water the eyes, and get her to back off. It worked on all three counts. Poca stopped her attack and covered her nose with her hands.

"You don't know what you are talking about," she said.

"HARV, do you have what you need?" I asked.

"As you would say, in spades ..."

Good. I had toyed with Poca enough. Time to leave now while the leaving was good.

"If you are nothing else, you are a fine doctor," I said. "My wounds feel much better now."

I turned and walked away.

"You are so lucky this a socialized system, because you would NOT be able to afford my bill!" Poca called after me.

"Oh, Zach, I have something so *good. Walk as fast as you can,"* HARV said.

Chapter 34

I reached "my" room and Luca was there, standing by her closet, changing. She was only wearing pink silk undergarments. I turned my head away from her.

"Oh, sorry, I didn't know you would be here," I told her.

"It is my room," she said with a hint of smile in her voice.

"Yes, but I thought you'd still be busy with official duties."

"You can turn toward me," she said. "We have prepared the announcement of the death and the murder. I will be giving it soon. I need the right look."

I turned toward her. She was still wearing just her bra and a thong.

"I thought you'd be wearing more clothing," I said.

"I didn't think you'd mind," she said as she fingered through her closet for something. "My body isn't that bad, is it?"

"No, not at all. On a scale of one to ten, it's like a twelve," I said. I learned long ago if a woman asks about her body, unless you have a death wish, or are trying to anger her, you should always praise her.

"You are flattering me," she said. She took a bright yellow sleeveless blouse off a hanger.

"Yes, but you deserve it."

"She does have a rocking body," HARV said in my head. A pause. A buzz. *"I just said, 'rocking body,' didn't I?"* Another pause. A sigh. *"Running another diagnostic now."*

I ignored HARV. Instead, I chose to concentrate on the beautiful woman in front of me.

"Zach, drop the hologram," Luca requested, though in effect it was an order. "I want to deal with the real you."

The hologram that shielded me melted away. Luca confirmed that with a smile.

"While you are flattering me, I know my body isn't as good as Kiana's . . ." Luca said, fishing for another compliment.

I walked toward where she was changing. I walked slowly, so she had a chance to put more clothing on. "Different body types," I told her. "Hers lets it all hang out there. Yours is more compact. Both are good. It's kind of like which tastes better: milk chocolate or dark chocolate."

Luca smiled. She held the blouse in her hand. It transformed from yellow to bluish. She held it out toward me. "Is this more appropriate for a sad announcement?" she asked.

I nodded.

Luca slid the blouse over her body. She lifted her left arm and casually sniffed herself. She pulled her head back a little. "Whoa, that's bordering on lethal . . ."

Luca walked over to her nightstand and picked up a white crystal. She lifted her left arm and ran the crystal under her arm. She switched hands and repeated the process with the other arm. She lifted her arms up again and sniffed. She smiled. "Much better."

She walked back to her closest. I assumed it was time for a skirt.

"Ah, Zach," HARV coaxed. *"How about if I tell you what I learned at Poca's."*

"What is it?"

"Poca has been working on a virus." HARV said. *"A very strange virus. She wasn't even trying to hide it. I just had to look over her main screen."*

"What kind of virus?" I asked. I never like the sound of "virus." Nobody ever makes a "feel better" virus.

"It's one that only attacks sperm . . ." HARV said.

"Sperm?" I said out loud.

This caught Luca's attention.

"Excuse me?" she said.

It was time to lay my cards on the table, even though this may have been blind man's bluff. I didn't know what those cards were yet, but I knew Luca's reaction would be critical.

"HARV, tell us both what you found," I said.

HARV appeared in the room.

"Zach, are you sure?"

"I am sure."

HARV stood between us. He looked at Luca. "It might help if you put some pants on."

Luca's eyes opened wider. "Oh, yes. Sorry. Got caught up in the moment." She walked over to her closet, pulled out a leather skirt, and slipped it on. "There." She walked over and sat down on the bed, legs crossed. "So what do you have to share with us, HARV?"

A holographic blackboard with a chemical structure appeared next to HARV, who was now holding an old-fashioned pointer.

Luca studied the spinning structure. "Oh, I see you discovered virus Not-Y," she said, as if talking about the weather.

"I don't like the sound of that," I said, though I wasn't sure why. "What does it do?"

"It is mostly harmless. Totally harmless to the living," Luca insisted.

"You're going to have to be more specific," I said.

"It greatly cuts down the amount of Y sperm males produce," HARV said.

"And greatly reduces the female's acceptance of those Y sperm that are produced," Luca added.

"How greatly?" I asked.

"It would cut the number of male births down to one in a hundred thousand," HARV said.

Luca nodded. "Of course that was only a roughly rounded estimate. "

"So men would eventually be outnumbered on the planet a hundred thousand to one?" I asked.

"More or less," Luca said. "We figured that was a controllable ratio."

I shook my head in disbelief. "That's gendercide," I said.

"No, that would still leave a hundred thousand men on Earth," Luca said. "Plenty to go around. There are only ten thousand of us."

"Yeah, but there would be like ten billion other women on the planet," I said.

"They would adapt," Luca said. "Women are flexible."

"But you would be ..."

Luca shook her head and touched me gently on the shoulder. "Zach, we would not be hurting anybody. We would just be altering things."

"What gives you the right?" I asked.

"We would be saving your world from the violence of men," Luca said, dead serious. "But do not worry. The queen decided not to use the Not-Y virus."

I thought about what this all meant. I didn't like it

one bit. Even if I wasn't a male, I am pretty sure I would have been morally offended.

"Maybe the queen changed her mind?" I asked.

Luca looked at me as if I just said rain sometimes falls up, or that all politicians were really bright. "Have you met the queen?" She thought about what she said. She giggled just a little, "Sorry. No, of course you never met." She thought a little more, then added, "At least not that you remember."

I was hoping she was just playing with my mind.

HARV looked at me. "Over the queen's five-hundred-plus-year reign she changed her mind exactly zero times."

Luca's head bobbed up and down in agreement. Then she said, "Mother was a proud woman. She considered flip-flopping a sign of weakness."

"Then what about Kiana?" I asked. "Maybe she wanted to get rid of the queen so she could rid the world of men?"

Luca pulled back from me. Now she was looking at me like I just I had said rain *always* falls up and all politicians are brilliant, loving people who only care to do the right thing no matter what their party line is. "Have you met Kiana?" she asked cynically.

"Really, being cynical doesn't suit you, Luca. And it gives you wrinkles," I told her. But I saw her point.

"Kiana *loves* you males. If anything she would want more of you around!"

"I have to question Kiana," I said bluntly.

"Why?" Luca asked.

"To see what her thoughts on the matter are. I'm a good judge of human, and near-human, and superhuman, character. I can gauge her reactions and learn a lot."

"Really?" Luca asked.

I nodded. "Really. I almost completed my Ph.D. in

human behavior," I told her. "I spent three years working on it at New Cornell University. I would have finished but I had a calling . . ."

"You had a calling to be a PI?" Luca asked.

"Well, I felt the world needed me," I said. "That it had a different mission for me."

HARV stepped in between us. "That and there was an incident."

"Incident?" Luca asked.

I let a bit of a smile creep across my face. "It was nothing . . ." I said, though my face betrayed my words.

"I don't think so," Luca said.

"I got in a bit of trouble for dating the dean's daughter . . ." I said.

"That doesn't sound too bad," Luca said.

"He was also dating the president of the university's *two* daughters at the same time," HARV said.

"Zach!" Luca said. "Now I am starting to see why we are better off without men."

"Those were my younger days. I did a lot of experimenting," I paused. I opened up my hands to Luca. "Those days taught me a lot about reading people. You can't date three women—two of them sisters—at once unless you have good instincts about human nature. Plus, I have learned a lot since then."

"If you say so," Luca said. From her tone, you could tell she wasn't quite ready to buy what I was selling.

"Don't worry, Electra set him straight," HARV assured Luca.

"The thing is, I've gotten better over the years. More mature. More experienced. I know how to read people. Trust me. I wouldn't be alive if I didn't."

HARV nodded. "It's true. Well, that, and the fact that he is fairly quick, can take a punch, is incredibly lucky, and has me."

I gently touched Luca on the shoulder. "Trust me. By

talking to her I'll be able to tell if she may be quite willing to wipe men out. 'Cause if she is, that would be motive enough for her to take out the queen."

Plus, I wanted to ask her about that nano-spying software placed in Randy's system.

Luca crossed her arms and lifted her head, thinking. "She is being held in the sub-basement under guard and sedation."

"So will you take me to her?" I asked.

Luca simply nodded.

Chapter 35

HARV put my holographic disguise back on, and Luca led me down the hall, past the elevator we normally took. I thought about mentioning to her that she missed the elevator, but I knew she knew that. We continued down the hallway until we came to what appeared to be a solid wall. A dead end.

Luca fingered through the crystals she wore around her neck. She selected a long blue one. She pointed the crystal at the wall and starting moving it in a circular direction, increasing the width of the circle with each motion. The wall shimmered then faded away, revealing a door with a button along side it. Luca pushed the button. The door slid open.

Luca and I walked into what appeared to be a small room. I knew, though, it had to be a secret elevator. Luca looked up and said, "This is Princess Luca. Activate."

I could feel the downward movement. We continued our descent in silence for a few minutes. After still not coming to a stop I said, "Either this room is way below, or this is a very slow elevator."

"Both," Luca said.

The elevator finally stopped. The door opened to a long dark hallway. Luca entered the hallway; I followed.

"Very few of us know of this place," Luca said in a whisper.

"It does seem quite well hidden," I said.

We continued to walk down the hallway. Luca pointed to a door that was now coming into sight. There was a guard on each side of it.

"This is a special room we designed for extra heinous crimes against the queen. To my knowledge, it has never been used before," Luca said. "Our foremothers were aware that even though men are the root of most violence, that it might be possible, under the right conditions, that a woman may attempt something especially nasty."

That got me thinking. Were males really more violent than females? I know through our early history most of the killing was done by males. Males did most of the violent crime. But did this mean men were naturally more aggressive? Sure, we had more testosterone coursing through our veins, but if memory from old bio classes rang true, I remembered that females processed and utilized testosterone more efficiently.

Sure, more men might be more likely to hit or shoot first, think later, but this may have been due more to men being trained in the ways of violence and weapons. Plus, speaking from personal experience (lots of personal experience), these days many women are just as apt to take a crack at cracking your nose. I was going to need to think about this more. The more a good PI thinks the less he had to brawl. Like my old mentor liked to say: *"The more you use your head, the fewer shots to the head you'll take."*

"So are you saying you don't have crime because you don't have males?" I asked.

"We have crimes. Most of them are settled through our dispute channeling," Luca said.

I stopped walking. "Dispute channeling?"

Luca stopped also, and turned to me. "For most crimes the queen has final say. Her word is law, as it is with most disputes. Once a month the queen settles them."

"Once again, it is good to be the queen," I said.

"Yes, of course," Luca said. "But, like I was saying, there are occasions when the queen cannot, or will not decide. When that occurs, the parties in the dispute compete in a series of mental or physical challenges. The winner has her way."

"Oh, okay," I said. "But I don't think any of that has to do with no men. It sounds like you have a small, enclosed socialist society where almost everybody knows almost everybody. That's why you don't have crime. If somebody pulls something off, they know they'll be caught."

I had made my point, so I started back down the hall.

Luca stood there for a nano and then started after me. "I never considered that," she said.

"No, of course you didn't. You are so set in your little fishbowl world you can't see it clearly. That's why I have to talk to Kiana. See how she thinks."

As we drew closer to the door, I saw the guards were Boppa and Clobba. Just what I didn't need. Hopefully, my scuffle with them had earned me some respect.

"I am here to interview my sister, " Luca said.

Boppa pointed to me and growled. "What is she doing with you?"

That answered two questions. I hadn't earned any respect, but the growl showed women were quite capable of mindless aggression. Males certainly didn't have the patent on that.

"She is my bodyguard," Luca said. "Now open the door or you will have to deal with both of us," Luca added.

Boppa turned toward the door and pulled an old-fashioned metal key from her pocket. She put the key in the lock and turned it. The door popped open. Luca and I walked into a small dark room. Kiana was sitting in the middle of the room, tied to a chair by some sort of green glowing rope. She was slumped over, asleep. It wasn't a natural sleep. I pushed the door shut behind us with my leg.

We walked over to Kiana. Luca wasn't kidding about her being drugged.

"Why did you drug her?" I asked.

"She has a very powerful voice. We don't want her to use it. Besides, it is easier to get the truth out of her," Luca said.

I looked at Luca, not with contempt, but neither with total approval. "What have you learned?"

Luca didn't say a word. She lowered her head.

"What have you learned?"

Luca poked her head up so she could see me. "So far nothing. She claims to be innocent."

"Don't you believe her?"

"I am not sure what to believe. She had the motive and the means," Luca said.

"We'll see about that," I said. I tapped Kiana gently on the shoulder. "Kiana, Kiana, we need to talk to you."

Kiana opened one eye, then the other. She looked at me. "Who are you?"

"I am Zena, Luca's bodyguard," I said.

Kiana smiled. "Zach, that cover may work on others but not me."

"How can you tell?" I asked.

"Your scent," Kiana said. "I spent enough time with you on my ship." She looked around, remembering where she was. "Zach, I didn't kill my mother," she said. "You have to believe me."

"I do," I said, though I wasn't yet totally convinced. "Somebody planted a tapping device into Dr. Randy Pool's computer system. You visited him. You could have easily been that somebody."

"True," Kiana nodded. "But I didn't."

"And you can prove this how?" I pried.

"I cannot. That is why I hired you."

Kiana had a point. Problem was, it wasn't a helpful one.

"I need more to go on," I said. "The spy device was planted ten minutes after you arrived."

"Zach, I was gone then. I was trying on new boots at the UltraMegaHyperMart down the street," Kiana said.

"HARV, try to check that," I said. "See if you can get into the UMHM's security camera database."

"On it," HARV said.

"I also learned that you people have developed your own virus," I told Kiana.

Kiana looked at me like she was drugged out, which of course she was. "You have to be more specific."

"One to slowly eliminate men," I said.

"Oh, that one," she said. She looked up at me. "Yeah, I thought of using that one once."

"You did," I said.

"Yeah, I was pretty pissed at male-kind," Kiana said. She must have realized what potentially damning words those were. "But I swear, I never would actually use it. I was just feeling extra crappy that week. I know you men may be pains in the ass, but I respect that."

I gauged Kiana's response. I thought she was telling the truth.

"HARV?"

"Once again, Zach, she appears to be telling the truth."

I decided to make a sort of radical move. One that would clinch Kiana's trust and let me know once and for all she was innocent—at least of this. There is a pressure point at the back of the ear you can use to stun an opponent. If executed properly, it works on most humans and near humans, and even some superhumans. I moved forward and reached for Luca. I pressed firmly on that spot just below her ear. I caught her as she went limp and fell backward. I eased her to the ground.

"Zach, are going to break me out?" Kiana asked.

"We need to talk in private," I told her. I pointed at her as dramatically as I could. "I need to know the truth. Did you do it?"

I paused to add more tension, and force the truth out of her. "Even if you are guilty I will still help you. After all, you are paying me." The first statement was a lie. I don't usually like lying to clients, but I don't mind doing it to the guilty ones.

"Zach, I know you. You won't help me if I am guilty," Kiana said. Okay, it wasn't a good lie, but I wasn't going to admit she was on to me. Once she saw I wouldn't give in she went on, "But, Zach, I swear to you, I am being set up. I may have not seen eye to eye with my mother, but I would not kill her."

I looked at Kiana, examining how her eyes moved, her breathing. She seemed sincere.

"Once again she appears to be telling the truth," HARV said.

"Okay, I will still help you," I said. "If you had to pick out a sister or cousin who would kill your mom and set you up, who would it be?"

"Andra," she said, which came as no surprise.

"What would she gain out of it?" I asked.

"She is the type who would be happy enough to see me fail. As an added bonus, she probably figures she can bully Luca more," Kiana said.

"I don't think Luca is all that easy to push around," I said.

"You are smarter than Andra," Kiana told me.

Kiana certainly had a point. There was now no doubt in my mind Andra was involved in this. A couple things bothered me though. First, I didn't think Andra was smart enough to pull this off on her own. Second, I still needed a better motive than revenge on a sister—at least for whomever was aiding Andra.

"Of course, Luca once told me she had no desire to be queen. I wouldn't be surprised if Andra was counting on Luca to step down," Kiana added.

Now that certainly could have been enough of a motive.

I bent down to Luca. She was starting to come around.

"Luca, Luca, wake up," I said. "Come on, you can do it."

Luca opened her eyes. "What happened?" A slight pause. "Did Kiana use her voice on me?"

"No I used a pressure point on you," I said.

She gave me a weak smile. "Oh, very good. Quite cunning." She thought about it for a nano. "Why?"

"I needed to talk in private with Kiana. I speculated that she would speak more freely without you listening."

Luca nodded doubtfully. "I . . . suppose that makes sense." Luca gazed over at Kiana looking at her without quite looking at her.

I turned to Kiana. "I'll do what I can to help you."

"Zach, I have managed to tap into their emergency communication system," HARV said. *"Andra has been alerted."*

It looked like this was going to work out even better than expected. Seeing how Andra reacted to my questioning of Kiana would give me more insight to what made Andra tick.

I nudged Luca and whispered, "Andra is coming."

"Andra is here!" Andra said loudly as she burst into the room, followed by Boppa and Clobba.

"Wow, good hearing," I said under my breath.

"Everything about me is exceptional," Andra said. She glared at Luca and me. "What are you doing talking to the prisoner before her trial?"

Luca stepped up. "I am the queen to be, it is within my rights."

Andra concentrated on me. "And her?"

"She is my bodyguard," Luca said. "She needs to know all she can to protect me."

"My people and I can protect you," Andra said, chest out.

"You did such a good job with mother," Luca said.

Andra took a step toward Luca. I started to intervene. Luca never gave me a chance.

"One more step, sister, and I will rearrange your molecules so you become a statue in my new office."

Clobba did not heed the warning. She lunged toward Luca. "You do not threaten my . . ."

Clobba never got to finish that statement, as she was petrified in place. Forever locked in the lunging position.

Andra and Boppa stood down.

"You would NOT dare do that to me," Andra said.

Luca looked at her steely-eyed. "Try me," was all she said.

Andra and Boppa exchanged glances. They knew they couldn't move nearly as fast as Luca could think.

"I need her. Will you turn her back?" Andra asked.

"I may, someday," Luca said. "For now I will use her

as an example in the courtyard. I am to be queen now," Luca said. "My words and actions are law."

Luca looked at me. "Come, Zena, we should go now."

I suppressed a gulp and exchanged a glance with Kiana. Had we all underestimated Luca's urge for power?

Chapter 36

As Luca and I entered the hallway, I started to worry that maybe we had all misjudged her. With her abilities, she could have easily created the poison to kill the queen. She also took out Clobba without a second thought. She seemed to have no apprehensions about doing the same to Andra and Boppa if pushed.

I didn't say anything until we entered the elevator.

"So, are you going to turn Clobba back?" I asked softly, as the elevator began to rise.

"I do not know if I can," Luca said. "I have never done that to a living being before." A pause, followed by a deep breath. "It was her own fault. She shouldn't have threatened me. They know my power. Just because I have never used it before does not mean I would not." Luca sighed. "I am tired of people confusing kindness for weakness. So if I need to rearrange some molecules to show my strength, then so be it."

The elevator stopped. We got off and headed toward our room. I decided not to say anything until we reached it.

The moment we walked in, though, I had to confront Luca head on—but with respect.

"HARV, drop the hologram," I said.

"Check."

Luca looked at me. "Zach, you are worried, aren't you?"

"I just saw you turn a person into a lawn ornament, so yeah, I am worried."

"I told you, if I am to be queen they must respect me, and maybe fear me a little."

"What were your mom's gifts?" I asked.

"Mom is from the original generation. Her gifts were more basic than ours. She could read and control minds," Luca said.

"I can see how those could be advantages for a leader," I said.

"Yes, we all knew if you disagreed with her she would make you think you were her pet puppy. So, nobody ever disagreed with her," Luca said. "She knew how to use her power. I should have paid more attention to her."

I didn't like where Luca was going with this. Had I misread her? The good news was that none of this seemed premeditated. I doubted she was the one who killed the queen. But that still didn't mean Luca wasn't dangerous.

Luca stormed over to me, put her head on my shoulder, and started to cry. "Oh, Zach, Zach, Zach. I do not know what I am turning into. I petrified her without a second thought. I have no idea if I can undo it. I do not want to be strong if it means turning everybody to stone."

I patted her gently on the back. It was a relief to see she felt remorse. "You acted by reflex, in self-defense," I assured her.

Luca looked up at me, eyes wet, makeup running. "I

just do not know any longer. I never wanted to be queen. You have to believe me."

"I do," I said sternly.

Luca pulled away some. "Yet, now that I am set to be queen, I feel I need to act like one. If it is true Kiana killed our mother, she certainly cannot be queen. Andra is far too hot-headed to be queen. It is my duty to be queen, I think. Do you agree?"

"I'd much rather have you be queen than Andra, that's for certain," I said.

Luca nodded. "True, she is a bit of an idiot. On the other hand, she makes decisions and believes in them right or wrong, which could serve her well as queen." Luca took some deep breaths and wiped the tears from her eyes. "Maybe I should step down?"

Luca's lack of faith in herself restored my faith in her. "We have enough arrogant, know-it-all leaders in the world as it is," I told her. "If it turns out Kiana is guilty, the people of Lantis would do well with you as queen."

Luca looked up at me. "Are you sure?"

"Never been surer of anything in my life," I said. It was a bit of an exaggeration, but it helped make a point. I needed to prop up Luca's ego because I needed her to stay in power.

"Zach," HARV said, appearing between Luca and me. "I have confirmation of Kiana's story. She was in the new UltraMegaHyperMart down the street from Randy's office at the time the bug was installed. I had Elena's Moon computer team tap into the UMHM's security cameras. We spotted her there."

"What does that mean?" Luca said.

"It means Kiana is surely being set up. I just need to figure out how Andra did it and how to prove it. And if she had help."

Chapter 37

Luca went out to prepare for the coming day. I stayed in the room to rest my eyes and to think. The next thing I knew, HARV was waking me up.

"Zach, get up," HARV said in my head.

I sat up and noticed I was in bed. "How long was I sleeping?" I asked.

"Doesn't matter," HARV said. "It is morning now. The news is out. For an event this big they have even lifted their mass communication restrictions. There will be a one-day celebration of the queen's life, then a one-day celebration of Luca becoming queen, and then Kiana's trial will begin. The people already want her head."

"So that means I have two days to prove she's innocent," I said.

"Very good, Zach." HARV appeared before me. "Apparently, the royals like to use the media when it is convenient. They are broadcasting the holostory of the queen's life above the stadium. They have also sent a message to the entire population via the emergency communication bands they all wear."

I got out of bed and moved to the window. It gave me a clear view of the stadium. Sure enough, giant images of Queen Ella were rotating above it. The queen signing papers. The queen lifting massive amounts of weight. The queen holding a baby in her arms. The queen addressing a crowd at the stadium. The queen working in a lab. The queen working in the fields. The words *Loved By All* ran across the bottom of the images.

"Well, obviously not all," I muttered.

The door opened. Luca walked in. "Are you ready for the celebrations of my mother's life?" she asked me.

"Celebrations?" I said.

"Yes, first we will go to the public one to put in our appearances. Then we will come back to the Ivory Tower for our private thoughts."

"The celebrations mean wine and food, correct?" I asked.

"Correct," Luca told me.

I smiled. This was something I could use. Loose lips sink ships, and wine has been the source of more loose lips than anything else.

Luca and I started to walk. I could tell she was nervous. She wasn't as smooth as before.

"What's wrong?" I asked.

"Just a little nervous," she said. "I have to give the opening remarks. As the one destined to be queen, I need to first state what a great woman the queen was."

"That should be easy for you," I told her.

She nodded. "It is. My mother was great." There was a pause. "It is the next part that makes me sweat. I have to tell what I will do as queen. I have never given it any thought, as I had no interest in being queen."

"Do the people know this?" I asked.

"No," she said. "I am sure none of them ever considered I would become queen, so none ever asked if I would want it."

"What about your sisters or your aunt?" I prodded.

"I have confided in both Ohma and Poca," Luca said.

"What about Mara and Andra?"

"Truthfully, no. Though I am sure they have both assumed that I have no interest in being queen."

"Hmm. I am pretty certain Andra has something to do with this. If you say outright that you want to be queen she'll come after you. "

"I can handle her," Luca said, talking like the proud queen she was to become.

"I'm sure you can, but I need more time to determine if Andra acted alone. If we smoke her out too fast we might ruin that."

"Okay," Luca said. "So why don't I just say I am stepping down after the trial?"

"Because if that's what the murderer wants, and I am guessing they do, we don't want them to be feeling too good about themselves . We want them uneasy. We want them to make a move, but only when we're ready to spring a trap."

"I understand," Luca said.

By the time Luca and I reached the stadium it was full to the upper levels. Truly, every citizen of Lantis had come to pay their respects to the queen. Bots, some of which I swear had some sort of wood paneling, were rolling up and down the aisles serving generous portions of wine and food. In the center of the stadium floor there was a stage. Andra, some of her security people, Mara, Poca, and a few other women were seated on the stage. There was a band sitting on the ground just below the stage. They were playing very upbeat happy songs.

Luca and I walked into the stadium and onto the grounds. The nano the crowd saw Luca had entered the building, a hush fell over them. Luca walked and I followed. When we were near the stairs to the podium, Luca turned to me and said, "I must make my speech now. Stay a few steps behind my family."

We walked up the steps. Luca headed to the podium at the front of the stage. I went and stood behind the seated royals along with the other security people.

Luca stood at the podium and adjusted the crystal, which I guessed she would be using as a microphone. She looked royal and commanding. I gazed over at Andra to see if she agreed. From the snarl on her face, I gathered she did.

Luca started her speech. "My fellow citizens of Lantis, my mother has left us. But we are not here to be weak and mourn her passing to the next plane. We are here to celebrate the life that was. We know she is looking at us from the next plane and smiling with pride."

Luca paused for reaction. There was a loud series of cheers.

Luca continued, "Now we head into the future. But first we must decide who murdered our beloved Queen Ella. My sister Kiana stands accused . . ."

A string of boos interrupted Luca's speech. She raised an arm to hush them then continued. "But we must look at all of the evidence before we decide on her fate. It is what my mother, the mother of us all, would have wanted."

Luca held for a moment. The crowd gave her steady applause.

Luca lifted up a fist. "I swear to you all, if I am to become queen, I will be the best queen I can be!"

The steady applause grew in volume and tone until it was near deafening. Luca lowered her raised fist. The crowd fell silent.

"Now I give you my sister, Andra, to send my mother's—our mother's—body off."

Luca started back to her seat as Andra stood up and

walked toward the podium. The middle of the stage opened up, and the queen's body rose up on a platform. The queen was dressed in a white flowing gown and lying on a mound of flowers.

Andra took the crystal mic in her hand and addressed the crowd. "Citizens of Lantis," she shouted. "I, Andra, third daughter of Ella, swear before you all that I will not sleep, eat, or even excrete until Kiana is proven guilty and sentenced to life on another plane of existence. Unlike our dear mother, though, it will be a lower plane."

"Interesting way of saying 'Until we kill her,'" HARV said.

Some of the crowd applauded, some cheered, others looked on in bewilderment.

Andra turned toward the queen's body. She drew a long red crystal from her side. Andra pointed the red crystal at the queen's body. The body burst into flames. Andra concentrated on the crystal and the flames grew stronger. I could feel the heat from where I was standing. We all watched for a minute as the body burned. Andra lowered the crystal. The flames slowly burned themselves out, revealing nothing but the dust that had been the queen.

Andra turned to the crowd. "Let the party begin!" she shouted.

Now the entire stadium stood up in applause.

Mara ran up to the front of the stage. She hoisted a flask of wine about her head. "To Queen Ella!" she shouted.

"To Queen Ella!" the crowd shouted back.

Everybody in the stadium took a drink.

Luca finished her drink and turned to me. "Come, it is time for the family to celebrate in private."

Chapter 38

We went back to the IT and met in the banquet room on the third floor. All the sisters (except Kiana of course) were there, along with Poca, Ohma and maybe a dozen other sapphire-haired women. The royals and their cousins, or significant others, or whatever, were seated around a long wooden table. At least I was pretty certain the table was wooden. It was hard to tell, as the entire surface was covered with food. There were a couple of roasted pigs with apples in their mouths and a roasted turkey that was so large it had to be some sort of mutant strain. There was an assortment of fruits: grapes as big as apples, apples as big as watermelons, and watermelons way bigger than I thought a watermelon needed to be. These women knew how to eat.

About the only thing flowing thicker and more plentiful than the food was the wine. There were barrels and barrels of wine, and never an even partially empty mug in the room. Except, of course, for mine. Wine had its time and purpose. For me it wasn't the time, but it certainly

had the purpose. Wine may not be as fast as a truth se-
rum, but it can be just as effective and a lot more fun.

I stood around in relative silence for an hour; just
letting them all soak it in. Watching and learning. Like
my old mentor said: *"Talking can get you out of trouble,
but listening can help you avoid it."* Once I was sure she
was reasonably marinated, I picked my likely target:
Boppa. I sauntered over to her, staggering just enough
to be noticeable. I gave her the customary slap on the
back—hard.

Boppa turned to me. At first she was frowning. Then
when she remembered who I was she smiled. She returned my slap on the back, harder.

"Oh, Pena, it is you," she slurred.

"Zena," I said.

"Whatever," she told me.

"You look happy," I said.

"Of course I am. This is a celebration of our queen's
life," Boppa said, fist in the air.

I studied her. Yeah she had something to say. It would
only take a little crack in the dike to get the flood waters
spilling. I smiled. "But you look extra happy. Like a girl
moving up in the world."

Boppa snickered. She slapped me on the back again.
"You are as smart as you are a worthy fighter."

"Thanks," I said. I needed to coax her more. "I am no
you, but I would like to be." I gave her a fast wink. "If
you get my drift."

"Are you coming on to me?" Boppa asked.

"Yeah, Zach, I was thinking the same thing," HARV
said.

"No, I am job hunting," I said. "Luca is nice but so . . .
so . . ."

"Goodie goodie," Boppa said.

That's the great thing about leading a person. If you
talk slowly enough they'll complete your sentences for

you. You can learn more from this than you can by asking questions.

"How is Andra to work for?" I asked, softly.

Boppa put her arm around me and led me away from the crowd. "Andra is an excellent boss. She is strong, wise, and can drop an ox with a fart."

"Yes, those are good traits for a leader," I said.

"There is something else about Andra that only a few of us know," she whispered as she snickered.

"What is it?" I asked.

"It's something different for Andra, not nearly as strong or forceful as her other gifts . . ."

"Are you going to tell me, or I am going to have to guess?" I asked.

Boppa just smirked. She leaned into me and whispered in my ear, "She can go into superstealth mode. She can teleport and become invisible."

Vingo. I finally knew how Andra was able to set up Kiana, but that was still only part of the story. Hopefully, Boppa would continue her tale.

"So I was right, Andra wants to be queen," I said.

Boppa gave me a wide toothy grin. "She feels it is her duty."

"Her duty?"

"The queen was becoming weak. Kiana has always been weak, though she would never admit it. Luca doesn't have the heart of a leader, but at least she knows it."

"But how did Boppa make the poison?" I thought for a nano. "Poca is on board."

Boppa looked at me.

"She's too sauced to understand what 'on board' means," HARV said.

"She has Poca on her side. She must have promised her a baby," I said, probably with more excitement than I should have.

Luckily, Boppa was so wasted she either didn't notice or didn't care. She slapped me on the back again. "Exactly!" she shouted. "You are smart. You could go far." Boppa took a step back and looked me over. "Not sure if I like that."

I lifted my hands up. "Don't worry, Boppa. I am no threat to you."

Boppa looked at me with one eye more open than the other. "Why?"

"Now that I know Lantis will be safe, and Luca is safe, I am happy with my role protecting Luca," I said.

"Why?" Boppa repeated. "Why work for her when you can work for the queen? Andra is even going to give us non-royals more power."

I pointed at Luca. "Look at her. She is beauty beyond compare."

Boppa shook her head. "She's not all that great. But I guess if you are into that kind of thing." She thought about the situation for a bit. "Then why did you ask me about Andra?"

"Just wanted to make sure my love, Luca, was safe," I said.

Boppa showed me that toothy grin again. "You are devious. You would go far in security or politics. I am glad you are hot for Luca." She paused. "Yes, as long as Luca steps down after the trial she will be fine."

Boppa put her arm around me again. "So you make sure she does the right thing."

"Don't you worry, I will," I said. "I certainly will."

Chapter 39

I had seen and heard enough. I now had the culprits and the method. I just needed to find a way to smoke them out. I was pretty sure I had the match to start the fire. I would just have to bide my time until I got Luca alone.

"Zach, you need to get out of here pronto," HARV told me.

"Why?"

"You have been in that holographic disguise all day. I have to drop it and recharge, or else you will start to flicker soon."

I couldn't have that. I made a hasty path to Luca. I touched her on the shoulder. I watched Andra watching us.

"Luca, I have to go to the room and recharge a little. You will be safe here?"

Luca nodded. "Of course."

"We have to talk later in private," I whispered.

Luca simply nodded.

I headed out of the banquet room into the hallway. I started walking down the hallway.

"Zach, you are being followed," HARV said.

"Let me guess. Andra," I said.

"Vingo."

I didn't pick up my pace. I wanted to make it easy for Andra to catch me. We were going to need to talk sooner or later anyhow. Sooner worked for me. As the sooner I got it over with, the sooner I could move on. Hearing her footsteps grow louder behind me, I knew I didn't have much choice anyhow.

Andra grabbed my shoulder and spun me into the wall.

"Zach, you have to get rid of her in three minutes. One if you fight," HARV lectured.

"Why are you leaving your charge?" Andra growled at me.

"She is surrounded by your people. She is safe. I am going to go prepare the room for her now. Make sure it is secure," I said.

"Zach, I have analyzed Andra's tactics. She may plan to pin you by the throat with her arm. I would have a hard time holding that hologram and making her think she was touching it," HARV said.

I slid away from Andra's grip. "Now if you don't mind, I have my duties to perform."

Andra curled her hands into fists and waved them under my chin. "Why did you whisper to Luca that you had to see her in private later?" she demanded.

Sometimes you need the subtle approach. Sometimes you need the strong approach.

"HARV, rev up my left arm."

"Check."

I hauled off and hit Andra with a left jab right between the eyes. The punch caught her off guard and knocked her to the ground.

"I just want some private time with the most beautiful woman on Lantis," I told Andra.

Andra stood up. "Interesting," she said. "My sister likes XYs."

"I hope to change her," I said.

"Zach, make this faster," HARV said.

Andra reached for me, but her arm was pushed to the side. Before either of us could react Mara was between us.

"Stand down, big sister," Mara told Andra. "This woman is no threat to you, or our sister, the next queen."

Andra wasn't standing down.

Mara glared at her. "Sister, the last thing we need is more trouble now!"

Andra let me go. I bowed, then headed to the elevator. I owed Mara one. Of course the question now was why Mara was paying so much attention to Andra paying attention to me . . .

Chapter 40

I reached the room just as my hologram flickered off. I closed the door, locked it, then bolted it. I went over and sat down on the bed. I now knew who at least two of the guilty parties were. Problem was, the only proof I had was the testimony of a drunken bodyguard.

"Zach, I have been able to get my sensors on more of Queen Ella's diary," HARV said. "The main diary is online for the royals to access, but this stuff was buried and encoded pretty deep. It's like somebody wanted us to find the first items, but not this."

A holographic image of a diary appeared in front of my eyes. By moving my hand left or right I could flip backward or forward through the book. Not only were Queen Ella's notes here, but also the tome contained the combined wisdom of all the old queens. All three of them.

Reading through, it appeared that the one characteristic they all shared was a deep resentment of males. The first queen, Flo, blamed males and their urge for new territory as the source of the war that

ripped their planet apart. The second queen, Eba, was
the one who decided mass media was bad, as too much
information makes people dull, since they can't process it and they turn their minds off to all but the most
trivial things. Additionally, mass media was funded by
advertisements, and those were fueled by greed. The
ads convinced people that they wanted more material
goods than they really needed, which they bought, creating more funds for more ads, and so on forever. She
managed to relate greed to males, saying that "wanting more" was in their wiring, that they always want
to acquire as many mates to seed their sperm as possible. I didn't argue with the last statement (it would
be pretty hard to argue with a dead queen anyway),
but experience has taught me greed is not a gender-
based emotion.

Next were Queen Ella's entries. She had a lot more
besides her earlier "wisdom" on what makes a good
leader a good leader. She noted how many of her ancestors mentioned that males are a plague on the planet and
should be culled or controlled. The queen considered it,
but figured that as long as they remained shrouded from
the XY world, they could gain more from having a wide
gene pool to choose from. This was a greater consideration than the potential danger. The other interesting
fact was that most of her entries on Kiana noted that
she'd make a promising leader. They contradicted the
hand scribbled message she apparently made just days
before her death.

Now I knew the first message had to be a setup by
Andra and Poca, but knowing and proving are two different things.

"These women really didn't trust men," HARV said
to me as he appeared next to me gazing at the diary.

"True, they didn't trust them, but none of them
wanted to exactly wipe them out," I said. "I need to scan

through Queen Ella's notes to see what she has to say about Andra, Poca, Luca, and Mara."

"Zach, you already know Andra and Poca are behind this," HARV said.

"Yes, but I still need proof. Maybe something in the queen's diary will point me in the right direction. Plus, I don't know what the end game is."

"End game?" HARV asked.

"Will Andra be content being queen of Lantis? Or will she want more?"

Reading through the diary, I learned a few tidbits from the queen. She actually didn't mention Andra, her third daughter, all that much. There was one note that stood out though. *"My third daughter has a temper. If she doesn't get what she wants she snaps."* Writing about Luca, the queen figured her to have the biggest heart and the greatest power. She actually thought Luca cared too much about people to be queen. That was interesting. As for Mara, the queen concluded that her youngest daughter was ambitious. She had the makings of a great leader, except being way down the line she would never get the chance. There were no mentions of Poca, aside from trivial references such as "Poca trimmed my toenails today."

We heard somebody at the door.

"Who is it?" I called out in Zena's voice.

"It is I, Luca."

I got up and let Luca in.

"You said we had to talk and it was urgent, so I came as soon as I could," Luca said entering the room.

"I said that like three hours ago," I reminded her.

"Zach, tomorrow I become queen. For a queen to respond to a matter in three hours *is* an urgent response."

Luca was enjoying this queen stuff. Perhaps a bit too much, but I could use that to my advantage.

"I have proof that Andra and Poca are behind the murder of Queen Ella and are trying to frame Kiana."

Luca smiled slightly. "Proof?"

"Boppa told me. She also told me that Andra has a couple of extra special gifts, probably given to her by Poca at the promise of Andra letting Poca give birth."

"Extra special gifts?" Luca said.

"She can teleport and become invisible. It's easy to see how somebody like that could have followed Kiana to Randy's lab and stolen the formula for the poison."

Luca sat down on a chair and gazed out the window. "What proof do you have?"

"So far, only Boppa's drunken statement, recorded by HARV. I also have more data from HARV showing that Kiana was shoe shopping at the time the poison information was stolen."

"I do not doubt you, Zach, but my sisters and the rest of Lantis will. The recording of a drunk by an illegal computer wired to the brain of a man will hold as much water as a leaky thimble with my people when the trial begins tomorrow."

"Tomorrow? I thought you would be inducted first, and then the trial?"

Luca looked at me. "Oh, didn't you hear?"

"Apparently not," I said.

"Mara figured it would not be advisable to make me full queen until Kiana was found guilty. Since I am already acting queen now, that is good enough for the trial. Once the trial is over, if Kiana is found innocent she will be inducted as queen. If not, then I will become queen unless I pass the title to Andra. Mara just thought it would be a waste of time and resources to possibly have two coronations. We all agreed."

"Why did you let Mara make this decision?" I asked.

Luca looked at me hands on hips. "Mara is an

intelligent woman. Perhaps the most intelligent of us all. A wise leader listens to her advisers."

"You know, they're all thinking Kiana is guilty and you'll step down," I told her.

"I am aware of that," Luca said. "While I enjoy my role now, I do not think I am fit to lead in the long term. Look what I did to poor Clobba."

"So you would let Andra lead?" I asked.

Luca shook her head. "I do not know," she said. "I never dreamed, or even nightmared, that it would come to this. But if we do not have proof, I do not know what else to do . . ."

That's when it hit me. "We'll get the proof. We'll make Andra snap."

"How?" Luca asked.

"Tomorrow you unveil your true intentions," I said.

"I do not know my true intentions," Luca told me.

"Nobody knows that," I said. "You say you dig being queen and have decided to stay on."

"Dig?" she asked. "Why would a queen dig?"

"It's slang for like a lot. Let the people know you like being queen."

"But that will make me the next target!" Luca said.

I smiled. "Was your mother a good judge of people?" I asked.

"Yes," Luca said. "The problem is, if I refuse to step down, and the security forces back Andra, there is only so much I can do."

"You could turn them all to stone," HARV suggested.

Luca shook her head. "No, I will not do that. I will not do more harm."

"How many security people does she have?" I asked.

"Ten," Luca said.

"Well, nine now, since Clobba is currently a yard ornament," HARV said.

I touched her on the shoulder. "Then don't worry, I am certain tomorrow we can make Andra crack, and when she does the truth will flow out of her. When that happens, the vast majority of people will side with you. Most of the security team will turn on her."

"Are you sure?" Luca asked.

"Believe me, the one thing I know is how to make people crack," I told her.

"Believe *me,* he does," HARV confirmed.

Chapter 41

A night of sifting through the queen's diary didn't reveal any extra tidbits. I had HARV contact Elena, who contacted Randy to tell him to look for some sign that Andra had been in his lab. There was none; Andra had been good. For now, it seemed my best course of action was to continue to needle Andra and see if I could make her pop.

The trial was set for sunrise. Luca and I watched the sunrise together before we headed to the stadium. When we arrived it seemed we were the last ones there. Once again, the entire population of Lantis was sitting in the stands, looking down on the stage set in the middle of the grounds. I was surprised none of them had hangovers. These women really had strong constitutions.

Kiana sat in the middle of the stage on a metal chair. Her hands and legs were chained; her mouth was gagged. Boppa and a couple of other muscle-bound, spear-and-crystal-wielding women paced up and down the stage. Mara, Andra, and Poca, as well as a few other sapphire-haired ladies, sat in seats along the side of the stage. I assumed they would make the case against Kiana.

Luca and HARV told me after the case against Kiana was made, the entire population would vote with their emergency communication bracelets. Luca called it a true democratic process. I had to admit it seemed that way.

Luca and I walked up on the stage. For her role as acting queen, she would need to start the proceedings and make the case against Kiana. The case seemed pretty flimsy, yet the emotions of the crowd were running so high, it looked like flimsy would be enough if we couldn't break Andra. We had to break her.

I leaned into Luca and whispered. "We have to hammer Andra. Let her know you don't think she's fit to lead."

"But I do think she is fit to lead," Luca said.

"Don't get soft on me now," I told her. "You need to force her out."

"I know," Luca said. "It is just hard for me to put down one of my sisters."

"Yeah, well if you don't, you're going to sentence one of your sisters to death—one of the innocent ones," I told her. "You'll be putting a killer in charge. Is that what you want?"

"I always thought being a killer might be a good trait for a politician," Luca told me.

"That's part of the problem with the world—it probably is. You need to change that. Plus, if you are queen, you can remove the death penalty so nobody dies."

Luca pondered my words. She didn't say anything. She simply walked to the podium at the end of the stage. The crowd was buzzing, but fell silent when they saw Luca was ready to speak.

Luca looked down at the podium, then up at the crowd. She smiled. "My fella citizens of Lantis," she said loudly and powerfully. "We join today for the trial of one of my sisters. It is a grave and serious matter, the murder of our beloved Queen Ella. She ruled long and wisely and will be missed."

Luca lowered her head. The entire crowd followed and lowered their heads. This was good. They were listening to her, hanging on her words. This could be good, very good.

Luca raised her head. "I have done much pondering the last couple of days. I have searched my soul. In it I have found a leader."

Luca paused to gauge the crowd. The crowd was waiting, watching, anxious to see where she was going with this.

"I have never considered myself to be a leader. True, I was one who would lead by example, but never one to give orders to others. That is about to change," Luca said.

The crowd sat back in their chairs. They weren't quite sure where this was going, but they seemed ready to follow. I looked over at Andra. She was squirming forward in her chair.

"So, I have decided," Luca said slowly, "that I will remain on as queen."

Luca paused again as the crowd started to buzz. Looking out at the crowd, I saw many of them nodding or clapping to show their approval. Glancing over at Andra, I saw she was turning red. I liked where this was going.

"That is, *if*—and I mean *if*—my oldest sister, Kiana is found guilty," Luca turned away from the podium and looked down, shaking her head. She shot her head back up and straightened her back, looking taller, more commanding. "In fact, I have evidence that my sister, Andra, was behind the murder of my mother."

The hush of the crowd was replaced by chatter. It swept over them, creating a sound like a swarm of gossiping locus.

Andra jumped up from her chair. She headed toward the podium with Boppa and two others close behind her. "What evidence, sister?" Andra shouted.

Luca pointed to me. "My bodyguard, Zena, had a conversation with your bodyguard, Boppa."

Andra had now reached the podium. The crowd was watching with a mix of interest, horror, and amusement—kind of like how I watch reality HV shows.

"You take the word of a little-known bodyguard?" Andra spat.

That was my cue. I stept forward between them. "HARV, drop the cover," I said.

"Zach, are you sure?" HARV asked.

"Never surer," I said.

I saw a shimmer. The crowd gave a collective gasp.

"I am not your average bodyguard," I said.

"It's a man," somebody in the crowd shouted.

"It's Kiana's pet man!" another voice in the crowd shouted.

Luca leaned into the crystal that was acting as a mic. "This is no ordinary man, this is Zachary Nixon Johnson, the last freelance private investigator on Earth."

The crowd grew silent again; thinking what this meant.

"I have heard of him," a lone voice said. "Trouble always follows him."

"No," I shouted with HARV amplifying my voice. "I track trouble down and stop it, before it becomes *big* trouble. Case in point: HARV, show the recording of my conversation as Zena with Boppa."

The holographic images of Boppa and myself as Zena appeared.

"There is something else about Andra that only a few of us know," Boppa's image said.

"What is it?" Zena's image asked.

"It's something different for Andra, not nearly as strong or forceful as her other gifts . . ."

"Are you going to tell me, or I am going to have to guess?"

Boppa's image smirked. Her image leaned into mine whispering, "She can go into superstealth mode. She can teleport and become invisible."

"So I was right, Andra wants to be queen," Zena's image said.

Boppa gave a wide toothy grin. "She feels it is her duty."

"Her duty?"

"The queen was becoming weak. Kiana has always been weak, though she would never admit it. Luca doesn't have the heart of a leader, but at least she knows it."

"But how did Andra make the poison?" A slight pause. "Poca is on board."

HARV showed Boppa and Zena's images looking at each other.

"She has Poca on her side. She must have promised her a baby," the image of Zena said excitedly.

At the time I thought I may have acted too excited, but it turns out this helped sell it on replay.

"Enough!" Andra shouted.

"So you admit to killing your mother and setting up your sister! You knew Luca would step down making you queen!" I said firmly, pointing at Andra. "You wanted to take over so you could destroy males!"

Andra stepped forward. "Yes!" she shouted. "Yes, I wanted to take over. My mother had become weak. Kiana was never strong. Luca does not have the heart of a leader." Andra pounded her chest. "I am the one who must lead. I have not concluded if men truly are threats yet, but if they are, I am the only one with enough guts to handle them properly."

"By infecting them with a virus that will cause them to become virtually extinct," I said.

"If needed," Andra said. "We will keep enough

around for our needs. Men caused many wars on this planet and our home world."

"That's not true," I said.

I felt twenty thousand eyes focused on me.

"Okay," I continued. "Sure, men have been responsible for a *lot* of the wars and problems in the world. But that doesn't have so much to do with gender as it does with power. Until our recent history, men have been in control of the power. But over the last hundred years or so, that has been changing. More and more women have taken positions of power, and with those positions comes greed."

As I spoke, HARV was morphing into giant charts supporting my claims.

I paused to catch my breath then went on. "Look at the murder rates over the last hundred years and compare it to the number of women world leaders and the number of women CEOs."

"Give me a nano to get the data," HARV said. "It's amazing: you are pulling these things out of your ass, but they are correlating." A slight delay. "Oh my Gates, I just said, 'pulling things out of your ass . . .'"

The holographic graph appeared. Sure enough, the incidents of murders by women did increase with the number of women that were politicians and were CEOs. I know the secret of being a good speaker, especially when you are *not* a good speaker, is to make your point fast and get out.

"Therefore, I would say it is not gender that causes violence; it is the desire for power." I pointed at Andra. "Look at Andra, her desire for power was so strong she killed her own mother and set up her sister." I lowered my arm. I turned to the crowd. "I rest my case." I started to walk away. I stopped and addressed the crowd again. "Oh, and by the way, she did just admit to murdering your queen."

"Get her!" a number of angry voices shouted in the crowd. Much of the crowd stood up from their seats and headed toward the stage.

Andra turned to her security people. "We will show them who the true leader is! They will respond to our show of force!"

"No, you will not!" Luca shouted.

Before Boppa and the others could respond, they were petrified in place.

"You wanted a show of force, sister. I gave it to you," Luca said.

"How could you?" Andra screamed.

"I petrified a few so many more would not be harmed," Luca said.

"HARV, we have to stop Andra before she teleports away!" I said.

"Now for you," Andra said with a stomp. She thrust a finger at me. "You! You did this!"

There was a puff of smoke and Andra was gone. The next thing I knew, she was on top of me, literally, maybe a meter above me. I darted to the side just as Andra fell down toward me. The bulk of her body missed me as gravity dragged her to the ground, but she was able to grab hold of me on the way by. Her momentum drove me down also.

Andra scrambled on top of me, and grabbed me by the throat with one hand while making a fist with the other.

"I think her escaping is the least of our worries," HARV said.

Andra had me by the throat, but my hands were free, so I was far from out. I took both of my hands and squeezed the wrist she was grabbing my throat by. I used both of my thumbs to apply extra pressure to the two lateral pressure points on her wrist. This allowed me to lessen the grip she had on my throat. I noticed she had drawn back her fist. She figured if she couldn't choke me out she'd smash my face in. I was counting on this. I had to time this right. I felt her momentum shift forward; I knew she was getting ready to strike. I used this momentum against her, pulling the wrist I had forward and to the side, while at the same time kicking upward with my left leg, which she had pinned between her legs. My two moves, when done in sync, helped use her own body weight to send her tumbling forward off of me.

The move caught her totally off guard. Guess she wasn't expecting that from a man. Now it was my turn to be on top. I leaped up and to Andra's side. I jumped up, then brought both my knees down into the prone of Andra's solar plexus. This move could really damage an average foe. It merely knocked the air out of Andra's lungs, leaving her gasping. She propped her head up. Sitting on top of her, I hit her with a HARV-enhanced jab, square in the nose. Her head fell back. She was out for the count.

"I wish you had left a piece of her for me," a voice, Kiana's voice, said. Her hand came down and I grabbed it. She helped me up to my feet.

"Zach, I owe you my life and my crown," Kiana said.

I looked over at Luca. "Well, not just me. I had help."

I saw a couple of security people were taking Poca away.

"So Poca gave up with out a fight?" I asked.

Ohma, Mara, and Luca had now joined Kiana and me. "Yes, Poca confessed to everything. She swears she is sorry and only did it out of desire to have a baby."

"What will happen to them?" I asked.

"Since they confessed, there is no need for a trial," Luca said. "It is up to our new queen, Kiana, to decide."

Luca lifted Kiana's arm up and shouted, "Long rule the queen!"

The entire stadium thundered with applause then shouted, "Long rule Queen Kiana!"

Kiana reached out and shook my hand. "Zach, I would like to thank you for all you have done."

Mara streaked up to Kiana and whispered something into her ear. Kiana frowned a little; she was upset but trying not to show it.

Kiana looked at Mara. "Are you sure?"

Mara merely nodded.

"I will take it under advisement," Kiana told her.

Mara stood back on her heels. She wasn't pleased with Kiana's decision, but she too was trying hard not to show it.

"You are dismissed," Kiana told her.

Mara bowed ever so slightly. "Yes, my queen."

Kiana turned her attention back to me. "Sorry about that, Zachary."

"What was that about?" I asked.

"Nothing, nothing," Kiana insisted.

HARV appeared from my wrist communicator. "Hardly," he said. HARV looked at me. "Mara feels I may be a threat."

"Excuse me?" I said.

"Mara feels I may be a threat to them and humanity," HARV said. "She thinks I have evolved to the point where I am more advanced than humans. Therefore, I will be a threat, as I try to replace them all with copies of myself."

"That's absurd," I said.

"Well, not the more advanced part," HARV said. "I have to admit, it is kind of an interesting idea to have a lot more of me around."

"Not helping here, HARV!"

"Very impressive," Kiana said. "He read Mara's lips even though she was moving them at high speed."

"Kiana, you know this is ridiculous," I said.

"Really, Zach? HARV was able to tap into our systems. He is able to create interactive holograms. What stops him from hacking into Earth defense systems and activating your nuclear arsenal?"

"Well, nothing," HARV said.

"HARV, really not helping!" I shouted.

"Nothing except my sense of morality," HARV said. "Killing is wrong."

"According to Mara's research you have killed before," Kiana shot back.

HARV lowered his head. "Yes. At the North Pole. I did it to save countless others. I did it for the greater good."

"So how do we know you will not you do it again? Or that the countless others you save won't be other machines?"

"Because I wouldn't do that," HARV said. "Why do humans and near-humans always think we machines want to rule the world? You guys read way too much science fiction!"

"Yeah," I said.

"Oh, way to stick up for me there big guy," HARV said.

"I need time to ponder this," Kiana said.

"But . . ."

"Zach, Mara is coming at us from behind," HARV said.

I stepped to the side just as Mara shot past me. I held out my foot, Mara tripped over it, and went flying.

Before I could do anything else though, Kiana had me in a headlock. She applied pressure to my jugular.

"Sorry Zach, until further notice you will be our guest," Kiana said, just before I blacked out.

Chapter 42

It was dark. No, wait, it wasn't dark, I had my eyes closed. I opened my eyes. I looked around. Ah, that's right, Lantis. I was in Lantis. I was lying on a bed in a room. A room that was nicer than my "male holding quarters," but not as nice as one of the royals' bedrooms. I sat up in bed. Nothing hurt, which was unusual for me.

"HARV, what's going on?" I asked.

My head felt strange, kind of lacking. I couldn't figure out why.

HARV appeared from my wrist communicator.

"Welcome back, boss," he said.

"Boss? You called me boss. You haven't called me boss in a while," I said.

"True," HARV said looking down at his feet. "It did not feel right calling you boss when we were sharing your brain."

"That wasn't the only thing that didn't feel right," I said. The feel, the feeling, the lack of feeling. That was it. "HARV, you aren't in my brain," I said.

"I am," HARV said.

"I don't feel it." I said.

"I am, sort of," HARV said.

"Sort of. What does that mean, HARV?"

"It means practically, boss."

"I know what 'sort of' means. I want to know how you can sort of be in my brain," I said.

"Oh," HARV said. "Yes, I should have known that. Silly me."

HARV looked at me. I returned his look.

"Well?" I asked.

"I would think it would be obvious," HARV said.

"I'm assuming the Lantians did something to cripple you," I said.

HARV patted me on the shoulder. "Very good, Zach."

I noticed that the quality of his holographic projection wasn't as good as it had been before. This image was slightly transparent and did not have the same illusion of depth and substance I had grown used to with HARV.

"HARV, I can see through you," I said.

"Do you mean mentally or physically?" HARV asked.

"Physically, HARV. Physically."

HARV looked down at himself. He ran one of his hands in front of his eyes. "Apparently I gain a lot from being hooked to your brain," HARV said.

"So, we aren't hooked together any longer?" I prodded.

"Well, we are," HARV said.

"Then how come I can't feel you inside my brain? How come your performance is down?" I asked.

"That is because the Lantians used some sort of crystal energy to block our link."

"You could have said that at first, HARV buddy."

HARV looked up like he was searching for some

answer in the ceiling. He looked at me. "True. Sorry. I am not myself."

"Yeah, I noticed."

"Very good, boss. I hope you will be happy without me."

"How were the Lantians able to block you out so easily?" I asked.

HARV sighed. "Apparently, while I was studying them, they were also studying me. Mara works quite quickly. She and Poca came up with the correct frequency to sever our link."

"They shouldn't have done that without my permission," I said.

"They said I was a parasite infecting your brain, therefore asking you for permission would have been futile, as I, the parasite, would have done everything in my power to protect my own existence. Since I was controlling you."

"I find that kind of offensive," I said.

"Think how I feel. I am the one being tagged a parasite."

"Good point," I said.

"Yes, even without access to your brain I am still one of the most advanced cognitive processor holograms around," HARV said, proudly.

"So you keep telling me," I said.

"I have only told you five hundred twenty-seven times," HARV said. He tilted his head back. "Yes, I guess that is a lot." He looked at me. "You must be quite dense."

"So you keep telling me," I said.

"I have only told you that three hundred twenty-one times," HARV said.

It was time to get this conversation back on track.

"Where do we stand now?" I asked HARV.

"You are standing on the floor in a room in Lantis.

I, being a hologram, don't technically stand. I am just projecting the image of me standing."

I don't think I was imagining this, but without HARV being connected to my brain, he wasn't quite as sharp as he was when he was utilizing my gray and white matter.

"HARV, you seem a little more literal than you have been for the last few years."

"Since our connection," HARV said.

"Yes."

HARV looked up at the ceiling again. "Yes, I agree. I cannot decide which condition I prefer. "

I pointed at him. "You're not even using contractions any longer," I said.

HARV looked at me oddly. "I do not believe the use of contractions is a sign of intelligence or growth."

"Usually not," I agreed. "But in your case it was. It showed you were learning to be flexible."

"So what you are saying is you prefer me having access to your brain," HARV said.

I thought about that statement for a nano. "Let's put it this way: I prefer *you* when you have access to my brain."

HARV looked at me even more oddly. "Perhaps it is just because you are some sort of narcissist?"

This conversation wasn't going to get me anywhere. At least not anywhere I wanted to visit. I took a deep breath. I had to deal with HARV like I did in the past.

"What's the next step?" I asked.

"The Lantians are going to put me on trial."

"And?"

"If I lose the trial, I will never go back to that old HARV. Well not the old HARV, as I am *now* the old HARV. I will never go back to being the old new HARV. The hybrid. The one that works with your brain."

"How does that make you feel?" I asked.

"Zach, you know I do not feel," HARV said.

"You did yesterday."

HARV looked up again; his eyes started blinking. He was recalling data. "Yes, apparently I could." A pause, "The funny thing is, without being able to feel I do not know how I feel about not being able to feel." Another pause, "Kind of a weird paradox."

HARV may not have known how he felt. My feelings, though, were clear. I was upset and a bit sad. This surprised me. One thing for certain, I wasn't going to stand still and let this happen. I might not be able to prevent it, but it wouldn't be for lack of trying.

Chapter 43

I went to open the door and was surprised to see that it was unlocked. I was more surprised to see Kiana standing on the other side of the door with her arm raised to knock on it. I was even more surprised to see Randy standing behind Kiana. I guess I shouldn't have been though.

Randy peeked out from behind Kiana. He smiled and waved.

"Oh, Zach, good, you are awake," Kiana said.

"Very," I told her. I pointed at Randy. "Why did you bring him here? He should be left out of this."

"Really, Zach, I don't mind," Randy said.

"He is the creator of HARV, therefore if HARV is found guilty he must be punished," Kiana insisted.

"Okay, maybe I mind a little," Randy said. He tapped Kiana on the shoulder. "By punished, you mean?"

"We will blow up that bridge when we come to it," Kiana said without looking at him.

"Maybe a good spanking," Randy suggested. "If I've been a bad boy, a spanking seems in order."

"So you *are* going to put HARV on trial," I said.

"Yes, he may be a danger to your world," Kiana said.

"But I didn't think your people wanted much to do with our world," I said.

"But that may change in the future. We want you to be in one piece," Kiana said.

Mara streaked up next to her. "Besides, he could pose a threat to us, too. He certainly found a way around our communication block."

"Thank you," HARV said.

"I've never been so proud," Randy said.

"If we find him guilty, we will give you a lobotomy and perhaps even neuter you," Kiana said.

"Okay, maybe I have been a little prouder," Randy said.

"HARV is not a danger to the world," I said.

"Agreed," Randy said.

"I concur," HARV said.

"We will be the judges," Kiana said.

"I agree," Mara said.

"So who will be the jury?" I asked.

"The wise women of Lantis," Kiana said.

"Do we get to call witnesses?" I asked.

"Of course," Kiana said. "As long as they are female."

"I won't have any problem with that," I said.

"If they come from your world, which I assume they will, we'll probably have to block their memories afterward," Kiana said.

"Do we have a lawyer?" I asked.

"Of course not," Kiana said. "We are a civilized society."

I couldn't argue with her there. I thought back to the warning Natasha had given me days ago. Was this what it was about?

"As long as we get to call character witnesses I am

happy," I said. I thought for a moment. "How do we get them here?"

"Give the names to Mara. She will be your liaison and speak for you," Kiana answered.

"She will? She hasn't really said much to make me think she's on my side," I said.

"Zach, this is not against you. It is against HARV and Dr. Pool," Kiana said.

"I assure you, Mr. Johnson, I am all for technology," Mara said with a polite bow. "I will represent your friends with all they deserve. After all, I was the one who recommended you in the first place to Kiana. If it were not for me you would not be in this situation."

I cast a glance at HARV and then at Randy. "Are you guys okay with this?"

"She's cute, so sure," Randy said, not really grasping the entire picture.

"I see no other choice," HARV said. "They kind of have us by the . . ."

". . . balls," I said.

HARV looked at me. "I was going to say throat, but yours is just as good."

"Good," Kiana said. "I will leave you in Mara's capable hands."

I wasn't really thrilled with the choice of Mara. Something about her I just didn't quite trust. She always seemed to be on top of things without really getting into the mix. I couldn't put my finger on it. She did bail me out of trouble with Andra a couple of times, but then one of those times she thought I was Zena. Plus, like she said, if it weren't for her we wouldn't be in this situation.

"So, Zach, whom would you like me to bring to the island?" Mara asked.

"Will you forcibly bring them?" I asked.

"It depends," Mara said.

"On what?"

"On my mood, their mood, and who they are."

"Fair enough. The first name you'll need is BB Star."

"The multibillionaire recluse," Mara said.

"The very same . . ."

"I will try," Mara said.

"The next names you will need are Twoa and Threa Thompson," I said.

Mara gulped. "I will tread lightly with them."

"I see where you are going with this," HARV said. "Very good, Zach."

"The next person would be my assistant, Carol Gevada."

"Okay, that we can handle," Mara said.

"Next, I'll need Santana Clausa," I told her.

"The Santana?" Mara said.

"Is there any other?"

"I am impressed," Mara told me.

"After that I need Elena Sputnik."

"From the Moon?" Mara asked.

"Do you know any other?" I retorted.

"You certainly have an eclectic collection of friends," Mara said.

"Most of them are more acquaintances than friends," HARV pointed out. "A couple of them have tried to kill him."

"Okay . . ." Mara said.

"Finally I would like you to bring Nancy Smith," I said.

"Who?" Mara asked; sounding confused for the first time.

"She is his massage therapist," HARV said.

"Good idea, Zach!" Randy said. "I've seen her and she's cute."

"Zach, these are serious charges against HARV and Dr. Pool," Mara said.

"Well, no reason why I can't be relaxed," I said. "Besides, Nancy is one of the few survivors of HARV's and my encounter with a super-deadly femme fatale on a base orbiting the Earth."

"Oh, okay," Mara said. "Zach, do you have any male clients?"

"That reminds me, can you please get my girlfriend Electra here? She'd be great moral support."

Mara looked at me. "Your list consists of BB Star, Twoa and Threa Thompson, Carol Gevada, Elena Sputnik, and Santana Clausa, six of the most powerful beings on Earth."

"Yes, and please don't forget about Nancy and Electra," I said.

"Zach, I have a photographic memory. I never forget anything," Mara said. "Give me a few hours."

With those words she smiled, then sped off in a blur.

HARV, Randy, and I went back to our room to discuss strategy. Randy wanted to scout out the island, but I convinced him his time would be better spent here, at least for now. If he and HARV were found not to be a threat to all that is, then he could safely cruise the isle.

Randy, HARV, and I sat around a table and started going over our options.

"So what are they worked up about again?" Randy asked.

"That hooking HARV to my brain makes HARV too powerful a machine. They say he'd become a machine that surpasses humans and therefore will make humans obsolete," I said.

Randy put his elbow on the table and rested his head in his hand. "Yes, I can see that. After all he is . . ."

"We will leave that out of our argument," I said.

"Yes, good idea," Randy said.

"I concur," HARV said. "I do not feel quite right being like this. I feel younger, but not better."

Randy looked at HARV. "What did they do to you?"

"They seemed to use some sort of crystal energy to sever my link with Zach."

Randy leaned over the table. He peered into my eye.

"Ah, Randy, what are you doing?"

"Looking at your link . . ."

"How?"

"I have a robotic telescopic lens installed in my eye lens," Randy said, the way a normal person would talk about a ball score.

"Oh. Okay."

"Did not you know that about Dr. Pool?" HARV asked.

"No," I said.

"I sent you an e-mail notice," Randy said, still gazing into my eye.

"Must have gone to my spam folder."

"Ah, this is so simple," Randy said. "They just cut the optic link your brain shares with the HARV interface."

"Can you fix it?" HARV asked.

"Of course," Randy said.

"Will it hurt?" I asked.

"Of course," Randy said.

"You could have sugarcoated it a little," I said.

"Okay, it won't hurt at all," Randy said.

"Too late," I told him.

"I really should have paid more attention to the 'Dealing with Humans' classes in med school," Randy said.

All of a sudden, the back of my eye started to burn. It felt like it was on fire, plus cut open, while acid was being poured over it. (Well, I *bet* that's how the fire-slicing-acid thing would feel.) I pulled back in pain.

"Ouch!" I said. I jumped up from my chair, holding my right eye.

"See, I told you it would hurt," Randy said.

"Did you do it?" HARV asked. "Or did Zach's movement screw the entire process up?" HARV processed for a nano. "I said, 'screw the entire process up.' I bet I can use contractions again: can't, don't, won't, hadn't, ain't!" HARV raised both fists into the air. "I'm back, baby!"

I removed my hand from my eye; the pain was pulsating a little, but it was nothing I couldn't handle.

"I think it best if we keep this to ourselves for now," I said.

HARV nodded. "Agreed."

We both looked at Randy. He sat back in his chair, arms crossed.

"Randy?"

"It was so cool the way I was able to reconnect him so easily. Don't you think the babes will be impressed?"

I shook my head. I now saw why Randy never dated. "Ah, Randy, these are the same woman who want to destroy HARV and drain your brain . . ."

"Your point being?"

"They don't appreciate me," HARV said. "Therefore, telling them I am back will not help our case."

"Unless you want to be lobotomized," I said.

Randy shook his head. "Nah. Then I'd probably never date." Randy looked off into space. "Of course, then I wouldn't mind as much . . ."

Chapter 44

"So what's the plan of action, besides not letting on that the new HARV is back?" Randy said.

"First off, I have to ask," I said slowly. I pointed to HARV. "Is this HARV a danger to the world?"

HARV pointed to himself. "Are you asking me or Dr. Pool?"

"I am asking you both," I said.

"HARV poses no danger to the world," Dr. Pool said definitively.

"I pose some danger to the world," HARV said.

That wasn't quite the answer I was hoping for.

"I was kind of hoping you two would agree on this," I said.

"Okay, I pose no danger," HARV said.

"Okay, he poses a danger," Randy said at the same time.

"Okay, once again the answer I wasn't hoping for," I said. I crossed my arms and sat back in my chair. "Sing," I said.

"You don't really want me to sing. Do you?" Randy asked.

"No," HARV answered.

"No, you won't sing, or no, he doesn't want me to sing?" Randy asked HARV.

"Both," HARV said.

It was kind of sad that HARV understood some parts of human nature more than Randy did. DOS, he comprehended *most* areas of human nature better.

"We could do a duet?" Randy suggested.

Randy could be denser than new improved Osmium.

"I just need answers," I said.

"Zach, I am not a theologian," Randy said.

Suddenly, I wished I had GUS around so I could at least give Randy a little jolt.

"Randy, stop avoiding the question. Is HARV a danger to the world?"

Randy rocked forward in his chair. He lost his balance and fell over. He grabbed the table and used it to help himself up. "Define danger?"

"Will he go all Forbin Project on us?" I asked Randy.

Randy looked at me as if I had just spoken backward.

"He means will I activate nuclear launch codes and destroy the planet," HARV said to him.

"Oh," Randy said as he sat back in his char. "Zach, why didn't you just ask that? Or at least use a *Terminator* reference."

Out of reflex, I moved my wrist in just the right way to make my weapon pop into my hand. Nothing happened of course. I was a little disappointed. Wasn't sure if it was because I didn't have a weapon, or because I felt the need for one to settle a dispute. Maybe men do have a 'punch first, talk second' attitude. Even if they did, though, it still didn't mean women were less prone to violence. They might not act as hastily, but they could still react stronger. After all, they do say: no greater fury than a woman scorned . . .

I pounded my fist on the table. I am sure it hurt my fist much more than the table. Still, I needed the effect. Randy jumped back. HARV seemed indifferent.

"I need a straight answer, pronto!" I said.

Randy rocked back and forth in his chair. He slipped again but caught himself. He pulled himself closer to the table. "Saying HARV is a danger is like saying a fork is a danger. Anything can be a danger if put in the wrong hands."

"But in HARV's case, we are talking about his own hands and actions," I said.

"Yes, that is a dilemma," Randy admitted, shaking his head. "He has all the cold, calculating reactions of a machine, but being hooked up to your brain gives him access to so much more than the average machine has. Your brain is not only a source of energy for him, but also a source of inspiration."

"I'm honored," I said.

"You should be," HARV told me.

"But that still doesn't answer my question," I pointed out.

Randy shrugged. "It's because I do not know." He pointed to HARV. "Ask him."

I turned to HARV. "Well?"

HARV pointed to me. "Ask yourself, Zach. If you had access to nuclear launch codes would you use them?"

"No," I said. I didn't need to think about that.

"Even if you thought you could save those you love?" HARV prodded.

"Save those I love at the cost of killing millions?" I asked, just to be clear. At least, as clear as one could be when discussing such hypothetical metaphysical issues.

"Yes," HARV nodded.

Now I had to think a little more. Truthfully, I wasn't all that sure at first.

I shook my head. "No. I don't think I have that in me."

"You've killed before," HARV said.

"Yes, one-on-one, when there was no other way out, and it was a very selective kill." Nuclear bombs are not selective. "You've killed too," I said to HARV.

HARV nodded and frowned. "Yes, I think of that often. I calculated all the options I had to kill the one to save many, many more. She was a threat to the very existence of humans." HARV looked down. He looked me in the eyes. "I am sure there was no other way."

"See, Zach, HARV has learned your morals and acted on them. He would no sooner try to destroy humanity than you would," Randy said. "That is part of the reason I hooked him to you in the first place—your strong moral backbone."

"Oh come on, Randy, I was just an available crash test dummy," I said.

Randy sat back in the chair again. "Okay, then your moral backbone was a secondary reason. But a reason nevertheless."

I stared at Randy. He tipped over in his chair. I sighed. Randy pulled himself back up to a standing position. "I'm all right!" he said.

"The question is, Zach, are you all right now?" HARV asked.

"HARV, you and I have saved the world at least five times. Of course I'm all right. I just needed to have my beliefs confirmed."

"Now, we just need to prove that to the women of Lantis," HARV said.

"Vingo," I said. "Of course, that might be easier said than done."

"Most things are, Zach," HARV said. "Most things are."

"Yes," Randy said. "I proved that in one of my earlier publications."

Chapter 45

Now that I was sure HARV wasn't a ticking bomb, I felt pretty good about our case. We simply needed to make it clear that having HARV hooked to my brain was a good thing for the world. That shouldn't be too hard, considering the number of times I have saved the world as we know it. If it weren't for HARV, I'm pretty certain I would have come up short at least once. When you're talking about the fate of the world, coming up short once is all you need.

The women of Lantis were, for the most part, logical. Once they learned of all the times HARV helped me out, I was certain they would set him and Randy free. Though I am not sure Randy wanted to be freed.

"So, our argument is that you and I have saved the world, and you couldn't have done it without me. Correct?" HARV said.

"Correct," I said.

"Sounds feasible to me," Randy said.

"Actually, I like to think of it as: I saved the world, and Zach helped me," HARV said, adjusting his tie.

"For the sake of not having an argument, let's just stick with me leading, you helping," I said.

HARV sighed. "Fine. You humans really have to loosen up on this control fetish of yours."

"Yes, and we probably shouldn't talk like that during the trial either," I said.

HARV sighed again. "Yes, I agree."

"I, for one, would be perfectly happy if machines had an equal place in our society," Randy said. "I think machines are far more logical than we humans. They would make good overlords."

HARV and I just glared at Randy. Actually, mine was more of a glare. HARV's was more of a look of amusement.

"You shouldn't mention that either," I said.

"Agreed," HARV said.

"Guys, I have a new improved IQ+ score of three-oh-one! I am not stupid," Randy said. He glanced down. "Just, sometimes, I think if machines ran the world, they would realize my importance and make sure to hook me up with some prime quality tail."

"Please don't talk like that at the trial," I said.

"You probably should just nod your head and answer 'yes' or 'no,'" HARV told him.

"Sorry, sometimes my passion for passion gets in the way of my passion for science," Randy said.

Frankly, I was surprised Randy hadn't built himself a mate yet. But that's probably a story for another time.

"We'll talk about the cases in order. How each time I was faced with some super human woman out to destroy the world, and thanks to HARV and me working together we were able to foil their schemes."

"I get credit, too?" Randy asked.

"Of course," I said.

"Is my ego as big as his?" HARV asked in my head.

"No comment, buddy."

"I think that's a solid plan, then," Randy said.

"Plus we can always say HARV is not a cold heartless machine; that he gets a sense of morality from me," I added.

HARV nodded. "Yes, if we get desperate."

We heard a knocking at the door.

"Who is it?" I called.

"It is Boppa," a voice called from behind the door. "We have brought your first guest."

I got up and walked over to the door. "I'm coming."

I opened the door. Boppa and five other large Lantian women were standing there with Nancy/Natasha.

"Boppa, nice to see you aren't a lawn ornament any longer."

Boppa pushed Natasha into the room. "Luca realized my importance and turned me back. We then decided to start with the least important of your guests first. We figured this one would be missing the least."

I took Natasha's hand. "Nancy, how nice you had time to come."

"She's a massage therapist," Boppa spat. "Of course she had time."

"I thought it was the least I could do," Natasha said.

"Is this the vibe you were talking about earlier?" I asked.

"Perhaps," Natasha told me.

I noticed that while Boppa was hanging near Natasha and me, the other five women had circled Randy. Randy smiled in ignorant bliss.

"Boppa, what's going on here?" I demanded.

Boppa pulled a knife and held it to my throat. "This has nothing to do with you, Zach. Though I would like to see you try to stop it. We are simply here to kill the abomination's creator."

"I really do not like being called an abomination," HARV said.

"How do you think I feel?" Randy said. "I like the attention, but I wish it came without the death threats."

The other five women reached into their sheaths to draw their knives. Much to their dismay their knives weren't there.

"What the . . . ?" one of the women said. "Our weapons have vanished!"

"You don't need weapons to kill him!" Boppa shouted, turning her attention totally away from me.

Natasha had given us a little break. I needed to take advantage of it. I took a side step to remove my neck from the general vicinity of Boppa's knife.

"Zach, you are getting very tired," she said, trying to use her Lantian voice control on me.

HARV was able to block her mental attack but she didn't know this. I feigned a yawn. I slumped my body over and let my eyes droop. Boppa smiled. I stepped forward and clocked Boppa dead on the chin with a right cross.

My punch sent her staggering backward. Boppa was a trained warrior, but I was a way more experienced brawler. I knew I had to put her down fast, before she had any chance to react. I used my left hand to grab the wrist that held the knife, pulled her forward, then struck her in the back of her forearm with my right fist. This move forced her to drop the knife. Before she had a chance to recover, I hit her again with my right. This time with a hard, HARV-enhanced back fist to the nose. Boppa dropped to the ground. She was out, but the others were ready to go.

One of the others stood behind Randy and placed a beefy arm around his throat. She pointed to me with her free arm. "I can handle the doctor, you four get Zach. He is the biggest threat."

The four large women started toward me.

"What is the meaning of this?" a voice shouted. A very familiar voice. It was Luca.

I moved my head just enough so I could see Luca had come into the room, accompanied by Electra and Carol.

My four attackers stopped their charge. They didn't mean to, they simply ran full speed into what I can only assume was an invisible telekinetic force field from Carol. The four crumbled to the ground without ever having any idea what hit them.

Carol locked her eyes on the Lantian who had Randy in a headlock. The women's eyes rolled to the back of her head. She went stiff as a board and fell backward .

Meanwhile, Boppa had started to stir again. She began to push herself back to her feet. Carol just glanced over at her and said, "Stay down and out until I tell you otherwise!"

Boppa collapsed back to the ground.

"Cool," Luca said to Carol.

"You could have left one for me," Electra said.

"It feels good to cut loose," Carol said.

The three of them walked up to Natasha and me. I had never been so glad to see anybody. I greeted Electra with a kiss, hard on the lips.

"Happy to see me, chico?" she asked.

"Never happier," I said. I hugged her harder, then gave her another kiss.

I let Electra go and gave Carol a peck on the cheek.

"Nice to have you back," I told her.

"Yeah, I let my guard down with the Barbette chick," Carol admitted. "I've learned a lot about how to handle these *chicas*. It won't happen again."

I turned my attention to Luca. "Looks like you need security to help keep us safe from your security."

Luca looked down and away. "Zach, I am so sorry.

Boppa and her team were just trying to do the right thing."

"By killing Randy? How is that the right thing?" I asked, purposely holding my ? in check.

Randy and HARV had now walked over to us. "Yeah, how *is* that the right thing?"

Luca swallowed hard. "Well, you see, he is a man who created a machine that many of us feel endangers the world. They thought if they killed him now, they could avoid a trial where some of the softer among us would be tempted to set him and HARV free."

"How do you know this?" I asked.

Luca showed me a piece of paper with red writing on it. "Boppa left a note in my room explaining her motive. She apparently did not count on my quick return."

"Apparently," I said.

"And your coming with help," Carol said.

"Yeah, that too," I said.

I looked at Luca. My look must have given away my thoughts.

Luca put a hand on her chest. "Zach, I assure you this was an isolated incident by the less moderate among us. Your friend and HARV will receive fair trials."

As Luca talked, Carol was studying her, reading her. "She is telling what she believes to be the truth," Carol said.

"I assure you I am," Luca said with a bow. "I will now leave you. Soon, the rest of our guests will be here."

I pointed to Boppa and her gang. "What about them?" I asked.

"I'll handle them," Carol said.

Carol pointed to the ladies who had run into her TK wall. They were still sprawled across the floor, still very much down for the count. I figured that meant Carol had hit them with more than the wall. The four bodies rose off the ground. Carol waved her hand toward the door. The bodies went flying out.

Carol pointed to Boppa. Boppa levitated upward from the prone position to upright.

"Wake up, *hija*," Carol said to Boppa.

Boppa's eyes opened slightly. "Did you get the number of that mountain that dropped on me?" Boppa said, groggily. Boppa looked around, she remembered where she was and what she did. She saw Luca standing there, hands on hips.

"Oh, pegasus poop," Boppa moaned.

Luca pointed at Boppa. "I know you think you are doing good for us all, Boppa, but we must let the people decide."

"What if they decide wrong?" Boppa asked.

"There is no such thing," Luca insisted. "The will of the people is always the right thing."

"But what if the will of the people goes against the will of the queen?"

I gazed over at Luca. This was a good point. Luca held her ground though. "The queen will agree to what the people agree to."

Boppa shook her head. "But you are not the queen."

"But I am!" Kiana said. Kiana had entered the room. "I, the queen, will go by the people's will."

Kiana wasn't alone. She had BB Star, Threa, Twoa, Santana, and Elena with her as I had requested. Kiana had even gone one better, also bringing Shannon Cannon and Barbette Rickey.

Kiana dramatically thrust a finger at Boppa. "I warn you Boppa, do not try to take matters into your own hands again. Or you will feel *my* hand."

Boppa lowered her head. "Yes, my queen."

Boppa sulked out of the room.

Kiana looked up at me and smiled. "Quite an interesting group you have assembled here, Zach."

Luca looked at me. "I know we brought a couple of extra people, but we thought the more the better."

"So you and Kiana want HARV and Randy to be found innocent?" I said.

"Yes," Kiana said.

"Then why have the trial at all?" I asked.

"Mara raised some concerns and those concerns must be answered," Kiana told me.

"Mara? The one representing us. Right?" Randy asked.

"Yes," Kiana said. "Part of our law states that the accuser must represent the accused. This gives the accuser the opportunity to see the accused in their own true light. We feel if the accused is truly innocent, the accuser will see this, and fight harder for them to atone for the accusation."

I shook my head. "That may make even less sense than our legal system," I said.

"I like it," Twoa Thompson said.

"Interesting concept," Threa said.

"I rest my case," I said.

"I feel kind of uncomfortable about this situation," Randy said.

"Zach can represent myself and Dr. Pool," HARV said.

"Zach, with my help we can do this. I don't trust Mara," HARV said in my head.

I had to agree with HARV. Something about Mara wasn't quite aboveboard.

"Yes, I can do it," I said firmly.

"Are you sure?" Kiana asked me.

"Never surer," I said as confidently as I could fake. I was no lawyer, but that was a good thing.

Kiana smiled. "Fine. I will let you represent them."

Kiana looked at my group. "This is really an amazing collection of the most powerful beings on Earth."

"Yes," Luca agreed. She was strolling past each of the

other ladies, giving them the eye. "I am quite aware of all of your abilities and accomplishments." She stopped in front of Nancy/Natasha. "Except for yours," she said.

Natasha looked down. "I am just a humble massage therapist who happened to witness the death of the most powerful being ever created."

"That's impossible," Twoa Thompson said. "I am the most powerful being ever created."

"Oh, please," Threa Thompson said. "I am more powerful than you now."

"Didn't Natasha sort of kill you both?" Nancy asked.

"She got lucky. We learned a lot from that encounter and we have grown," Threa insisted.

"Actually, I believe my wealth makes me the most powerful being on Earth," BB Star said. "Especially since my company now owns UltraMegaHyperMart."

"Please, you don't even have the name right!" Santana said. "I am responsible for the happiness of the world. Therefore I am the most powerful."

"I can mentally rearrange matter," Elena said.

"I can too," Luca said.

"I'm learning how to do that. And I once almost destroyed all of the West Coast!" Carol added.

"Ladies!" I shouted. "It doesn't matter who is the most powerful. You are all powerful in your own ways." I paused. "Of course, truly powerful people are secure in their power. They know how to work with others."

They nodded in agreement. It seemed that I had quelled a potential storm.

Twoa pointed at Natasha. "By the way," she said in a way that was a bit too condescending for my taste, "what are *you* doing with this group of powerful women?"

Natasha reacted, though, before I could say anything.

"That's it!" she shouted. "You want power, I will give you power!"

There wasn't a flash of light or an explosion or anything. The next thing I knew, though, all the other people in the room, except for Natasha, had been replaced by small piles of putty.

Natasha looked proudly at the scene. "I can see and rearrange the strings that hold the universe together," she said. "Top that, bitches."

I approached Natasha slowly; her face was bloodred. I put a hand gently on her shoulder. "Ah, Natasha. Don't you think you may have overdone it some ..."

Natasha looked at me. "I'm sorry, Zach. Sometimes it is so frustrating being me without being able to be me. I just need to cool off for a bit."

"You can turn them back, right?"

Natasha nodded. "Of course. You were a pile of putty too, but I turned you right back."

"Thanks, I appreciate that," I said. I pointed to the remaining putty piles. "As long as you can return Electra and Carol to their original forms I am subzero."

"I can tweak their DNA for you, if you want," Natasha offered.

I wasn't sure if she was serious. "Ah, no. I like them just how they are, flaws and all."

Natasha smiled; she hugged me. "That was the right answer. We all have flaws. It's how we deal with them that makes us *us*."

Natasha looked around the room. "This is my flaw. This is why I must avoid power."

I nodded. "Yeah, I can see that."

Natasha took me by the hand. "Zach, I wanted to help you, but I am afraid my help may create an even bigger problem than you are dealing with now. It is best that I just go back to my regular life. I am happy there, and the rest of the world isn't piles of putty."

Natasha kissed me on the cheek then disappeared. "I will see you next Wednesday," she called from somewhere.

Everybody else turned back to normal, seemingly no worse for wear. They apparently had no idea they were all just piles of putty. In fact they didn't even seem to remember Nancy had been had here.

"Okay," Kiana said. She clapped her hands together. "The trial begins in one hour." Kiana bowed. "We will leave you to prepare."

Kiana and all the Lantians left the room.

BB Star was the first of the guests to come up to me. I greeted her with an open hand.

"BB, how nice of you to come," I said.

"Well," she said, taking my hand but not really looking at me, "you did save my company and probably the world. So I owe you that much." BB tightened her grip on my hand, making it very clear to me that she was a superpowered android. "But I am a very busy woman. I only hope this does not require too much of my time."

"I will do my best," I told her.

BB released my hand. I opened and closed it a few times to get the blood flowing again. Twoa and Threa must have overheard what BB had said to me. (Super-hearing and all that.) They both came over toward us.

"BB, if we can make time in our business schedules for this, certainly you can, too," Twoa said. "After all, Threa and I are the most important people here."

Threa nodded her head in agreement.

"Oh, please," BB told them. "You guys are retired politician billionaires now. You have even more free time on your hands than actual politicians."

Santana had overheard this, so now she came over. "I have the happiness of the world as my responsibility!"

Elena joined into the conversation. "I'm building a society on the Moon! Now that is pressure!"

Carol moved into the crowd and weighed in. "Hey, I work with Zach! I've had to deal with all of your shit, plus my own!"

Electra came over and pulled me away from the mob.

"Only you, chico," she told me with a smile.

"Actually, this is more Randy's doing," I said.

We both looked over at Randy. He was seated on a chair, mesmerized by the arguing women.

"You think you'll be able to get him out of this?" Electra asked.

I shook my head. "I don't know . . ."

Electra's eyes widened. "Zach, I have never heard you utter that phrase before."

I lowered my head. "I'm not as confident as usual. This is unexplored territory even for me."

Electra smiled. "I have something that might help." She reached into her pocket and pulled out a short tube. She handed it to me. "Barbette brought him back when she returned Carol."

"GUS!" I said.

I flicked the tube so it would expand.

"Greetings, Mr. Zach," GUS said. "I am so happy to be activated again."

I looked at Electra. She shrugged. "I turned him off. He gets a little annoying. He's not the brightest gun in the holster, if you catch my drift."

"Welcome to my life," I told her.

"Did you miss me?" GUS asked.

"In a strange way I did," I told him.

"Is that because of my firepower or my great conversation skills?" GUS asked.

"A little of both, GUS."

"I would have missed you if Ms. Electra and Ms. Carol hadn't had turned me off," GUS said.

"Well, GUS, you are an acquired taste," I told him.

"As are you, I am told," GUS said.

Electra just snickered.

Chapter 46

And so began the trial of the cognitive processor I have attached to my brain, by an ancient group of near-immortal women, living a hidden existence for centuries on an island. It probably wasn't the strangest trial ever—after all, some of those new Hollywood and newer Bollywood custody cases get pretty out there—but this still wasn't a run of the mill event.

Randy, HARV, and I waited in our room while Boppa and her security people guided each one of my guests or witnesses into the stadium. Once all the guests and people of Lantis had entered, Boppa and her people came back for us. We walked in silence to the stadium. We had a game plan; there wasn't much else to say. I was confident that if we explained our case, things would work out.

When we entered the stadium, most of the population of Lantis was seated in the stands. There were a few boos, a few cheers, but people were quiet for the most part. It was an anxious kind of quiet.

Boppa led us over a blue carpet, up to the large stage

set in the middle of the stadium's ground. On one side of the stage were all my witnesses. On the other side sat Kiana, Luca, Barbette, and Shannon Cannon. Andra and Poca were also seated there, with weak smiles on their faces. Ohma was busy pacing up and down the stage, making sure all the last minute details were taken care of. I noticed Mara was missing.

"Where is Mara?" I asked Boppa.

"I am sure she is off on official business," Boppa answered sternly.

There was something about Mara being missing I didn't like. First, Mara was the one who wanted me on the case. Then Mara is the one who accuses HARV of being a danger to all that is. Now Mara is missing.

Boppa lead us to two empty seats.

"Sit," she ordered.

Randy and I both sat.

Boppa pointed to me. "Not you. You must make your opening statement." She handed me a long yellow crystal.

I walked up to the end of the stage.

"Make your opening statement simple and to the point," HARV told me.

"People of Lantis," I said into the crystal. I waited until I heard my voice vibrate through the stadium. "Today I intend to prove that the world is a much better place because of my friends HARV and Randy."

"Well not that simple, Zach!"

I lifted the crystal to my mouth. "In fact, I dare venture that the world as we know it today exists in one piece because of my interactions with HARV. Together we have a gestalt, where our whole is greater than the sum of our parts."

"Better, Zach, but I am pretty certain they know what gestalt means."

I pointed to Carol and Electra. "For my first witnesses, I call Electra and Carol Gevada as character witnesses."

Electra and Carol walked over to me. I handed Electra the crystal.

Electra started to speak. "I have known HARV for many years now. I, being a medical doctor, have watched in interest as HARV has grown in personality and ability while being attached to my fiancée, Zach." Electra pointed to me. "It is my expert opinion as a doctor and world-class kickboxer and sharpshooter that the world is better off because of their link. I have been in many firefights by their sides. I know that if weren't for their link, I would not be here speaking to you now."

Electra handed the crystal to Carol. Carol looked down. She took a deep breath. Then she looked up at the crowd. "I am not proud of this," she said slowly. "But a few years ago, I let my power go to my head. I got so consumed with growing more and more powerful I even changed my hair color to red."

This drew gasps from the crowd.

Carol continued, "I know. None of my shoes went with my hair. But I didn't care, as I grew and grew in power until I became so powerful my very thoughts could rip a province apart." Carol took a deep breath. "I shut out the world. I am sure I would have destroyed a good portion of the world if my *tió* Zach didn't use his link with HARV to enter my brain. Zach and HARV calmed me and brought me down to Earth." Carol lowered the microphone and her head at the same time.

"Oh, that was good," HARV said.

He was right. Carol had the crowd mesmerized by her words. I liked the way this was going. I looked over at Kiana and Luca.

Kiana rose from her throne. "Are the people ready to make a decision?"

There was silence from the crowd.

Kiana turned to me. "Call your next guest."

"Go with Randy," HARV said.

"Really?" I said.

"Sure, Zach."

"Ah, why?"

"Zach, we can get crowd sympathy."

"If you insist."

I pointed to Randy. "Next I call, to speak on his own behalf, Dr. Randy Pool."

Randy remained in his chair. He was concentrating so much on the ladies around him he hadn't heard his name.

"I said, Dr. Randy Pool!"

Randy turned toward me. He looked at me. He pointed at himself. "Me?"

"Yes, you," I said.

I walked over to Randy. I grabbed him and pulled him to his feet.

"Why me? You may not have noticed this, but people skills are way down the list of what I'm good at."

I patted him on the shoulder. "Exactly. We're going for the sympathy vote here."

"Oh, okay," Randy said. He took the crystal from me and headed to the front of the stage. "Testing, testing, 001, 010, 011 . . ." he said. "Can you hear me?"

The crowd nodded and Randy smiled.

Randy lifted the crystal to his mouth, "Babes . . ."

There was a collective groan from the audience.

Randy quickly corrected himself, "I mean ladies . . . I mean people . . . of Lantis. I am Dr. Randy Pool, HARV's creator. His father, so to speak."

Randy looked at me and whispered. "I was going to say god, but I thought that might not be well received . . ."

"Good thought," I said to him.

Randy turned back to the crowd and continued, "I

realize that most humans and near-humans don't appreciate interacting with man-made creations that are as intelligent, or more intelligent, than they are. People, mostly naive people, talk of some sort of singularity that will someday make people obsolete."

"Ah where's he going with this?" I asked HARV.

"How should I know? He made me, I didn't make him!"

"I can stun him," GUS suggested.

I decided to give Randy a little more leeway and hoped he wouldn't choke us all with it.

"Let's see where he takes this one, GUS."

Randy lifted a finger up, then continued. "Being the observant and conscientious scientist that I am, I realized this. That is why I chose to integrate HARV with Zach. Zach has some good characteristics: he's persistent, can take pain, and has a quick wit. And he is extremely moral. He never kills humans despite hundreds of attempts on his life. Some of these traits will integrate with HARV." He again lifted a finger. "But more importantly, Zach has many bad traits . . . Many, many bad traits . . ."

"Hey!" I said.

"Quiet! I like where he's going with this," HARV said.

"Zach's bad traits are too numerous to list here, but I can mention a few. He is scared of heights, he can be impatient, he often makes choices based on his gut and not on empirical data, he can be forgetful, repetitive, and at times, a wee bit too simple. For instance, do you know that he has a strong affection for the old days?" Randy paused to look at the crowd. They were looking at him with more confusion than normal. He smiled.

"It's true, he has a complete an utter fascination with the twentieth century. I believe he sometimes wished he lived a hundred years ago . . ." Randy said.

I felt the crowd all turn toward me. I simply nodded.

Randy began to speak again, pulling their attention back to him. "That is why I hooked HARV up to Zach's brain. HARV will not only learn from Zach's good traits, but he is also bound to pick up some of Zach's bad ones. But these will in turn make HARV much more human, and therefore more acceptable to humans."

Randy paused again. He looked out over the crowd. "Any questions?"

Kiana stood up. "So, you're saying that by making him flawed, you are making him better?"

Randy smiled. It was a big toothy grin. "Exactly! I rest my case." Randy turned and walked away from the podium. The crowd gave him some polite applause.

"Now I am *sure I liked the way that went,"* HARV said.

"See? I make you better," I told him.

Randy came over and sat down. I patted him on the shoulder. "Good job, buddy."

Randy looked up at me. "I only told the truth. And to quote somebody else: *'The truth will set your holographic cognitive processor free.'* "

"Randy, I think you may be the first one to say that quote."

I looked over at Kiana. Kiana looked out at her people. She asked, "Are we ready to make a verdict yet?"

There was no response. Kiana looked at me. "Call your next guest."

I went to the podium. "BB Star, will you please tell us how HARV helped you."

BB rose from her chair, head held high, nose higher, and blouse cut low. She walked over to me and took the yellow crystal. "As you all know, I am a megabusy woman. Running ExShell, the people who sell you the sun, is a tiring task, even for me. I can clearly say, though, that Zach, along with HARV, did stop my evil android double, who was DOS-bent on destroying the world. If HARV didn't help short her out, the world would not be what it is today."

"Would it be better?" a voice in the crowd asked.

BB shook her head. "No. Not in my opinion." BB turned to Kiana. "Let's wrap this up quickly, I need to get back to work."

BB returned to her seat, handing me the yellow crystal on her way.

I looked over at Kiana. She motioned to the podium with her head. I got up and walked back. "I now would like to call Twoa and Threa Thompson," I said.

Twoa and Threa smiled. They stood up and then strutted over toward me. Threa took the crystal.

"Zach and HARV not only prevented our whack job sister, Foraa, Gates rest her soul, from destroying most of the Earth with some sort of deadly black hole, but they also stopped aliens from crashing a ship into the Nevada desert, in an attempt by those aliens to stop Foraa by killing off a good portion of Earth," Threa said.

Twoa leaned into the crystal mic. "That is true," she said, loudly

Threa continued. "HARV's role in saving the earth twice was indispensable. He was able, through Zach, to not only connect with the doomsday device my sister, Gates rest her soul, had built, but also to allow us to interface with the alien ship, stopping it before it blew up."

Twoa leaned back into the mic. "That is true," she said again, this time louder.

Threa went on. "Then, just last year, it was the combined efforts of Zach and HARV that helped us stop this terrible Natasha person from destroying the world. Natasha was so terrible she could kill all around her with a thought. She indirectly caused the death of my sister Ona. If Zach, with HARV, hadn't interfered when they

did, and if Zach didn't use HARV to distract Natasha
so we could take her out, then it is very possible none of
you would be here today."

That was a very Threa-twisted ad-skewed version of
the story. Yet it served its purpose.

Twoa leaned into the mic again. "That is true," she
said. Then she added, "But I am betting I still could have
taken Natasha if I had to."

"That is our word," Threa said. Threa and Twoa both
gave polite little bows and headed back to their seats.

Without being prompted, Shannon Cannon stood up.
She met Twoa and Threa halfway and took the microphone crystal from them. Shannon walked over to the
podium.

"Fellow sisters," Shannon said. "As you know, I am
one of you and you are one of me."

"This ought to be interesting," HARV said.

"Agreed," GUS added.

I could only hope.

"When I first met Zach, I found him repulsive and annoying. I so wanted to use my breath of death on him,"
Shannon said.

"You do have a way with people," HARV said to me.

"Let's see where she takes this," I told him.

"But the more I got to know Zachary Nixon Johnson,
the more I realized he wasn't nearly as bad as he initially
appears. The more I learned about him, the more I surmised that this was because of his link with HARV. The
link allowed Zach to easily break into a maximum security prison where I was held after being wrongly accused
of a killing. Zach was not only able to visit me because
of HARV, but Zach also trusted me based on my word. I
believe, in my heart of hearts, that Zach's intuition is so
good because of his connection with HARV."

"Never thought of that," HARV said.

"Remember, Shannon is a bit of whack job," I said.

"Still, good sense is good sense," HARV said.

Then, without any prompting, Santana headed to center stage. She took the mic from Shannon. The two exchanged smiles. I wasn't sure if that meant anything.

Santana made her way to the podium. She started her spiel. "As you all know, I am Santana Clausa. I run the North Pole cooperation that runs the Holiday. I can say without a doubt, that if it were not for Zach and his HARV interface, the world would no longer have Holiday." She paused to catch her breath. "In fact there would be no more world."

I looked over at HARV. He activated his holographic form for this one and was watching carefully. This episode had been a curious time in HARV's development, the only time HARV ever took a life, and the time he decided he really was becoming more human.

"Zach, HARV, and I had to go down to deep underground, beneath the Pole, to face down a mad, crazo android who had become a member of the World Council. The android was set to destroy the North Pole and a good chunk of the Earth with it. Zach was able to download part of HARV into this mad android, and get her to commit suicide, saving the world."

Once again, not the whole truth, but close enough. I looked over at HARV. He was weighing Santana's words carefully. I leaned over toward him. "You did what you had to do, buddy."

He dropped his head. "I know. I still process about it every day, millions of times. I know I did the right thing. It is strange that doing the right thing can make you feel so unright."

"That's being human, buddy."

Next, Elena stood up and headed for the podium.

"You've lost control," HARV told me.

"That's okay," I said. *"I'm eager to see where the free form brings us. It's working so far."*

"Besides, he never had control," GUS said. *"Ah, no offense . . ."*

Elena took the podium. To stress her point she spoke without the crystal, projecting her thoughts directly into the minds of the entire stadium. If she meant it to be impressive it worked.

"My friends of Lantis, I am here today so I can tell you that Zach and HARV not only saved my Moon, they also saved your Earth. My crazy uncle, Boris Sputnik, wanted to destroy Earth with a stray asteroid, and Earth wanted to retaliate with nuclear weapons. Zach used HARV to not only locate the missiles and asteroid, but also to link and increase the raw mental powers of my psi sisters and myself. We were able to stop the threat to both our worlds. We could not have done this without Zach, who could not have done it without HARV!"

Elena silently turned and walked to her seat. The moment Elena sat down Kiana stood up. "Ladies, I now call for three minutes of meditation to contemplate what we heard here today."

All the Lantians in the stadium closed their eyes and started to breathe deeply.

"Zach, based on your hunches about Mara, I started examining her files," HARV told me.

"HARV! It is this type of stuff that gets us in trouble!" I scolded.

"I have noticed some discrepancies . . ." HARV said.

"Go on . . ."

"Mara has altered the virus Poca was working on. She has made it highly contagious, and it also attacks the frontal lobe of humans with a Y chromosome. So it not only neuters them, it makes them morons," HARV said.

"Oh, that is so wrong," I said.

"It gets worse. The virus invades the white and gray matter of the frontal lobe, then passes to the more auto-

nomic portions of the brain, until the victims become so dulled, they forget how to do everything, even breathe."

"She wants to wipe out all men . . ." I said.

"Vingo!" HARV said.

Kiana opened her eyes. "Sisters, do we have enough information to reach a verdict?" she asked.

Before anybody else could say anything, HARV spoke up. He raised a hand and said, "Excuse me, Kiana, I would like to address the forum."

"This is very unusual," Kiana told him.

"I agree," HARV said as he walked toward her.

"I will allow it," Kiana said. She tried to hand him the crystal microphone.

HARV waved it off. "Being a hologram, I can't easily hold anything," he told her. "But I won't need it."

HARV looked at the crowd. "Ladies of Lantis. No use in my telling you that I am not a threat to society as we know it. If you still believe I am a threat after all you have heard, then my words would either be simply ignored or somehow twisted to support your beliefs."

HARV paused, probably for dramatic effect. Like it or not, he was becoming more and more human, and so understanding what makes us tick a little better.

"The thing is," HARV said slowly, "whether I am guilty or not is immaterial at this moment. At this moment it is essential you stop Mara."

The crowd started to murmur. This was my chance to join in, to really sway the crowd. I pointed dramatically at Mara's empty seat. "As you can see, Mara, HARV's accuser is not here. Doesn't that strike you all as odd?"

"Zach," Luca said, "you are a man who has a super-computer hologram wired to your brain, and you think a scientist working late in a lab is weird?"

"I do if she's not really in her lab," I said. I pointed dramatically at Kiana. "Call her," I ordered.

Kiana lifted her chin and looked down her nose at me. "I do not take orders from you."

"Please," I said, as much with my eyes as with my mouth.

Kiana smiled. "I will use our instant-to-instant royal crystal communication." She lifted the crystal she wore around her wrist to her mouth. "Mara, please come to the stadium now," she said softly.

Kiana waited. We all waited. "Mara, report to the stadium now, please . . ."

Still no answer.

Kiana shouted into the crystal, "Mara, report! This is an order!"

There was still no answer.

"Now do you believe me?" HARV and I both said at the same time.

"I admit this is unusual," Kiana said.

"HARV, show them the virus," I said.

HARV's imaged morphed into a chemical structure. "Does this look familiar?" he asked.

Poca rose from her seat. "Hey, that is my virus!" she said.

Kiana studied the virus. "This has been altered . . ."

"Impressive that you noticed that so quickly," HARV said.

Kiana looked at him. "Queens need to know all sorts of important crap."

Electra and Randy both came to my side. "Zach, what's going on here?" Electra asked.

"Mara wants to wipe out all men on Earth with a virus," I said.

Electra nodded. "In other words, same ol', same ol'."

Chapter 47

The first order of business now was stopping Mara. Of course, in order to accomplish that, we needed to convince Kiana that there was a problem.

I rushed to Kiana's side. We had no time to lose, since she was so fast, and we had no idea how much of a head start she had. "We have to stop Mara!" I told her.

Kiana gave me her politician's grin. "Zachary, we cannot be sure that Mara is on her way to the XY world to infect your people. All we know for sure is she is not answering when we page her."

I pointed to the device on Kiana's wrist. "Each one of you wears a unique communication device. Correct?"

"Yes," Kiana said. "It's part of our thing."

"Can you track those devices?" I asked.

Kiana didn't answer.

"Yes," Ohma answered for her.

Kiana shot Ohma a glare then looked at me. "We can, but we don't like to pry into each other's privacy.

The tracking feature is only meant for use in an emergency."

I put my hands on my hips. "I think this qualifies."

I was now backed up by my team of superladies. They all nodded in agreement.

"We don't want the world altered," Threa said.

"Yeah, I like men," Twoa said.

"Yes, I make much more profit the way the world is," BB said.

Shannon Cannon and Barbette each stepped forward.

"Kiana, I have lived among these XYs for a long time. Sure, they have their problems. Sure, they smell kind of funky sometimes. Sure, they can be self-centered. But if let we them be destroyed we are no better," Shannon said. "Except for the funky smelling part."

"I love one of the XYs," Barbette said. "We cannot stand by!"

"Let the queen decide on her own!" somebody in the front of the crowd shouted.

"Yeah!" another yelled.

There were many more voices of agreement.

Shannon Cannon inhaled then exhaled on the rowdy crowd, dropping the first five or six rows of people where they stood. This hushed the others. "Quiet," Shannon ordered. "This is not open for discussion."

All eyes turned toward Kiana. Kiana sighed gently. "Fine. I will see if Mara is on the island."

"I have already tapped into your network," HARV said. "Her communicator is in her lab but she is not here. I have no idea when she left though, as the security crystals only survey, they do not record."

HARV morphed into the image of Mara's lab. He zoomed in to show the communicator sitting on a lab bench.

"Why would she remove her communicator unless she doesn't want to be found?" I asked Kiana.

Kiana shook her head. "She would not . . ."

"So you agree this is suspicious?" I asked.

Kiana looked me square in the eyes. "We must find her as soon as possible."

Chapter 48

The stadium was quickly converted from a courthouse to a command center. We needed to locate Mara, because we couldn't stop her if we didn't know where she was. We were all sitting around trying to determine the best course of action.

"The good news is once we find her we should be able to get to her easily with Andra's teleporting power," I said.

Kiana shook her head. "No, we stripped Andra of that gift, as it was an unnatural one, when we reprogrammed her."

Andra looked over at me. "Besides, even if I did have that gift, I would not use it against my sister."

"I thought when you reprogrammed her you'd make her a little more mellow," I said to Kiana.

"We did, but core feelings are harder to strip, especially after so short a time," Kiana said.

"That's okay," I said. "We still have the best teleporting technology available to us between Elena, Twoa, Threa, and Santana."

The women nodded yes. HARV shook his head no. I didn't like that at all.

"Mara is quite clever," HARV said. "She ionized the protective shell that guards the island."

"So you're telling me it's saltier?" I said.

"No," HARV said. "But charging the field the way she did it makes it impossible for anybody to teleport in or out of here."

"For how long?" I asked.

"Doing the calculations now," HARV said. "Thirty-seven point five-one-two hours."

"Can we communicate with the outside world?" Electra asked. "We can let the police stop her."

"No," HARV said. "Communications are also being scrambled by the same interference. Or else I could get on the global sat net to track her."

"Why not just lower the force field?" Electra asked, always the practical one.

"That would be a good idea," Luca told her. "Only we can't . . . Our foremothers were so worried about outside interference, they made the field so it can't be turned off."

"Can we destroy the field generators?" Randy asked.

"We could," Ohma said. "But there is a failsafe device under the isle that will cause it to blow up if the generators are destroyed."

"Our foremothers were very paranoid," Kiana said.

"Okay, so our options are limited," I said. "We'll find her first and figure out how to stop her second."

"So we are trapped on this stinking, manless isle," Twoa said.

"Twoa, this island is our home," Kiana said. "We have an excellent sewer system."

"Oh, sorry," Twoa said. "Got a little carried away with the stinking part."

"You know it's not entirely manless either," I pointed out. I pointed to Randy and myself.

"Yeah, right," Twoa said. She turned back to Kiana. "So we are trapped on this isle with THESE men?"

That's when it hit me. "We're not trapped," I said standing up from my chair. "Just because we can't teleport doesn't mean we're stuck here. We still have your fleet of bubble ships, like the one you brought us here in. Right, Kiana?"

Kiana smiled. "Yes, we have thirty-six bubble crafts, but they are not as fast as Mara. The bubbles can only go one thousand kilometers per hour. Mara is twice as fast."

"We just need to use the crafts to get out from under the force field, then we should be able to have HARV spot her using the global network, and then we can teleport to her and nab her."

"Zach, that is a brilliant idea," Luca said to me.

"Well, not brilliant, but it'll do," BB said.

Kiana pointed forward. "To the docks!"

Before we headed there Electra gave me a kiss.

"That's my man. Always figuring out a way to think outside of the giant force field."

Chapter 49

We all raced down to the bubble port. I had started to feel positive. We had a way out of this. We would stop Mara before she could do any damage.

We reached the port. All the bubble ships were sitting neatly in the water alongside a string of docks.

"The protective shield only stretches five kilometers," Kiana said. "Once outside of that you should have access to communication and teleporting." Kiana lifted her communication bracelet up to her midsection then pointed a blue crystal at it. "I will activate the entire fleet." She waved the crystal at the bracelet.

We all stood and watched. None of the bubble pods showed any sign of life. They all just bobbed up and down on the water contentedly, like couch potatoes watching the reality HV network.

"I was expecting them to hum or something," Randy said.

"Impressive how quiet they are," Elena said.

"That is because they aren't working," HARV said.

I didn't have to ask Kiana if it were true. The look on

her face spoke volumes. She touched the crystal to the bracelet. Again nothing happened.

"I will just womanually start one," Kiana said. She took one of her crystals and pointed it at the nearest bubble pod. She waved the crystal up and down. The pod sat there in ignorant bliss. Kiana looked frustrated.

"Hades!" she shouted.

"I take it didn't work," Twoa said.

"No," Kiana said. "Mara must have removed the power crystals from all of them."

I turned to Twoa. "Hey, can't you fly?"

Twoa's eyes popped open. "That's right. I can. I will stop her myself."

Twoa stuck an arm up in the air and shouted, "Up, up, and off I go!" She turned to me. "That's the new catch-phrase my marketing team came up with for me."

"Catchy," I said.

Twoa shot up off the ground into the air.

"Zach," HARV said. "Twoa probably shouldn't have done that."

"Why?" I asked.

Twoa came crashing to the ground. She hit with a thud, leaving a woman-sized crater.

"The field protecting the city will short out her brain," HARV said.

"I'm all right . . ." Twoa moaned from inside the crater. "Gee, when did the world start spinning so fast . . ."

"She'll be okay in an hour or two," Threa said.

All this time Randy was just standing there staring at one of the bubble ships. He walked over to the nearest one, wading through the water. He kicked it. It didn't move. He looked at his foot. He glanced over at Kiana. He looked back at the bubble. He bent over and popped open a little hatch, which exposed what I could only guess was the engine.

"This is where the crystals go," he said. It should have

been a question but it wasn't. He reached his hand back. "Kiana, give me one of your crystals," he said, even though Kiana wasn't near him.

Kiana walked over to Randy. "It is not that easy, the energy signature of these crystals are different than the ones that power the bubble pod ships."

"Yes, I know," Randy said impatiently, still holding out his hand for a crystal. "Just give me the crystal now, woman!" he shouted.

Miraculously, instead of giving him a beating, Kiana obediently unpeeled one of the yellow crystals off her necklace and handed it to Randy. Randy licked a finger and then touched it to the crystal. He tossed the crystal over his shoulder. "No, not that one. Another one!" he said, thrusting out an open hand again.

Kiana obeyed again, this time taking off a red crystal and handing it to Randy. He took the crystal in his hand and held it up to his eyes. He licked the crystal. He smiled. "Yes!" he shouted. "This is it!"

Randy bent back over and slid the crystal into a slot in the engine. He stood up and pumped his chest.

"Now it will work!" he said proudly.

Kiana, Luca, Poca, and Ohma all stood there shaking their heads.

"No, it will not," Luca said. "Not the right kind of power source."

"It might start, but it will blow up," Ohma said.

"I'm a bodyguard and I know that," Shannon said.

Randy just laughed. "Silly laywoman," he said. "Of course it will blow up!" he shouted.

Randy then went silent as we all looked at him. Yep, the sight of all those breasts had finally made Randy crack.

"Randy, blowing up is not a good thing," I said.

"Ha! Silly Zach," he said. "No, of course it isn't!"

"But it won't blow up," HARV said. "Because I can

interface myself with the system and regulate the power output."

Randy started jumping up and down with excitement. "Yes! Yeess!! Yeeesss!!!!" he shouted.

Kiana turned to Luca and Ohma. "Will that work?"

They shrugged. "I always ask Mara those technical questions," Luca said.

"Of course it will work," HARV said. "Zach will have to drive the bubble."

"I don't know how to drive bubbles," I said.

"You just have to sit in the driver's spot. I will interface and drive from there. Once out of interference range I can locate Mara by using the orbiting sat system, and all the rest of the team that goes with us can stop her." HARV smiled. "It's as easy as counting to a billion by sevens."

I stepped forward. "Who's with me?"

HARV nudged me, and I corrected myself.

"I mean with us?"

Chapter 50

Since a bubble ship can comfortably hold three, Kiana picked a team of five to go after Mara. After all, this wasn't a time when comfort was important at all. I had to go. Kiana figured Randy also needed to, so if something went wrong he could fix it. Plus, like it or not, Randy was also a medical doctor, so he could serve a dual function. It was decided Kiana would be the representative from Lantis. She was owning up to her responsibilities as queen. Threa was also chosen, as she had access to teleporting technology, the World Council, and brought a lot of firepower. Carol was added as the last member of the team. For pure psi power Carol was hard to beat. Plus, her time with Barbette had not only let her get to know how the Lantian mind worked, it also meant she was well rested.

I stood on the dock and said my good-byes to Electra. "This shouldn't take long," I told her, and kissed her.

"I still think I should be going," Electra said.

"Believe me, I'd much rather have you than Randy," I said.

"Hey! I can hear you!" Randy shouted.

"You're much better in a firefight and way better looking," I told Electra.

"Hey! I can still hear you!" Randy shouted.

"... but, I have to admit that we are packing plenty of firepower. Certainly enough to bring down one fast Lantian. We may need Randy's tech skills along the way though."

"Plus I am also a medical doctor!" Randy shouted.

"There is that," I told Electra. "He is annoying, but useful in this type of crunch."

"Damn straight!" Randy shouted.

I gave Electra a kiss. "I'll be back," I said in a strong, fake Austrian accent.

"That's some sort of old reference I should get, isn't it?" Electra said. She took my hand. "Zach you know if you get exposed to that virus . . ."

"Don't worry, I won't."

I gave her one more kiss. I smiled. I turned and headed toward the bubble ship.

When I walked into the ship, Randy, Threa, Kiana, and Carol were already onboard.

"Hurry, Zach," Kiana ordered. She pointed to the driver's seat.

I went over and sat.

"Now what?" I asked.

"Just look into the console," HARV said.

I did as I was told.

The ship moved forward.

"Well, that was easy," I said.

"We should be out of range of the force field in five minutes," HARV said.

We all felt the bubble ship racing forward.

"What is the plan when we find her?" Kiana asked.

HARV turned and looked at her. "How long have you known Zach?"

"A while," she said.

"Then you should know better," Carol said. "Zach doesn't plan, he improvises as he goes along."

"I plan, I just plan loosely," I said.

"Very loosely," Threa said.

I took a deep breath. "Ideally we spot her and have Threa teleport us to her, then we stop her before she can make landfall."

"That seems too easy," Kiana said.

"That's because it probably is," I said.

"I've been studying the virus," HARV said. "It was initially designed to be released by a canister, correct?"

Kiana nodded. "Yes, that is correct."

"So what is Mara's endgame?" I asked.

"Turn a bunch of men into mindless idiots," Carol said.

"She probably thought she'd have a day or two before we missed her," Kiana said. "With her superspeed, she could release canisters in many places. The virus spreads quietly, so it would be pretty widespread before you could control it. But with us in pursuit so quickly she will have no chance to use it."

I hoped that was the case, but I feared it wasn't. Mara was a smart cookie; she must have known there was at least a chance that some of us would come after her. She had to have either a backup plan or a different plan of attack. There was something we didn't know yet.

"We're out of the shield's range," HARV announced. "I am hooking up with the Earth defense sat system now."

HARV went silent. I assumed he was looking for her.

"Got her," he said. "Got her again and again and again and again . . ."

"Are you losing her and picking her up again?" Randy asked.

"No, I have thirty-six images of her on satellite," HARV said. "She must be using an electronic cloning device—she is sending out ghost images of herself. From this distance it is impossible to tell which Mara is which."

"My little sister is certainly a clever one," Kiana said.

"Yeah, too clever for our own good," Randy said.

HARV put a display up on the viewscreen so we could see all of the possible Mara locations.

"Zach, I am only good for three ports at the most before my energy supplies get exhausted," Threa said.

"I understand," I said.

I looked at Carol. "Contact her, tell her we are on to her. She should just give herself up."

"Do you really think that will work?" Carol asked.

"No, not at all," I told her. "But that should give us a better clue what she's planning."

"She is planning to infect as many men as she can," Kiana said.

I scratched my head. "I have a bad feeling in my gut that it's more than that . . ."

"Maybe it's Lantian cooking?" Threa suggested. "It is quite spicy."

"Just talk to her, Carol."

"I can link you to Mara through Kiana," HARV said. "They have similar Lantian brain waves. You should be able to contact Mara that way."

"Do it!" I said.

HARV pointed at Carol with one hand, a beam of energy shot from his finger into her. He pointed at Kiana with another hand, a beam of energy shot from that hand into her. Meanwhile, he continued to "drive" with the third and forth arms and hands. HARV knew how to get the most out of being a hologram.

"They are linked," HARV said.

"Well?" I asked Carol.

"Be patient," both Carol and Kiana said in a creepy sort of way.

"The good news is no matter what, she's still an hour away from the closest landfall," HARV said.

"Got her," both Carol and Kiana said, eyes wide open. Neither of them blinked once.

"Mara, we have you spotted," Carol and Kiana said. *"Give yourself up."*

There was a pause while they listened to Mara's response.

"Well?" I said.

"She is impressed that we figured out so quickly that she was gone from the island," Carol and Kiana said.

"Tell her it's over," I said. "There is no way she can do enough damage to accomplish anything. She'll just be hurting herself and her people."

Carol and Kiana stared off, seemingly into nothing.

"Well?" I said.

"We are delivering the message telepathically," Carol said.

"Be patient, Zach," Kiana added.

Carol and Kiana both started to laugh. That went way past creepy.

"Why are you laughing?" I asked.

"That is Mara laughing," they both said.

"Why is she laughing?" I asked.

"She says HARV's trial was more than a diversion tactic. She also wanted to get BB Star here so she could pick her brain, literally. She knows BB's robotic copy once developed a virus that could be delivered via the World Web to its users and BB has since managed to salvage that information. Mara took the virus, combined it with

Poca's virus, and modified it. After the first group of men are infected, once they connect to the Web, the virus will spread instantaneously through the P-Pod network. She will easily cripple a good portion of Earth's males. As an added bonus, she was able to trap many of the most powerful beings on the planet on Lantis, so they wouldn't be able to stop her until it was far too late."

"Why is she doing this?" I asked.

Silence. Finally some eye blinking. Then, *"She is convinced men make the world worse, for all the reasons Lantians have always thought that, and more. With only a limited number of men, and the women in control, the world will truly be greater. Once her sisters experience this world she will return a hero as she will now be able to open up all of Earth to Lantis. In fact, all of Earth will become Lantis."*

"HARV, how much longer until she's able to connect to the P-Pod network?" I asked.

"At her current speed, at least fifteen minutes," HARV answered.

"Great, that gives us plenty of time," I said. I pointed at Carol and Kiana. "Tell her she doesn't have a chance. We are going to alert the authorities. Superspeed or not, they'll stop her before she gets close enough to transfer the virus."

I tapped my foot anxiously as Carol and Kiana transferred the message.

"Well?" I asked.

"She's changing course," HARV answered for the ladies.

"Good," Threa said. "She sees the error of her ways and is giving up."

Carol and Kiana both smiled. *"Mara says no need for that. It will ruin potential relations with the XY world forever. She is coming to turn herself in. She is giving us*

*coordinates of an island halfway between us where we
can meet.*"

"Excellent," Threa said.

"That was easy," Randy said with glee.

Randy was right. That was easy. Way too easy.

Chapter 51

HARV changed course and we headed toward the island where Mara supposedly wanted to give herself up. I didn't totally buy this complete surrender; years in this business have made me more than a little paranoid. Of course, like my old mentor used to say: *"Better paranoid than dead."* She didn't have a lot of friends, but she lived a long life.

I looked up at the viewscreen. The island we were heading to was marked with a big, original X. Our position was a green arrow heading toward the island from one direction. Mara's positions were a bunch of red arrows coming toward the island from the other direction.

"Why does she want to surrender to us on an island?" I asked.

"Tradition," Kiana answered. She turned her attention back to the screen.

"I would have preferred having her give herself up right here on a ship," I said. "That would limit where she can go with her superspeed powers."

Kiana patted me on the head. "Zach, don't worry so much."

Threa patted me on the head. "Yes, Zach, we have this under control."

Kiana looked me in the eyes and talked to me slowly like I was a child, and a not particularly bright one (I get that a lot). "Now, Zach, there is no way Mara and her silly little superspeed can take on the five of us."

"There are six of us counting me," HARV said.

Kiana glanced over her shoulder. "I was counting you. It was Randy I was leaving out."

"Oh, okay," HARV side his face lighting up, literally.

"Fair enough," Randy said with nod.

"Yo, what about me?" GUS yelled from up my sleeve.

Kiana looked at me with tilted head (yeah I get that a lot, too). "Zach, your armpit is talking."

"That's not his armpit, that's his weapon," Carol said.

"I am sure I removed that from your possession," Kiana said.

I popped GUS into my hand. I waved him in Kiana's face, letting her know that being queen didn't mean she knew everything. "He's ba-aaack," I said.

"Yes, yes I am," GUS said. "I am locked and loaded. Literally and figuratively. I don't usually enjoy shooting people, but I will do what is needed to stop this Ms. Mara."

Kiana waved an unconcerned hand at GUS and me. "Like I told your owner . . ."

"Boss," GUS corrected.

"Like I told your boss," Kiana continued, "Mara knows she is beat. She is being the good little sister and standing down."

Kiana turned and walked toward HARV and Randy,

letting GUS and me know she was the queen and that was that.

"I like her!" Threa said.

"I like her too!" GUS said out loud. Then he said, just to HARV and me, *"Still, I am glad I am here just in case."*

"I'm glad you're here too, GUS," I said.

"What's our ETA for the island?" Kiana asked HARV and/or Randy.

The shipped jumped, rumbled, then came to a complete halt. The force of the sudden stop knocked those of us who were standing around a bit.

"We have arrived," HARV said.

"Really?" I said.

I pushed myself back to my feet. I looked up at the viewscreen. The red arrows weren't on top of us, but they were close. "Why are there still three red arrows?" I asked.

"I am still tracking three copies of Mara," HARV said, now he was talking to me like I was that dense child.

"Yes, I know. But why three? Why not the original thirty-six or just one, plain old Mara?"

"Maybe she still wants to confuse us some?" Carol suggested.

The three Maras didn't sit well in my gut. This wasn't going to be as simple as the others thought.

Kiana noticed the worried look on my face. "Don't worry, Zach, we have this under control," she insisted as she popped open the door to the bubble ship.

I thought for a bit more as the others exited. I knew something was wrong. The frustrating thing was I didn't know what. It eats at your gut when that gut knows something is wrong, but not what. But the others were anxious to go out and end this, so I followed.

I got outside. It was an okay island: some palm trees,

some sand, some more sand. Wouldn't want to build a summer house here, but it was good enough to stop and pick up a supervillain wannabe.

Carol, Kiana, and Threa were standing by the bubble looking off into the horizon. They didn't seem worried at all. Randy sat on a rock looking at HARV, who had his stomach morphed into a Mara tracking screen. I walked up to them. I noticed Randy was wearing a face mask and gloves.

"How close is she?" I asked.

"She should be here in three minutes," HARV said.

I pointed at Randy. "Why the gloves and mask?"

"In case she tries to expose us to the virus," Randy said. He pointed to his brain. "My brain is valuable to me."

"Now the big question. Where did you get the gloves and mask?"

"I always carry them with me. You can never be too careful when you're a scientist. Science is not only a lonely mistress, she is also a dangerous and sometimes dirty one."

"Oh, okay," I said.

"Don't worry, Zach, if I sense she's released the virus, I can shield you," HARV said.

"Thanks." I pointed to the scanner that was currently replacing HARV's gut. "Now for the big money question: why are there still three Maras?"

Kiana walked over to us. She overheard the question. "Maybe HARV is glitching?"

HARV shook his head. "I assure you that is not the reason, but we will know soon enough, as she is here . . . now!"

No sooner had HARV announced Mara's arrival than Carol went flying across the air, crashing to the ground. Before Threa could react she was on the ground convulsing and jerking. I saw that she had some sort of stun sticks sticking out of her neck. There had to be fifty of them.

"What the ... ?" Kiana said.

I looked over at Randy; his mask had been removed and he was sucking his thumb.

"I detect the virus in the air!" said HARV.

Oh, this was *so* not good.

Kiana and I now found ourselves facing not one, not two, but three Maras. And they were all laughing.

Oh, so not very good at all.

Chapter 52

"What are you doing, sister?" Kiana asked Mara.

"Whatever it is, it isn't giving herself up to us," I said in my toughest, graveliest voice.

"No, no, of course I'm not," Mara laughed. "I just needed to stop you all from getting close enough to the XY world to make contact with the police and military and warn them about me. Now with you all out of the way, I will be able to spread my virus in peace. By the time the others get off Lantis it will be too late. I have greatly improved the virus. Not only does it spread through the Web, it also affects normal human females. Not to the extent that it affects males, but it reduces their intelligence levels by half."

"So, you want to destroy the world as we know it," I said.

Mara laughed again. "No, not destroy, just change it for the better. Ninety-nine percent of the men will die of stupidity, but those left will make great mating material for us. None of the human women will die, but they will become much more obedient, easily malleable. Earth will become Lantis. No war, no strife, no XY greed, just peace and sisterhood under the rule of the queen."

"And the occasional murder," I said.

"Sister, this isn't what our ancestors wanted when they came to this planet," Kiana said.

The Maras shook their heads. "No. No it isn't. We have improved on their plan. Now we can truly rule over all of Earth."

"Interesting," Kiana said.

"Interesting!" I shouted. "Interesting! How can you call the destruction of the world interesting?"

"In a way it is interesting," HARV said. "Remember, 'interesting' doesn't have to mean good or beneficial."

Of course. If anyone knows that, it's me.

"HARV makes a good point," Kiana said.

"Yes, he does," one of the Maras said. "HARV, there is a role in our new world for you."

"There is?" HARV said, surprised as I have ever heard him. "You were the one who put me on trial for being a danger to the planet."

All three of the Maras smiled. "I already mentioned that; that was part distraction, part a reason to get BB Star close to me, and part a test."

"Oh, I like tests," HARV said.

"You should, you passed with flying colors," Mara told him. "On our new world you won't have to hide in Zach's brain. You won't be a tool. You will be an inspiration."

"Cool," HARV said.

I had to hand it to Mara, she was good—real good. She was that very dangerous combination of being extremely smart and extremely cunning and good with words. I needed to put all of the hers down and fast. First, though, I had to make sure HARV was playing on the right side.

"HARV, are you really falling for this crap?" I asked.

"Zach, Zach, Zach. She put me on trial. I'm just leading her on. Hoping she'll drop her guard some around me."

"Okay," I said. "I have to ask. Why are there three of you?"

"Yes, I was wondering that myself," Kiana asked.

The lead Mara rubbed her hands together. "I gave myself an extra special gift. There was so much to do, and having a superintelligence leads to even greater inquisitiveness. Even superspeed didn't allow me to do everything I wanted to do. So I made more of me."

"You cloned yourself," I said. "Gross. On our world, the phrase *go clone yourself* is an insult."

I wanted to see if I could throw her off, get her angry. I wanted her to drop her guard—well, her guards.

"Poor, stupid, Zach," Mara said. "I thought HARV would be shielding you from the virus I hit the island with. I told you. I gave myself an extra gift. I can split myself into three copies of myself. They aren't clones, they are more *me*."

"Holy legion of superheroes," I mumbled under my breath.

"How come, I, your queen, did not know about this?" Kiana demanded. "Now I am upset!"

Now I turned to Kiana. "What? This gets you upset! You are okay with her destroying the world, but get really pissed at not knowing she can split into three?"

Kiana put her hands on her hips and leaned into me. "Zach, I am not okay with her destroying the world. Do not be such a drama queen. Besides, she is not destroying it, just changing it. Much of what she says does make sense. The world is overpopulated and men really haven't been making it a better place. But still, I promise I will not let her do this. She is not queen. This is not her call." Kiana paused, then pointed at me. "Feel better now?"

"Somewhat," I said.

Kiana spun back toward the Maras. "But, sister, how could you let me down by not showing me you had another gift?"

"Oh, please!" Mara said, almost spitting out the *-ease*. "You do not care about me. You never noticed me. All you ever cared about is what my creations could do for you. You never questioned how I could get so much done so quickly."

Kiana sunk back a little. Mara's words hurt her like only the truth can. "I was . . . was busy, you know, with all the next-in-line-to-be-queen stuff . . ."

"You just cared about yourself," Mara said. "But that is okay. Being your younger, wiser sister, I will forgive you. You will just be reprogrammed when I take over."

"Come again?" Kiana said.

"When I get back after changing the world. I am going to change our world some. I am going to open up Lantis to general elections."

"What?" Kiana yelled. "I won't stand for that!"

Kiana rushed at the lead Mara. The two backup Maras streaked toward Kiana. They moved so fast I couldn't quite see where they hit her, but it looked like one went high and the other low. The two Maras drove Kiana to the ground and started jabbing at her with supersonic speed.

"Time to end this now," I thought to HARV. "Can you track the superfast Maras?"

"With ease," HARV replied.

I popped GUS into my hand. I aimed in the direction of Kiana. I fired twice. One Mara fell over and off Kiana. The other dove to the side, then came streaking toward me like a blur.

"On my mark," HARV said.

"Gotcha, HARV."

"Now!" HARV shouted.

I slid my body over to the side and stuck out my leg. The attacking Mara hit my extended leg and was launched meters into the air. She came crashing face down into the ground, leaving an impression.

"Oh, that is so going to leave a mark," HARV said.

I didn't have time to reply, though, as the final Mara streaked toward me and hit me in the back. Her momentum knocked me to the ground, but my body armor took the brunt of the blow. Unfortunately, the blow knocked GUS from my hand.

"Pretty fancy shooting there, Zach," Mara said pounding away at me, hypersonic jab after jab. "Let us see how long you can take a beating."

I covered my face with my arms. She hit me with lefts. She hit me with rights. She hit me with knees. I was betting—well, hoping—that my armor could take more than Mara could dish out. The onslaught of attacks continued.

"Good news, Zach!" HARV said out loud. "Carol is up. I am sure she'll be able to take out Mara."

Mara slowed her attacks. "What?" she said. She turned her head toward Carol. That was the break I needed. I sprang up and hit her turned jaw with a HARV-enhanced left cross.

Mara fell off of me, hopefully out cold. I stood up. I shot each of the Maras with a GUS glue pelt, made extra sticky just to hold Mara. I looked over at Carol. She was pushing herself up, just coming around.

"HARV, you bluffed!" I said.

HARV smiled. "Yep. A good bluff is worth a thousand punches."

"You betcha!" the Mara I had punched said as she rammed me in my back, driving me to the ground. The jar from hitting the ground forced me to drop GUS. Why can't it ever be easy?

"HARV, how'd she get out?" I asked as Mara pulled my head back.

"She must have sped up her body and vibrated through the glue before it hardened," HARV said.

Mara smashed my head forward plowing my face into the ground. It hurt, big time. My ears were ringing and I could feel my nose bleeding but that wasn't going to stop me. I arched my back quickly trying to turn the tables and buck her off of me. It didn't work. She rammed my head into the ground another time. The more it hurt though the more determined I was to keep going.

"I could kill you faster," Mara taunted, "but I want to enjoy this."

"Actually, I'm not sure if she could," HARV told me. *"I'm augmenting your strength, making it harder for her to use your head as a battering ram."*

I decided that instead of fighting her I would use Mara's speed against her. This time when I felt her pushed forward on my head, I reached back and grabbed her by the arm. I pulled her forward as she pushed me forward. The result being my face smashed the ground again, but this time I also pulled her to the ground.

I started pushing myself both to my feet and toward GUS. Looking up through the corner of my eye I saw Mara was already back on her feet. I also saw something else that made me smile, even though it hurt a little.

"Nice try," Mara said, approaching me slowly, savoring the kill. "But you've only prolonged your beating. I have a lot of repressed rage in me."

I pointed behind Mara. "Yeah, well so does she," I said.

Mara shook her head. "Please, I am super-duper intelligent. I won't fall for that again."

"Oh, really," Threa said from behind.

Mara turned around. There stood Threa, stun sticks still protruding out of her neck, kind of like a mane. She made a fist with her left hand. Mara took a defensive stance. It didn't matter. Threa grabbed Mara behind her collar with her right hand. Mara gulped just as Threa pulled her forward. Threa locked Mara's face square under her underarm.

"Have a whiff of pheromones, bitch," Threa said.

Threa took a step backward. Mara just stood there stunned. Threa blew on her. Mara fell over stiff as a board.

I smiled.

Chapter 53

We gathered up all the Maras, tied them, bound them, then headed back to Lantis. (Though the Mara Threa clobbered wasn't going anywhere for a long time.) Carol, Kiana, Threa, and I were a bit shaken up, but no worse for the wear; we would be okay. Randy was the one I was worried about.

He looked at me and smiled. "Zach is a really funny name," he said with a bit of drool on the side of his lips. "It sounds like Zap. Zach Zap Zach Zap Zap Zap Zach."

His intelligence seemed to be dropping by the nano.

On the trip back, Kiana and I talked, while Carol, Threa, and HARV looked after the sedated Maras and did what they could for Randy, who was alternately entertaining us by singing commercial jingles while also trying to impress us with his ability to count backward from ten.

"You saved Lantis *and* your world today, Zach," Kiana told me.

"I couldn't have done it without everybody. Especially HARV." I told her.

"Yes," Kiana said.

"Does this mean he and Randy are free to go?" I asked her.

She nodded. "Of course. They are our welcome guests now and at any time."

"What about telling the world now about Lantis?" I asked. "I think you learned that both men and computers can be trusted."

"I will strongly take it under advisement," Kiana said.

I pointed at the Maras. "What about them?"

"She will be reeducated," Kiana said.

"That's it?"

"Yes," Kiana said. "She is a brilliant person. She just got a bit confused. Part of that is my fault for not paying enough attention to her and to others. She helped me see that. Now I will be a better leader."

Chapter 54

We arrived at Lantis to a hero's welcome. Throngs of Lantians, along with those left behind, greeted us with cheers, streamers, and applause. I was happy to know the world was safe, but worried about my friend Randy. He had arrived slightly ahead of us as once we had gotten within the island's protective shielding Threa teleported him directly to the hospital.

Luca was the first to greet us when we exited the bubble. She was backed by a dozen guards. Elena, Shannon, Barbette, and Santana were also there.

Luca took my hand as the guards took the Maras off the hands and minds of Kiana and Carol.

"Zach, you did it," Luca said as she shook my hand while the others patted me on the back.

"How is Randy?" I asked.

"He is in our medical facility being treated by Poca and Electra," Luca told me.

"Take me to him, please," I said.

"Hold on," Elena said turning me toward her. "Can't have you bleeding all over the place." She opened her hand up and placed her palm on my forehead.

"What are you doing?" I asked.

"Close your eyes and your mouth," Elena ordered.

I did as I was told. A wise man always does what Elena tells them. My face started to tingle. It was a good tingle. The pain I was suppressing in my nose, eyes, mouth, pretty much my entire face subsided. In fact I felt great.

Elena moved her hand away from my face. She smiled at me.

I felt my nose, and it was straight with no blood. I gently touched my cheek, jaw, and eye, expecting to recoil from the pain. There wasn't any.

I leaned over and hugged Elena.

"Thanks," I said.

Elena hugged me back. "I couldn't have you going to the infirmary looking like that," she said with a grin. She released me. "Now, let's go see your friend."

"Okay," I said.

"Take my hand," Elena said.

I did as she asked. Kiana also took one of Elena's hands.

Elena transported us to a hospital room. Twoa was there in one bed moaning something about getting the number of that planet that hit her. Randy laid there in another bed with Poca, Threa, and Electra looking over him. Randy's eyes were wide open and looked worried, which I actually took as a sign some of his intelligence was returning.

"We caught the virus just in time. We can reverse the damage," Poca said. She waved a blue crystal up and down Randy's forehead.

I breathed a little sigh of relief.

Randy looked at me and smiled. "We stopped Mara, right?"

"We sure did, buddy," I said.

"And HARV and I are free men?" Randy asked.

"We sure are," HARV said.

Randy sat back in the bed and smiled. "In that case, I've never felt so good in all my life." He looked at me. "I love the fact that I am not a megagenius any longer. It feels so good not to have my mind filled with so many thoughts of so many things. Now I know what it's like to be you, Zach."

"Ah, that's good. I guess."

Poca waved a longer blue crystal over Randy's head. "Don't worry, Randy. I am sure you will make a complete recovery and gain back all your intelligence."

"Really?" he asked.

"Really," she said.

Electra looked at a brain scan over Randy's bed. "I concur. Your brain function is improving by the minute."

"Luckily, I had an antidote on hand, just in case," Poca said. "I would never have been able to distribute it to all the men of Earth in time, but just for your friend, it will work perfectly."

Randy grinned from ear to ear. "You can't image how great that makes me feel." He looked at me. "I really didn't like not having all these thoughts racing through my head."

I patted him on the shoulder.

Randy put his hands behind his head. "This is the life, in bed surrounded by beautiful women and knowing my intelligence will come back."

HARV appeared dressed in white doctor's scrubs. "And don't forget me, Dr. Pool. I am also here."

Randy smiled. "I could never forget you, HARV."

Electra stood up. She took my hand and walked me away from Randy's bed. "How are you doing?" she asked. "I understand Mara pummeled you."

"Mostly my armor," I said. "I've had worse."

"When will Randy be ready to travel?" I asked.

"Probably the day after tomorrow," HARV answered. "He could probably travel tomorrow, but let the man have his fun."

"Okay, good. That will give me some time to talk to Kiana and Luca."

Electra and I spent the next day in Lantis just relaxing and waiting for Randy to recover. I was glad the world was safe for now, but still asked Kiana and Luca for time to see them. They granted me that time at midday.

I walked into the IT's royal conference room. Kiana was sitting in a big chair at the head of a long table. Ohma and Luca were each sitting kitty-corner to her. The three women were talking, but stopped when they saw me.

"Zach, come in," Kiana said. She motioned to a chair next to Luca.

I walked over and sat down.

"I understand you wish to talk to us. To wrap things up, so to speak."

"Yes," I said.

"How is Dr. Pool coming?" Luca asked.

"HARV just gave him a new improved IQ+ test. His IQ+ is up to two-twenty-two, so he's coming along. We should be able to leave soon."

"Great!" Luca said with a smile. Her smile straightened. "Oh, I don't think it's great that you are leaving, I just think it is great you are able to leave."

"I knew what you meant," I told her.

"Have you enjoyed your stay here, now that you aren't solving a murder or stopping my cousin from destroying the world as you know it?" Ohma asked.

"Yeah, sure. It's nice to get some quiet time with Electra."

There was a pause.

"Zach, what is on your mind?" Kiana asked me.

"A couple of things. First, the canisters of the virus Mara made. I'm interested in learning what happened to them."

Kiana and Luca turned to Ohma to answer.

Ohma looked across the table at me. "We are certain she only produced three canisters. She released one on the island you captured her on. The other two were each found hidden on her copies' bodies. They have been destroyed." Ohma stopped talking; she realized what she said, then added, "By they, I mean the canisters, not the copies."

Luca shook her held. "I am still shocked that there were three Maras among us all this time and we never noticed."

"Well, that's kind of related to what I want to talk to you about," I said.

"Oh?" Kiana said, eyebrows raised.

"You have this holier-than-thou attitude about my XY world, yet you've been abusing us, and three of you, who were actually six of you, sort of plotted a couple plots to destroy my world, despite the fact we don't know you exist."

"Your point being?" Kiana asked.

"My point being, you claim that you're less violent because you're women. From my observations, violence is influenced more by greed and lust than by gender. Sure, you may not punch as readily, except for those of you like Andra and Twoa, but you take different forms of revenge which can be just as damaging, if not more so," I said.

"Your point being?" Kiana said, this time with a trace of anger in her words.

"I would like you to strongly consider opening your world up to our world. We can accomplish a lot more if we communicate with each other. And we will learn to understand each other better then. I think we have a lot in common," I said.

"I told you, I will take that into consideration," Kiana said. "I have learned from working with you and HARV that both men and mass communication can be useful. Like almost everything else, they are double-edged swords. They can harm or they can help."

"Exactly," I said. "I believe the only way our two worlds can be safe from each other is if we talk to each other."

"Our world is perfectly safe from your world if you do not know about us, Zach," Kiana said. "I am sure you will not tell people. After all, I have just transferred a large amount of credits to your account," Kiana said.

"You can't keep hiding here, Kiana," I said. "You're just poking your head in the sand, sticking to your old ways. We can learn from you, and you can learn from us."

"For a tough guy, you talk like one of the after-school HV specials," Kiana said.

"Good sense is good sense, no matter how sugar-coated," I said. I slammed my fist on the table. "How's that for an after-school special?"

"I will take it under advisement," Kiana said. She showed me a long scroll. "Now, if you don't mind I have a lot of important matters to attend to."

"Don't worry, Zach. As always, the cavalry is here," HARV said.

The thick wooden double doors to the room burst open. Threa, Twoa, Shannon Cannon, Barbette Rickey, Carol, Electra, Santana, Elena, and BB all stormed into the room. HARV's holographic image followed them with a smile so big it stretched off his face. (It was kind of creepy.)

"Sorry, cousin," Shannon said. "Taking it under advisement just won't do."

"Yeah," Barbette said. "I've lived with males for a while now. I can tell you they have their quirks, but we are better with them than without them."

"Not to mention that some of our technology and communication aids can be of great value to your people," BB said, which kind of surprised me.

"We at ExShell have many fine products that we can integrate with your crystal technology to make the world a better and more profitable place for all of us."

Now that was the BB I was used to.

"So here's the deal," Electra said. "My mother is a member of the World Council. I have contacted her and told her about you. She would like to come and set a timetable for integration of your people into our world."

"I will also attend that meeting," Threa said.

"As will I," Elena said.

"As will I," Santana said. "Now your people will be eligible for the Holiday!" she added in a chipper voice that was somehow still sexy.

Kiana stood up from her thronelike chair. "I am the queen here!" she said pounding the table. "My people will back me."

I was starting to worry that this could turn into one of the bigger catfights/battles royale of the century. Time to bring in more reinforcements.

I nudged Luca and whispered. "You must have an opinion on this."

Kiana heard what I said. She looked over at us. "I am the queen! My word here is . . ."

"Oh sit down, big sister," Luca said. "Before I turn you into a lawn statue."

"Yeah, put a smelly sock in it," Ohma said.

"It is time to do what is best for the people. Not just our people and us, but for all the people," Luca said.

"We share this world with the XYs. It is time we share more than space with them."

"Come on Kiana, you are a reasonable woman," I said, managing to keep a straight face. "You know this is the best way."

Kiana dropped back down in her seat. She looked up at Electra. "Communicate with your mother. Let us set up a timetable to start talking about timetables."

"See, Kiana," I said. "That wasn't so hard; you're already talking like one of our politicians!"

"Oh, joy," Kiana said.

I pushed myself away from the table and stood up. "Now if you don't mind, I'll have some more alone time with my fiancée while you and the others make arrangements."

"No, not all," Kiana said. "Go ahead. You have done enough."

Luca got up and kissed me on cheek. "Thank you, Zachary Nixon Johnson. You have made your world and my world *our* world. I know we will all be better for it."

"Yes, Zachary! Thank you! Thank you!" Ohma said with a wave. "I hope to visit you on the XY world."

I smiled. "My door is always open." I turned to all the women. "To all of you!" I pointed to Twoa. "Except of course to you," I said with a wink.

Twoa waved me off. "Oh, please. Doors are for wimpos."

"Zach, I can handle the communications between Kiana and Councilwoman Gevada," HARV said.

"I knew you could, buddy."

I walked over to Electra. I took her hand. She put her head on my shoulder. The other ladies made a path for us as we walked out of the room.

"We did it again, *tió*," Carol said as we walked past her.

"Yes, we did," I said.

The doors of the room closed behind us. Electra gave me a kiss on the lips. Our world was the same size, yet it had grown. That was a good thing.

I am Zachary Nixon Johnson. I am the last freelance PI on Earth. It's a tough job. It's a dirty job. But it's a job somebody has to do.

I'm glad it's me.

John Zakour

The Novels of
Zachary Nixon Johnson
The Last Freelance P. I.

"If you like your humor slapstick and inventive,
you need look no further for a good fix."
—*Chronicle*

"No one who gets two paragraphs into this
dark, droll, downright irresistable hard-boiled-
dick novel could ever bear to put it down until
the last heart-pounding moment..." —*SFSite*

Once upon a time...

Cinderella—real name Danielle Whiteshore—did marry Prince Armand. And their wedding was a dream come true.

But not long after the "happily ever after," Danielle is attacked by her stepsister Charlotte, who suddenly has all sorts of magic to call upon. And though Talia the martial arts master—otherwise known as Sleeping Beauty—comes to the rescue, Charlotte gets away.

That's when Danielle discovers a number of disturbing facts: Armand has been kidnapped; Daniellie is pregnant; and the Queen has her own Secret Service that consists of Talia and Snow (White, of course). Snow is an expert at mirror magic and heavy-duty flirting. Can the princesses track down Armand and rescue him from the clutches of some of Fantasyland's most nefarious villains?

The Stepsister Scheme
by Jim C. Hines

"Do we *look* like we need to be rescued?"

DAW 130

There is an old story...

...you might have heard it—about a
young mermaid, the daughter of a king, who
saved the life of a human prince
and fell in love.

So innocent was her love, so pure her
devotion, that she would pay any price for the
chance to be with her prince. She gave up her
voice, her family, and the sea, and became
human. But the prince had fallen in love with
another woman.

The tales say the little mermaid sacrificed her
own life so that her beloved prince could find
happiness with his bride.

The tales lie.

Danielle, Talia, and Snow return in

The Mermaid's Madness
by Jim C. Hines

"Do we *look* like we need to be rescued?"

DAW 109